D0992330

Angels Among Us

Mysteries of Sparrow Island™

ANGELS AMONG US

Ellen Harris

Guideposts Books

CARMEL, NEW YORK

For Raymond Fay Harris, in remembrance.

TO CANADA

SAN JUAN ISLAND

SHAW

LOPEZ

San Juan ISLANDS

SPARROW ISLAND*

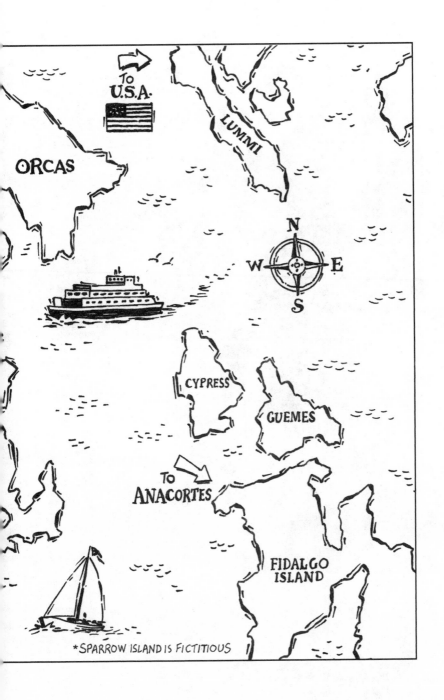

To U.S.A.

LUMMI

ORCAS

N W E S

CYPRESS

GUEMES

To ANACORTES

FIDALGO ISLAND

*SPARROW ISLAND IS FICTITIOUS

PROLOGUE

A LIGHT RAIN FELL, EACH droplet leaving a dark spatter mark as unique as a snowflake on the gray pavement of the off-ramp. Tony Malachy stepped off the ferry and onto Sparrow Island. He set his backpack down and stretched. He was in no hurry. It was important to be observant, to take in every detail. It had taken so much to get this far. Nothing was to be gained by rushing things.

He'd heard about this place all his life and about the people here too. How open and trusting they were. How welcoming they were to strangers. Now here he was, ready to put that reputation to the test.

He pulled back the hood of his parka and let the cold rain hit his face. Even the rain here seemed different—fresh and unsullied. He closed his eyes and took in a great breath of air. It smelled of evergreen. He wondered if it was like this all the time or if it was just because it was the Christmas season. Even now, on a workday Wednesday morning, with Christmas yet eleven days away, there was a festive feeling in the air. Everywhere he looked there were wreaths on door fronts and boughs of greenery overarching doorways and adorning lampposts.

He hoisted his backpack onto his shoulders and started up the hill toward the picturesque little town of Green Harbor. He thought of stopping to pull out his map to locate the bed-and-breakfast that held his reservation but decided he'd just amble about for a while getting to know the lay of the land.

As he moved away from the water, the stinging wind funneling between the shoreline and the big ferry gave way to a gentle breeze that lifted his blond curly hair. It was just cool enough to be exhilarating. Or maybe the way he felt had nothing to do with the temperature.

He had a good vibe. He was almost certain he'd get what he'd come here for. It wasn't a sure thing of course, and there was an outside chance it would all go sour on him, but big rewards called for big risks. And if all went well, he'd get what he'd always wanted. The very thought of it made his cheeks tingle and a smile spread across his handsome face. Yes, indeed, he was in the right place at the right time. He just knew it.

He'd done his homework. He had a notebook full of feverishly scribbled notes in his backpack, the product of hours spent online and in the public library back home. He knew the name and address of every woman on the island in the target age range. Now he just had to narrow it down. And he had no doubt he'd find the right one. He knew enough to get started and if people here were as friendly as he'd been led to believe, it shouldn't be that difficult. By the time his ten-day stay here was over, he'd be leaving Sparrow Island a much richer man.

CHAPTER ❦ ONE

THE AROMA OF BAKING cookies and mingled spices wafted toward Abby as she opened the laundry room door from the garage. The fragrance was so strong it felt like it might lift her right off her feet and carry her along like a cartoon character following her nose. She shed her damp jacket and spread it out on two pegs of the coat rack so it could dry and went into the kitchen.

"What in the world!" she exclaimed as she stopped short in the doorway. Every surface was covered with baking trays, cooling racks and freezer containers.

Mary doled out a spoonful of dough into the last empty space on a cookie sheet. "Hey there, how was your day?" she asked distractedly. Then without waiting for an answer, she turned her wheelchair and picked up the cookie sheet. "Finnegan, oven," she said.

Mary's devoted service dog, always on the alert and eager to please, looked at her as she pointed toward the oven door. "Open," she repeated.

Finnegan grabbed hold of the leather strap dangling from the oven handle with his teeth and backed away until the door started to tilt. He continued pulling until his nose was on the floor and the door was all the way open. Mary pulled out one cookie sheet and set it on the stovetop. She slipped another one in and closed the door.

"When did you teach him to open the oven?" Abby asked. "I didn't know he could do that."

"It's new," Mary said. "We've been working on it for a couple of weeks. It really helps when I have my hands full."

"So now he's your service dog *and* your baking assistant," Abby said. "And it looks like you need all the help you can get," she added, surveying the kitchen again. "Mary, what *is* all this?"

"Christmas baking, Abby," Mary said. "I told you this morning it was time for us to get going on it. Isn't that why you're home early?"

"Well, yes," Abby said hesitantly. "But I thought you had in mind a couple of batches of cookies and maybe a few loaves of banana bread."

"Oh no, no," Mary said, shaking her head. "I mean, yes, those too. But that's just for openers. I wanted to bake gifts for the neighbors, and we can make some things ahead for Christmas dinner at Stanton Farm with Mom and Dad. And I'd like to freeze a few things for just-in-case gifts. You know, for people I might have accidentally forgotten who show up with a gift in their hands. That's happened to me a couple of times and I've been just mortified." She put her hand to her forehead and then rushed on. "And for the bake sale at church and for all the get-togethers."

"Okay, okay," Abby said, laughing and throwing up her hands. She pulled an apron from the hook inside the pantry and pushed up the sleeves of her sweater. "That explains this extravaganza."

"Are you kidding?" Mary asked. "I haven't even started. This is just for my craft group tomorrow. We're meeting here and I wanted to have a variety of desserts to serve." Mary picked up the timer from the kitchen counter and gave the dial a spin. "Could you stir that fudge on the back burner?" she asked as she wheeled back around toward the table. "I've got the cinnamon-apple bread done, oatmeal-raisin cookies in the oven, that batch of fudge and tea cookies already stored in those containers. Next I want to do a couple of batches of divinity fudge."

"Like Mom used to make?" Abby asked, smiling as she remembered the white fluffy confection. If she closed her eyes, she could almost taste it melting on her tongue. As far as she could remember, their mother never made that treat except at Christmastime so it was inextricably linked to the season—a sweet taste that evoked sweet memories.

"*Just* like Mom used to make," Mary said. "At least I hope it'll turn out as good as hers; it's her recipe." Mary pointed back to the stovetop. "That fudge ought to be about ready. Would you check the temperature on the candy thermometer?"

Abby did as instructed, and as she bent over the pan the smell of the rich chocolate made her feel light-headed. "It's ready," she confirmed. "But I've got to tell you, I need to get something to eat before we go on with this. I skipped lunch today so I could take off early, and all these goodies are making my stomach rumble."

"I have cold-cut sandwiches made for us," Mary said, sliding three cookies off the sheet and into a freezer container with quick strokes of the spatula. "And a nice salad. Help me get the fudge spread in these trays and we'll take a dinner break."

Abby managed to get through the task without succumbing to the temptation to do more than lick the spoon. While she cleared off one end of the table, Mary brought out their supper and fiddled with the table setting. Even in the midst of this chaos, Mary took the trouble to set a nice table.

Ordinarily, Abby appreciated these finer domestic touches, but she was so hungry she would have reverted to her old ways if Mary weren't around. When she'd been a research scientist back at Cornell, she'd often returned from a workday with barely the energy left to heat up a can of soup, which she'd usually eaten standing up at the kitchen counter.

"Would you look at that?" Mary said after grace was said and they'd begun eating. She pointed to the wall calendar with her fork, then speared a bite of greens.

Abby looked at the color-coded month of December and laughed. "I don't think we're going to be able to fit many more things on there, though I'll point out there's a lot more of your red than my green."

"That's your own fault Abby. You've had just as many invitations as I have."

"Yes, I know," Abby said. "And part of me would love to go to every single event, but I'm not like you Mary. I need some alone time to stay on an even keel. And with the holiday open house at the museum less than a week away now, I want to make sure I'm not overcommitting. It wouldn't do for the Associate Curator to be too tired to mingle with all our guests, now would it?"

"No, it wouldn't," Mary said. She reached over to pat Abby's hand. "You'll be the life of the party, Abby."

"Well, I don't know about the life of the party," Abby said with a grin. "You're the social butterfly in the family. But I do have that new dress I'm looking forward to wearing. And I would like to be at my best, so I need to pace myself."

Mary smiled, but then gave a heavy sigh, moving her salad around in the bowl with her fork as if searching for something. "I'll tell you the truth Abby, I think I'm eager to fill up my calendar so I don't have time to dwell on the kids' not being here for the holidays."

"I know, Mary," Abby said, her voice soft. "But you know they'd come if they could."

"Oh yes," Mary said. "I understand perfectly, really I do. I know Nancy and Benjamin have to watch their finances. After all, they have two children to bring up. And I know it's very expensive for them to fly out here all the way from Florida. And now they have their own Christmas traditions to observe. And Zack can't just pick up and come out here in the middle of an engagement. He'll only have a few days off. His jazz band's booked all through the holidays in a club in Chicago . . ." her voice trailed off.

"But understanding the situation doesn't mean you can't be disappointed about not seeing them, does it?" Abby said.

"No, no it doesn't," Mary answered. She lifted her teacup, but didn't drink. "I imagine Zack will have Christmas dinner with Lily's family and I'm happy about that."

"Well, I would think you would be. Everyone knows you're hoping they'll fall in love—or realize they already have—and get married. That's no secret."

"Okay," Mary said. "I confess; you've got me. Is that so awful? Yes, I love Lily. For lots of reasons, not the least of which is that she brought Finnegan to me," she said, glancing over at the beautiful yellow Labrador, golden retriever mix. "If it hadn't been for her patience and understanding I don't know if

I'd have come to realize what a gift a service dog could be to my life. Especially this special dog, right, Finnegan?"

The dog looked up at Mary and panted, which gave him an expression so closely resembling a human smile, it made Abby and Mary both giggle.

"And," Mary continued, "as you say, I can see that Zack is already in love with Lily and I think she feels the same way. But it's going to take more time together for them to finally tell one another. And his vagabond musician's life is not exactly relationship-friendly."

"True," Abby said as she got up to fetch more hot water for tea.

"And Lily can't be expected to stay in limbo, forever waiting for him to make a commitment. That's just not fair," Mary continued.

"Kind of like Henry must feel," Abby murmured under her breath as she picked up the teakettle.

Mary's beau, Sergeant Henry Cobb of the San Juan Sheriff's Department, had been patiently waiting for quite some time for Mary to admit how much she cared for him.

"What was that?" Mary asked.

"Oh nothing," Abby answered brightly. "I was just saying, you're absolutely right. It's not fair to keep a person waiting for an unreasonable time."

Mary narrowed her eyes. Abby could feel her gaze boring in on her, but she poured more hot water into each of their cups and tried her best to look nonchalant.

Mary didn't press the issue. "Anyway," she said, steering the conversation back into more comfortable territory, "I think Zack may actually be about ready to make some changes in his life. He tells me one of the guys in the quartet has been hinting that he may want to leave the group soon. He's married now and would like to start a family, and the touring just isn't compatible with the kind of family life he wants."

"Oh?" Abby asked. "That's the first I've heard that. But couldn't they just replace him? I mean, there are a lot of talented musicians out there."

"Well, yes, I suppose they could," Mary said. "But to tell the truth I don't think he's the only one getting tired of the road. Zack seems to have lost a little of his enthusiasm for it too. Not for the music, certainly, but for the constant travel. It was exciting at first, seeing all the new places, but I think it's getting old."

"I can understand that," Abby said. "I used to love to travel. I was always thrilled when my boss back at Cornell chose me for far-off research projects. I'm glad I've had a chance to see so much of the world. But, I tell you, as I get older I'm becoming a real homebody. Especially since I've moved back here to Sparrow Island."

"Well, as you know, I've always been that way," Mary said. "It's just the way I am. I like my routine and I love being in familiar surroundings. That's one reason I didn't accept Nancy's invitation to go to Tampa to spend Christmas with them. First of all, I didn't want to disrupt their Christmas activities. And frankly, I just couldn't bear the thought of being away from home. I'd love to have them all here, but since they can't be, that's all the more reason to keep busy and enjoy all the holiday festivities here on the island. Then I won't have time to miss them."

"Well, I'd say you're giving it a valiant try," Abby said, pointing to the calendar. "It looks like you've got something every day and half the nights from now until Christmas."

"Yes," Mary agreed, looking at the calendar. "Between that

and helping Candace get all the Christmas orders out at Island Blooms, I'm going to be a busy camper."

Finnegan lifted his head from the floor where he was resting and gave a little whine.

"You, too, Finnegan," Mary said to him. "We're going to have a Merry Christmas—and a very *busy* one, right?"

The dog gave one sharp bark and twitched his tail before putting his head back down and gazing adoringly at Mary.

"COULD YOU GET THE EGGS OUT of the fridge and start separating them?" Mary asked after they'd finished eating and done the few dinner dishes. "We need to get the divinity going next."

Abby reached for the refrigerator door, but just then the doorbell rang. "Were you expecting someone?" she asked.

"No," Mary said, pulling a recipe card from the wooden box that held all the family recipes. "It could be someone dropping off things for the craft fair. I told several people they could bring things here and we'd take a load to Little Flock Church tomorrow in my van."

Abby went to the door. She looked though the small window in the doorframe and saw a tall, slender young man waiting on the front steps. The light over the door caught his blond, curly hair and turned it into a nebula around his head. Abby had never seen him before.

"Hello," she said when she'd opened the door, making it more of a question than a greeting.

"Hi," the young man said. "I'm here on a mission from Terza at The Bird Nest. I'm a guest there and I volunteered to bring these over for her. She says I'm to give them to Mary Reynolds." He held up a couple of bulging plastic bags. "Are you Mrs. Reynolds?"

"No, I'm Abby, Abby Stanton, Mary's sister."

"Tony Malachy," the young man said. He hefted the plastic bags again to show he had no free hand to offer.

"Please, come in," Abby said, opening the door wide. "Mary's in the kitchen right through here." Abby showed him in, thinking it rather odd that Terza was using a guest to do her errands. She introduced him to Mary and told her why he was there.

"Nice to meet you," Tony said with a nod. "I see you two are as busy as Terza," he said. "She and Martin are cooking up a storm. That's why she finally agreed to let me do this errand for her," he said, gesturing again with the bags. "She says these are the lanterns your craft group's going to paint for the craft fair at your church, Mrs. Reynolds. Where would you like me to put them?"

"It's Mary, please," she told him. "Just hand them to Abby and she'll put them in my craft room. Thank you so much for bringing them over."

Abby took the bags from him and carried them into Mary's overflowing craft room. Apparently, a few people had already taken Mary up on her offer to transport their donations to the church. Abby took a few minutes to rearrange the bags and boxes lining the walls to make sure nothing was obstructing Mary's wheelchair path. Then she walked back into the kitchen expecting to say good-bye to the young man and see him out.

But when she got there, she found him spreading his wet jacket over the back of a chair by the heat vent.

Mary had the teakettle going. "Tony's soaked," she said to Abby. "I've insisted he have a cup of tea and warm up a few minutes before he sets out again."

"Definitely," Abby said, getting a cup from the cupboard

and setting the tea chest in front of Tony. "There's a nice selection here. Pick something that appeals to you."

Abby still thought it rather odd that Terza had allowed a guest to do errands for her, but it was a hectic time of season and maybe the young man had wanted to be helpful. He seemed very amiable. Abby set about doing a friendly inquest.

She learned that Tony was here on a little vacation, as a gift from "someone special" in his life.

"A sort of holiday holiday," he joked. "I've heard about this place all my life and always wanted to visit, but I've never had the chance until now."

"And so far, what do you think of our little island?" Mary asked.

"Well, I only arrived yesterday. But so far, it's everything I've always thought it would be," Tony said. "Everyone here is so friendly and it's beautiful. Especially all decked out for Christmas."

"Every season here has its charms," Abby said.

"Say, is that divinity you're making?" he asked, as he watched Abby assemble ingredients.

"Why yes," Abby said. "Our mother's recipe. It's a special Christmas treat for us."

"Me too," Tony said, his eyes widening in surprise. "My grandmother used to make it, but only at . . ."

". . . Christmastime," Abby and Mary both finished in unison.

"Yes, only then," Tony said. "Would it be okay if I helped?" he asked. "This brings back such good memories."

"Sure," Abby said, giving Mary a glance and getting a nod. "The more the merrier."

The three set about the preparations for making the divinity.

"I hope I'll have a chance to experience the island in the other seasons," Tony said, after he'd donned the apron Abby got for him. He handed over the bowl of egg whites he'd separated to Mary.

She snapped the beaters into the mixer. "Every season has something special about it," she said.

"Well, if what I've seen so far is any indication . . ." he said smiling. "I gave myself a walking tour of the town yesterday. And first thing in the morning I'm going exploring farther out. You'll have to tell me all about the island so I won't miss anything."

The three spent the rest of the evening making not two, but four batches of divinity and a batch of ginger cookies to boot. All the while they talked easily about one thing or another.

Tony finally said his goodnights when the last cookie was packed up and the myriad bowls, pots and cookie sheets had each been washed and put away. Abby walked him to the door and stood on the front porch, her heavy cardigan sweater pulled around her against the chill of the evening.

Tony put the bag of goodies that Mary had insisted he take into the basket of the bicycle Terza and Martin kept for guests and zipped his jacket up to his chin. The rain had completely stopped and the cloud cover had moved out, making for a rare moonlit winter's night. Wet branches and leaves glistened and the puddles in the driveway looked like a series of shimmering mirages stretching out to the street.

"Thanks for a great evening and thanks for these," Tony said, gesturing toward the bag as he straddled the bike. "I'm sure I'll find someone to share them with."

He pedaled off into the night, the pale light of the moon catching on his hair. As Abby watched, she felt like she'd just said good-bye to an old friend instead of someone she'd only known for a few hours

"What a nice young man," Mary said when Abby came back into the kitchen.

"Yes, yes, he is that," Abby said, smiling. "And I have to say, it was nice to have him here. He was very pleasant and a great help too. But there was something else about him—I can't quite put words to it—he just seems . . ."

"Charming?" Mary said, raising her eyebrows and putting both hands out toward Abby, palms up.

Abby laughed. "Yes, charming will do. It still seems rather odd to me, though. That Terza would have a guest out running errands for her. Doesn't that seem strange to you?"

"Oh, I don't know," Mary said. "I hadn't really thought about it. I know Terza has her hands full right now. And you saw how eager he is to help. She probably accepted his help for the same reason we did."

"Yes, you're right," Abby said. "That's probably it. In any case, I don't know if it was him or making the divinity, but I have to say, I'm feeling more in the Christmas spirit now."

"Me too," Mary said, a broad smile lighting up her face. "It's going to be a very special Christmas here on Sparrow Island. I just know it."

Finnegan got up from where he was resting on the kitchen floor and walked to Mary's chair. He made a show of turning himself around and sat down next to her as if in solidarity. He gave Abby an expectant stare.

"Yes," Abby told him. "A Merry Christmas for all, dogs included."

CHAPTER ❧ TWO

ABBY ARRIVED AT THE Sparrow Island Nature Museum bright and early Friday morning. The clear weather from the previous evening was holding. Visitors often expressed surprise about the climate in the San Juans, even people from the nearby mainland. They seemed to expect the same days-on-end overcast and drizzle they might find in Seattle. But the islands were in the rain shadow of the Olympic Mountains. Those formidable peaks reached up and wrung much of the rain from the clouds before they could shower down on the islands. This gave the San Juans a lot of sunshiny days. Two hundred and forty-seven per year to be exact, at least according to a boast of the Chamber of Commerce.

But even at that, splendid sunny days like this one was shaping up to be were rare during the winter months. Abby rued the idea of wasting this day indoors, but she had a lot of work to do to get ready for the Christmas open house and it was coming up fast. Still, she thought if she worked hard all morning maybe she could steal a few minutes at lunchtime for a quick walk on one of the trails in the conservatory.

❧ 15 ❧

Abby had been serious when she'd told Mary she was trying to allow some alone time in her holiday schedule. She was self-aware enough to know she'd begin to feel out of sorts and unsettled after a few days away from nature.

As it was, she was delaying the observation and counting of a flock of old-squaws that were wintering in the fjordlike sound off Orcas Island. She'd been out just once to see them, and it had been quite a spectacle. There were about a hundred of them, but the noise had made it sound like two hundred. With their black and white plumage and distinctive quill tails, the sea ducks had been easy to pick out of the raft of scoters they had chosen as traveling companions.

Abby had enjoyed watching them dive, and had held her breath, along with her fellow bird watchers, waiting for each bird to resurface from the deep water. They were capable of going down to a depth of two hundred feet below the surface, and put on quite a show for the humans.

She'd also wanted to get some pictures of a flock of snow buntings that had nested in an open area of the conservatory grounds. With their downy feathers, these birds sometimes looked like a swirling cloud as they moved across the sky. It took shooting a lot of photos to capture them at just the right angle to showcase their delicate beauty.

She was pulling her bag out of the backseat of her car when Wilma Washburn's minivan pulled into the lot. A festive evergreen wreath was tethered to the front grill and the red ribbon on the bottom of it fluttered as Wilma slowed to pull into a parking spot next to Abby.

Wilma was usually the first one at the museum each morning and Abby glanced at her watch, wondering if she herself had gotten here earlier than she'd imagined.

"Good morning, Abby," Wilma said as she got out of the van. "I'm running late this morning. I can't believe it." She pulled at the collar of her coat to free a strand of dark hair that had worked loose from the tight bun she wore at the nape of her neck.

"Looks to me like you're right on time," Abby remarked. "You're just not *early* like you usually are," she added with a laugh.

Wilma pulled her bag out of the van and hoisted it on her shoulder. "I just can't believe how far behind I am. Christmas has really crept up on me this year. I have so much to do yet. I don't know how I'll ever get it all done in time."

Abby was a bit taken aback. Normally Wilma Washburn was one of the most unflappable people she had ever encountered. For her, this was a state of near frenzy. "Me too," Abby commiserated. "I haven't finished my Christmas shopping or gotten my cards out even, and it's just, what . . ."—Abby ticked off a count on her fingers—"I can't believe it! Nine days until Christmas."

As the two walked toward the entrance of the museum, a moped puttered into the parking lot. The biker was wearing a metallic helmet, and for a moment it caught a direct ray from the morning sun and splintered the light. Both women watched as the rider parked and peeled off the helmet. Abby immediately recognized the blond curls. It was Tony Malachy.

Abby called to him and he looked in her direction. A smile of recognition spread across his face and he trotted over. "Hello there. Didn't think I'd get to see you again this soon," he said. "But the Chois went on and on about this place. I had the moped reserved and as soon as I picked it up, I decided I'd better make this my very first stop. Are you open yet?"

"Well, not officially," Abby said, looking at her watch. "But I think we can let you in a few minutes early," Abby told him. "I hope it lives up to the Chois' recommendation. We like to think it's pretty special." She introduced Wilma, and the three continued on toward the museum.

Tony chattered amiably. Abby expected to have to carry the conversation, but to her surprise, Wilma jumped right in. Normally quite taciturn, Wilma seemed very comfortable with the young man. At first she was telling him about the museum, but once inside, the talk became more specific. Wilma told him to be sure to take time at the Native American exhibit. Tony asked a few more questions and soon Wilma was telling him about her tribal heritage and about her family.

They were still talking when Abby went into her office, smiling and shaking her head. Would wonders never cease? Wilma had probably said more words in the last ten minutes than Abby had heard her say all month. Tony seemed to have a gift for putting people at ease.

Abby settled behind her desk and sat for a moment, staring at her closed door. Her smile faded. What was it about this young man that made people open up to him like that? Even Wilma Washburn, of all people. Abby felt a slight sense of unease, but pushed it away. She had absolutely no reason to be suspicious of him. He had wonderful manners and a warm, friendly personality.

But the skeptic in her reared its head. She thought back over the conversations she and Mary had enjoyed with Tony the previous evening. What had they really learned about this young man? That he was here on vacation. That he lived in Spokane. Wait, was that what he said? That he lived there or that he was born there? What else? Abby tapped her fingers on her chin, her signature thinking gesture. That was about the extent of it, really. The rest was just chatter.

He, on the other hand, had learned quite a bit about her and Mary, Abby realized in retrospect. And about others on the island as well. He'd asked a lot of questions. An awful lot of questions. Maybe he was just a naturally curious person. Abby could identify with that. She had that tendency herself. But maybe it was something else. Something less innocuous.

Abby made up her mind to get to know Tony better. She liked the young man enormously. But there was something in his easy charm that seemed almost too good to be true. One could be welcoming and accepting without throwing caution completely to the wind.

"THESE LANTERNS are going to sell out immediately," Mary said as she watched Ana Dominguez stroke red paint onto the white rice paper. "Wherever did you learn to do that Ana?"

"The calligraphy?" Ana asked. "Why from Terza, of course. I only know how to do a few words. This one says peace, and the one over there in green says happiness."

"Well, they're lovely and I know they'll go like hotcakes," Mary said, wheeling around to the craft table where she had laid out a series of charts. "Where shall we put those for the sale?" she asked Patricia Hale who was leaning over the table studying the charts of the presentation of the craft fair merchandise.

The pastor's young wife drew a pencil out of her casually bundled red hair and made a few marks across the top of a page. "How about if we suspend a rod from the ceiling here and hang them all along it? That will show them to good advantage, and we'll save the table space we need."

"Oh, that'll be lovely," Mary said. "They'll look so festive hanging all in a row. I have a feeling this is going to be the best craft fair the Little Flock Church has ever had. Look at all these beautiful things. And this is only a small part of it."

Everyone murmured agreement. "And what a blessing," Patricia said. "We're in need of a few repairs around the church, and we want to do gift baskets for all the elderly and shut-ins on the island. Plus, we want to provide Christmas dinner for a few families who've fallen on hard times. We can really use the proceeds from the sale to do a lot of good this year."

Mary's craft room was filled with activity, with sorters and workers spilling out into the hallway and the den. Everyone talked of Christmas plans and activities, and a few admitted to feeling stressed about how much they had yet to do.

"I felt that way too, at least until yesterday," Ana said.

"What happened to change things?" Patricia said. "Did you get a lot accomplished since then?"

"Well, yes and no," Ana said. "I've been working on a wall hanging that I absolutely *have* to get finished and shipped by early next week. This is for a regular customer, and he's counting on it for a gift for his wife on Christmas morning. I was really getting worried about getting it done in time. I went to the shop yesterday morning to work on it, and as I was carrying some supplies in from my truck, a young man who's staying at the Chois' happened by on the sidewalk. He helped me carry some things in."

"Was his name Tony?" Mary asked.

"Yes, how did you know?" Ana answered.

"I'll tell you later, go on with your story," Mary said, smiling.

"Well, this young man, Tony," she said, with a nod in Mary's direction, "asked if he could watch me work for a few minutes. He said he'd seen the wall hanging in my window and was interested in how I did it." Ana nodded and Mary noted that a blush crept into her cheeks. "Actually, he said he was enchanted by it, can you imagine?" Ana said, rolling her eyes and giving a little giggle. "*Enchanted.* Anyway," she said, clearing her throat, "he watched for a little while and we passed the time talking about the island and this and that, then he says I don't seem to be enjoying working on this piece. It surprised me when he said that, but then I realized I wasn't enjoying working on it. I was so uptight about getting it done, that it had become a chore."

"That's not like you, Ana," Patricia said. "You usually find such joy in your work."

"That's true," Ana said, nodding vigorously. "But lately, I've had so many orders that I can hardly keep up. Still, what kind of person would I be to complain about my success?"

"You never complain, Ana," Mary said. "You're one of the most positive people I know."

"Thank you for saying so, Mary," Ana said, giving her head a little shake. "But we have a saying where I come from, *irse a pique*—to sink yourself. Here, I think you say someone is going off the deep end. That's what I've been doing, going off the deep end *and* sinking myself. But anyway, as Tony watched me work, he started to comment on what I was doing. He talked about the beauty in the intricacy of the knots I was making, but then he said there was also beauty in the open work. It got me thinking, and suddenly it came to me that I could modify the design and get it done more quickly. And to tell the truth, I think it's going to be prettier than my original design. I think I'll have it finished by tonight."

"Lucky for you he came along when he did," Edmonia Lewis said. Edmonia, in addition to being the most sought after hairdresser in town and the owner of Silver Scissors Salon, was also a renowned island potter. As she talked, she unpacked the bowls and vases she had donated for the sale.

"I'm not sure luck had anything to do with it," Mary said. "Maybe he was sent." She told the group about the previous evening's visit from Tony. "Isn't he the nicest young man?" she asked Ana, before rushing on. "Abby and I were saying how his visit really came at just the right time. He seemed to be bringing Christmas joy right along with him."

"Where is he from and what's he doing on Sparrow Island?" Edmonia asked.

"Well, I do know he's from Spokane," Mary answered, "at least I think that's what he said." She tilted her head to one side and frowned, then shook it and went on. "Well, anyway, he said this trip to the island was a gift from someone close. A Christmas gift, I think."

Edmonia looked up from her work. "Really? You know, as much as we love our island, that seems like sort of a strange gift, doesn't it? I mean, Christmas is usually a time when people want to be *with* their families and friends, not sending them away."

Mary cocked her head to the side again. She hadn't thought of it like that, but she had to admit that what Edmonia said was certainly true. Only the night before hadn't she been saying how much she'd miss her children at Christmas?

"Well, whatever his story and however he ended up here, we'll have to make sure he feels he's among friends for Christmas, won't we?" Patricia Hale asked. "In true Sparrow Island fashion?"

The others all murmured their assent, then went back to laughing and talking together as they worked.

ABBY WAS PROUD of how much she had been able to accomplish in the last two hours. She'd made numerous phone calls, answered at least a dozen emails and had everything all squared away as far as the food for the open house was concerned.

She picked up a clipboard from the end of her desk and went out into the museum to draw a sketch of where the food tables should be set up and to make a list of what was yet to be done regarding decorations, cleaning and polishing. She was surprised to see that Tony was still there.

He and Hugo Baron, Abby's boss and friend, were involved in an animated conversation. Abby saw Hugo clap Tony on the shoulder and let out a huge Hugo-sized laugh. Abby watched them, observing every nuance. Hugo was friendly by nature, but it usually took a little while before he got this chummy.

But if that surprised her, it paled in comparison to the next thing that happened. Tony got ready to leave and called out a good-bye to Abby across the main room of the museum. Abby waved, then heard Wilma Washburn say, "Don't forget, Tony, dinner at my house tonight. We'll expect you about six."

"I wouldn't miss it," Tony replied. "May I bring something?"

"Just yourself," Wilma said. "It'll be a simple meal. But I'd like you to meet my family."

"See you then," Tony said. "I look forward to it."

He gave another little salute in Abby's direction and went out the door. Wilma gazed after him, a contented smile on her face.

Wilma Washburn was a lovely woman and Abby was very fond of her. Once you earned her friendship, she was loyal to the end and gave her trust completely. But she was normally a bit on the stoic side, particularly with strangers.

"Abby, my dear, you look like someone could knock you

over with a feather," Hugo said as he strolled over. "And that's not a good thing for an ornithologist, is it?"

"What?" Abby said, still staring toward the museum doors. "Oh no, no it's not," she stammered, smiling absently at Hugo's little joke. She lowered her voice. "I can't believe what I saw. Wilma asked Tony Malachy to dinner? She just met him a couple of hours ago."

"Well, yes," Hugo said, as if the thought had only now occurred to him. He spoke quietly, satisfied that Wilma wouldn't overhear them. "But he's a fascinating young fellow. And he was so interested in everything about the island. I guess his enthusiasm's contagious."

"Yes, that's true," Abby mused, looking again in the direction of the doors as they turned to walk back toward their offices.

"Okay, let's hear it," Hugo said. "What's really troubling you? I know you. When you get that look, you're stewing about something."

"It's nothing," Abby said, batting a hand in the air."

Hugo shrugged and started to walk away.

"Except . . ." Abby said, stopping him in his tracks.

He turned back toward her and stepped close. He bent his head down and looked at her searchingly. His blue eyes focused in on her and she let out a sigh.

"I know it sounds terrible. It's Christmas and this goes right against the spirit of the season, but sad as it is, I'm afraid in this world today a little caution is called for. What do we really know about this young man? And why is he *so* curious about our little island and the people here?"

"Oh, Abby," Hugo said, with a hint of disappointment in his voice. "I'm afraid you're letting your scientist's skepticism run away with you. I appreciate that you want to protect your friends, but until this young man gives us any reason to think we should do otherwise, we should welcome his interest in our little corner of the world. I have a good feeling about him."

Abby smiled letting her shoulders slump. "I guess so. I do like him a lot. He's friendly and personable and his interest seems genuine."

"And if we think so, there's no reason in the world Wilma wouldn't think so too. So there you have it," Hugo said, putting both hands out, palms up and giving a shrug.

"You're right. Of course you're right," Abby said, with a quick affirmative nod. She tapped her pencil on the clipboard. "I'll have to be sure to invite him to the open house. He'd probably like that."

"That's the spirit," Hugo said, his voice booming. He walked away heading for his office humming along to the music playing over the museum's system. *Angels we have heard on high, sweetly singing o'er the plains. . . .*

CHAPTER ❦ THREE

ABBY AWOKE TO A COLD, drizzly Saturday morning. She padded to the window, the floorboards cold underneath her bare feet. She pulled the curtain aside and looked out into the backyard. The temperatures had changed overnight. A cold rain had pelted the warm ground, shrouding everything in fog and mist. It was beautiful and peaceful, but despite the scene before her, Abby's mind started to race with thoughts of errands to run and things to check off her perpetual to-do list.

She sighed and went to her dresser and pulled out a pair of warm socks and put them on. She pulled a fleece robe on over her pajamas, then crawled back into bed. She took her gratitude journal and her Bible from the bedside stand and reached for her glasses. Abby knew when she got this caught up in tedious worldly concerns it was time for her to slow down and turn to the source of her faith.

She'd left her booklet of guided devotions downstairs so she decided to try her mother's method of selecting a reading for the day. She ran her thumb along the edge of the Bible's gilt-edged pages and let them flutter, then inserted her index finger as the pages flipped by. She half expected she'd end up with an Advent reading, one that would help get her mind focused toward the miracle of the season. But she'd picked instead a gentle treatise on how human beings are to treat one another.

Abby had read this passage many times and knew it by rote, but suddenly a few words seemed to fly from the page and go straight to her heart. "For I was hungry and you gave me something to eat, I was thirsty and you gave me something to drink, I was a stranger and you invited me in" (Matthew 25:35).

Abby closed the Bible and ran her hands along the embossed cover. She thought of Tony Malachy and the pleasant evening she and Mary had spent with him, and of Wilma's offer of hospitality to the young man. But then she had to look, too, at her own suspicions. She had welcomed him in, but with mental reservations. She bowed her head and sat very still in the gray morning light and prayed for an open heart.

She opened her gratitude journal and wrote: *I am grateful for meeting a nice young man who seems to spread good feeling wherever he goes.* She paused, let out a sigh then scratched her pen across the page adding, *and for the challenge his presence creates for me to be a more welcoming and accepting person.*

Abby heard Mary moving around in the kitchen and talking in a low voice to Finnegan. She pulled back the covers. Her to-do list still ran long, but she felt in a much better frame of mind to deal with it now.

She went down the stairs and found Mary turning her chair from one side to another as if she couldn't decide which way to go. "Morning Mary, how're you feeling?"

"Good morning, Abby," Mary said absently, "I'm trying to get some breakfast going, but I need to feed Finnegan and I have to get dressed right away. I told Patricia I'd be over at church by nine to help price the rest of the items for the craft fair."

"You're not setting up today are you?" Abby asked.

"No, we just have to finish pricing everything. We can't set up until early Monday morning because we have the potluck at the church Sunday and we need the hall for that. But we want to have everything that's come in so far priced so all we have to do is set it out on the tables Monday morning. It's more complicated than you might think. We have so much and more coming in and limited table space. It takes a lot of planning. Honestly, I just feel all at sixes and sevens. I can't seem to get my mind organized today."

"Have you done your devotions?" Abby asked.

"Not yet," Mary answered, looking up at Abby and putting both hands to her cheeks. "So much to do," she said finally.

"I'll feed Finnegan and get breakfast started," Abby said. "You go in and get dressed and do your readings and prayers. That's not just one more thing to do, you know. That's the thing we do that makes it easier and more rewarding to do all the other things!"

"Yes, you're absolutely right," Mary said firmly. "Thank you for reminding me of that." She turned her chair toward the doorway. "Just do something simple for breakfast, Abby. A nice bowl of hot oatmeal with juice and coffee would be fine with me."

"Sounds good to me too," Abby said. "But don't forget to leave me Finnegan."

Mary stopped and looked at the dog. He was following

along beside her chair on the chance that his services might be needed. "Off the clock, boy," she said, reaching out to pat his tawny head. "Go to Abby, she'll give you breakfast."

The dog twitched his tail and Abby stepped over to his bowl. He gave one last look at Mary as if to ask if she was sure he couldn't be of some assistance and she pointed again toward Abby. At that moment, a white fluff of fur wound languidly around the doorframe. The cat stopped and stretched, then looked around expectantly.

"Blossom doesn't have to be told twice," Abby said, reaching into the pantry and getting a scoop of the cat's food and filling her bowl.

Finnegan trotted over to his bowl and began crunching his kibbles. Blossom, giving him a disdainful look as if his eagerness showed a decided lack of dignity, approached at a more regal pace. Her soft white fur barely registered the movement as she glided across the floor.

The animals' needs met, Abby turned her hand to getting the human inhabitants of the household fed. She put oatmeal on to boil. No instant foods were allowed in this house; Mary still preferred the old-fashioned kind. As the oatmeal cooked she made coffee and set the table, complete with matching napkins and placemats, the way Mary liked it. Any small thing she could do to bring Mary a measure of comfort was worth the effort.

This would be the first Christmas Mary had spent without seeing either of her children since Nancy was born. Abby knew it would be difficult, even with Mary's attempts to pack the season full of activities and distractions.

Abby pulled a small notebook from the pocket of her robe and made a new entry. If she had time and could find them, she'd put some of the outside Christmas decorations up. Despite Mary's suggestion that they skip the hassle of putting them up this year, Abby knew it would brighten her spirits to see them lighting up their usual spots.

She looked over her list as she stirred the oatmeal. Lots of things to do, but if she worked at it she could probably get most of it done today. And it was still eight days until Christmas. Plenty of time. Of course, the list kept growing as the days ticked by, so maybe she'd only be staying even.

Mary came out a little while later looking like a new woman. She had chosen a cheery bright red sweater with a candy cane motif and a rich red broomstick skirt. Her makeup, as usual, was expertly applied and her silver hair meticulously coiffed. Mary was still a striking woman, and being in the chair had done nothing to blunt her fashion sense. She even had a matching bag tied onto the side of her chair; it, too, was decorated with candy canes.

Abby stared at her for a moment, then pulled the little notebook from her pocket again and added *get my hair cut* to her growing list.

AFTER MARY AND FINNEGAN had left, Abby did the dishes and made her bed. She resisted the temptation to turn on her laptop and read her e-mail. That was the kind of thing that could completely derail her schedule.

She showered and dressed, choosing a no-nonsense working outfit of jeans, a turtleneck and a Cornell sweatshirt. She still had a collection of these from all the years she had spent there working in the laboratory. She was glad to have them because every time she pulled one on, she thought fondly of all her friends and co-workers back in New York.

She missed them—some of them she missed fiercely—but she couldn't say she'd ever had a moment's regret about her decision to move back to Sparrow Island after Mary's accident. She felt blessed to have this time with her parents and with Mary. And her job at the museum and conservatory had proved more satisfying than she could ever have imagined when Hugo had first approached her with the offer.

She cast a longing glance at her birding vest draped over the back of the chair in the corner of her room. She wondered if it was warm enough outside for her to wear just the vest over her sweatshirt. She loved having everything she needed in its many pockets and being able to leave her coat and purse and her cumbersome backpack behind. She squinted at the digital thermometer Hugo had given her for Christmas last year. The instrument was accurate to within tenths of a degree. The readout on the inside display in the windowsill was relayed from an outdoor sensor.

Abby frowned, but then snatched up the vest. It was still a bit chilly, but she could always throw her parka and bag in the back of the car in case they were needed.

She slipped the vest on and loaded the pockets with tissues, her wallet, her checkbook and a pen. She glanced again at her to-do list, figuring out her plan of attack, before slipping it, too, into a pocket.

She clattered down the stairs and went out the back door. A shiver stuttered up her spine as the cool morning air enveloped her. It was bracing, but she'd be okay once she got moving. The vest and sweatshirt would do nicely.

She headed to the storage shed in Mary's yard and shouldered open the stubborn door. The flat gray morning light barely penetrated the small windows laced with cobwebs. Abby squinted into the dim corners. She pulled a penlight from her vest pocket and aimed it at the shelves.

There, on the very top, were two boxes marked OUT-DOOR CHRISTMAS in a strong, upright hand Abby recognized as Jacob's. Mary's husband had been a meticulous man. Abby looked around and thought of how unhappy he would be at the state of this cluttered shed. She needed the ladder to get to the decorations, but it was wedged in behind the lawnmower and the old charcoal barbeque grill she and Mary had abandoned in favor of the more convenient gas one now on the deck.

Abby sighed. Not such an easy project. She put away her flashlight and closed up the shed. Maybe if she had time later on she'd give it another go. Maybe get her dad to come over and give her a hand with getting the ladder out. But she had higher priorities today and she needed to get a move on.

AS ABBY DROVE into Green Harbor, the Christmas decorations began to capture her attention. She had to admit in all the rush she'd become very unobservant. They'd all become just part of the background to her. But one of the things Tony had talked about as they'd all made divinity together was the beauty of the displays he'd seen on his self-guided walking tour of the town on the day he'd arrived. It had made Abby want to look with fresh eyes.

She turned off her normal route and came in on Harbor Seal Road, paying special attention to the holiday decorations on each house. Beautiful evergreen wreaths and swags featuring bright red bows; lampposts festooned with garland and more bows; shrubbery covered in nets of lights and yard trees sporting string upon string of multicolored bulbs. Several had their outdoor lights on against the gloom of the morning.

The sight of so many candles in windows made Abby catch her breath. It was such a poignant image, particularly in a seafaring town where the loved ones of sailors had for centuries kept a candle burning in the window to light safe passage home from the sea.

Abby slowed as she passed a street just beyond the Medical Center. She looked up the short block, which ended in a turnabout. An involuntary laugh broke the silence inside her car. She glanced in her rearview mirror and quickly flipped on her turn signal.

Tony had told them about this cul-de-sac, and it was everything he'd said it was—and more. Apparently everyone in the neighborhood had gotten together and decided to do this, or perhaps friendly competition had spurred it on and it had just gotten out of hand. Either way, it was a sight to behold. The houses were practically obscured by strings of lights, lawn reindeer, Santas and sleighs and gigantic blow-up snowmen. It was a regular tinsel town. It was tacky beyond belief, and ordinarily Abby would not have approved of such excess, but she thought of what Tony had said about it and she smiled approvingly. "Think of what fun they must be having," he'd said. "Think about all the neighbors out talking to one another in November, planning this. All the adults must feel like children again. And the kids must think it's absolutely magical."

Abby had to agree. Even in daylight hours, the place was enchanting. She would have to be sure to bring Mary back at night to see the spectacle. As she reached the end of the cul-de-sac and turned back toward the street, she caught sight of

Trevor Carlson and his teenaged daughter—what was her name again? Stacey, that was it. Abby knew them both, though not well. They had volunteered to help out with a few projects around the museum and conservatory.

Their house was at the corner of Harbor Seal Road and Pelican Court, just at the entrance—and the exit—for this phenomenal light show.

The two came to the very edge of their yard and Abby slowed as she watched Trevor hammer a short iron stanchion into the ground. As she pulled alongside, he was pounding a spike through a flange at the bottom to stabilize it. Stacey was standing beside him holding a small laminated poster.

Abby slowed to a stop and pushed the button to lower her passenger window. "Hi Trevor, Stacey," she greeted them.

Both went into a crouch and lowered their heads to peer into the car. "Dr. Stanton!" Stacey said. "Hello." She pushed the long blonde hair spilling from underneath her knitted cap back behind her shoulders and came toward the car. Trevor put down the hammer and joined her. "Abby," he said, "Merry Christmas!"

"And to you and yours," Abby said. "This is just amazing," she said, gesturing around the circle. Don't tell me you're adding yet another element to it."

"Not exactly," Trevor said. He turned to his daughter. "Show her the sign, Stacey."

The girl flattened the sign and passed it through the car window. IF YOU HAVE ENJOYED THE LIGHTS, HELP US BRIGHTEN SOMEONE ELSE'S WORLD, it read in colorful marker. ALL PROCEEDS GO TO THE LOCAL FOOD BANK.

Stacey trotted over to fetch the large round popcorn can that had been sitting on the ground beside the stanchion.

"Dad's gonna mount that on the post," she said as she came back and resumed her crouch. "And see here, there's a slit cut in it so people can make a donation if they want. I'm going to tape the sign right to the can."

"What a great idea!" Abby said, passing the sign back to her.

"Yeah, it is, isn't it?" Trevor said. "Wish I could say we had this in mind all along, but the truth is, we were just all having fun here. It started off as a lighthearted rivalry between two of us and just spread. Guess we're all just going through a second childhood or something. We hadn't thought of it much beyond that. But then a couple of days ago this young man who's here on a visit came by . . ."

Abby put up a hand to stop him. "Don't tell me. Let me guess. He was tall with blond, curly hair, right?"

"Yes, how did you know?" Stacey asked. "Do you know Tony?"

"I do," Abby said, shaking her head in wonder. "So this was all his idea?"

"Well, not exactly," Trevor said, frowning. "I mean he didn't suggest it, but I guess he got us to thinking how we might make it benefit someone else. And this is what we came up with."

"Well, it's a great idea," Abby said, reaching into her vest pocket. She folded a five-dollar bill and passed it to Stacey. "Let me be the one to start it off."

"Thanks," Stacey said, feeding the bill through the slot.

"I'll let you get back to work," Abby said, putting the car back into gear. "And I'll spread the word."

Abby drove away, still smiling.

Her first stop in town was the marina. She parked and pulled a large sack filled with strings of lights and batteries from the back of the car. She slipped her key into a vest pocket and headed out to deliver the goods to her father and little Bobby McDonald. The two of them had gotten it into their heads that they were going to rig up her father's humble fishing boat for the annual parade of boats on Christmas Eve. And their plans were growing ever more grandiose as the days went by.

Abby enjoyed the stroll down to the dock, the crisp air made her nose tingle and put some pep in her step.

Out of the corner of her eye she caught sight of a bird sailing in and coming to rest on the water just down from the dock. She quickly snatched her small folding binoculars from a breast pocket and trained them on the spot. This was a skill beginning birders had to practice—that of getting the target bird into the field of sight and adjusting their eyes. But to Abby it was second nature. She focused in on the small, short-tailed bird and smiled.

Yes, it was indeed a short-tailed shearwater. These birds were rare in the San Juans aside from certain "invasion" years when they made forays into the waters and were seen regularly for a season.

This was exciting. A birder from the last group that had visited the island around the first of November had thought that he'd seen a short-tailed shearwater. He hadn't been sure enough to report a sighting, but he'd told Abby about it.

Abby watched the bird for a few more minutes until the noise of a boat motor starting up frightened it to flight. She saw the uniform pale coloring of the underwings and confirmed the identification. She drew out her notebook and made a notation. Yet one more thing to add to her job list, but a welcome one. A count of a rare shearwater invasion.

Her father and Bobby were so involved in what they were doing they didn't even hear her greeting when she approached.

She stood on the dock for a moment, the heavy sack dangling from her hand and cleared her throat theatrically until they both turned to look at her.

"How's it going?" she asked.

"Well, we've hit a few snags, but we're getting there," her father said.

"Just wait," Bobby said. "It'll be the best one when it's all done."

His words were strong, but Abby sensed some tension in her young friend. "Are you okay, Bobby? You look a little frustrated."

"Well, I guess I am a little," he said, picking up a tablet of graph paper from the seat of the boat and passing it over to her. "We've got the plan all figured out, but we just can't get it all to work. But we won't give up and I think we can still take the prize. Right Mr. Stanton?"

"We'll certainly do our best, Bobby," her father answered.

Abby looked at the diagram Bobby handed her. It involved a complex network of pipes and wire that would be used to suspend lights in a latticework all around the boat.

"Rube Goldberg would be proud," she mumbled under her breath. But it wasn't quite far enough under to escape Bobby's sharp ears and overactive curiosity.

"Who's Ruby Goldberg?" he asked.

"Rube Goldberg," her father answered. "He's a fellow who used to make cartoon drawings of complicated contraptions that were way more complex than they had to be to do simple tasks. I think Abby's teasing us a little."

"Maybe just a little," Abby said, a smile playing around her lips as she handed the tablet back to Bobby. "In any case, here are the lights and batteries you asked for." She stepped closer to the vessel and used her fingertip to flick one of the wires stretched taut to suspend the strands of lights, making it sing. "You know, if this thing keeps growing, you're going to have to allow some room on the boat for a portable generator to power all the lights."

Her father and Bobby looked at one another, then down at the drawing, and back to one another again. They each gave a knowing nod.

"Oh, for pity's sake, I was kidding," Abby said. She rolled her eyes, but they ignored her. "Well, good luck to you. Carry on," she shrugged and turned to go. She got two halfhearted waves in return and was almost to the end of the dock before she heard them call out in unison, "Thank you, Abby!"

She lifted her hand in a backward wave and reached into her vest pocket for her shopping list. First she'd hit Beach Bag Books to get a WWII biography for her father, then she'd walk over to In Stitches for some knitting supplies for Mary. Her step was light and she strolled along feeling a premature sense of accomplishment. Then her phone rang. She stopped short and fished it out of her pocket, frowning down at the number on the display. Abby still sometimes felt like she was on a leash with this cell phone and she guarded the number jealously. The readout showed Mary's cell and Abby clicked it on immediately.

"Mary, is everything okay?"

"Yes, everything's fine, Abby," Mary answered. "But what are you up to right now?"

"I'm just walking up from the marina and on my way to do some Christmas shopping. Why? Do you need something?"

"Could you come by the church for a few minutes, please? Patricia and I would like to show you something."

"Can it wait until lunchtime?" Abby asked thinking of her list, still unblemished by checkmarks.

"Well, it's kind of important," Mary answered. "It should only take a few minutes, but I think you'll be really interested in this."

Abby sighed. "Okay, I'm on my way."

She closed the phone and put it back in her pocket. She did an about-face and headed toward Little Flock Church, picking up her pace. Mary had probably found something adorable in the craft contributions that she wanted to show her—most likely something with birds on it. But if it made Mary happy, Abby could certainly take a few minutes to give her that satisfaction. Abby thought of her mother's oft-heard admonition never to get so busy that we take care of things and shortchange people.

Abby arrived at the church hall slightly winded. She found a couple of volunteers busy pricing items and putting them back into a series of cardboard boxes. But she saw no sign of Mary or Patricia.

"Corrine?" Abby called to one of the volunteers. "Do you know where Mary and Patricia are? They just called wanting me to come over to look at something." Abby frowned and looked around the room as if Mary and Patricia might be hiding somewhere.

"Patricia and Mary are in the storeroom," she said, pointing toward the door at the end of the room. "They've been in there for a while."

Now Abby's curiosity was aroused. What in the world would Mary and Patricia be doing in the storeroom? Nothing they needed for the craft fair was there. The tables and chairs were all kept in racks that were left at the far end of the recreational room, and the everyday supplies were in the kitchen.

Abby opened the door and called out. She saw Mary and Patricia in the dim circle of light provided by one bare bulb. The room smelled musty and was chockablock with old church furnishings and cardboard boxes.

Mary and Patricia were staring at an old pew that was turned with the backside toward the door. They were both obviously intent on whatever was there and were engaged in a murmured conversation.

"Hi Abby," Mary called when she caught sight of her. "Come around here and look at these. You won't believe it!"

Abby positioned herself alongside the two women and almost gasped when she saw what they were looking at. Several paintings in gilded frames were set up along the length of the pew. Each featured an angel and each possessed some transcending quality that seemed to steal Abby's breath away.

"Oh my," Abby said.

"Exactly," Mary said.

Abby looked down the row again. They were obviously all by the same artist. They were unsigned, but the style was distinctive.

"Someone donated these for the craft sale?" Abby asked, incredulously.

"No, no," Patricia said, waving both hands in a crisscross fashion. "We found them. Way back here in the storeroom behind all these old pews." She pointed back to the darkest corner of the storage room and Abby noticed that Patricia's turtleneck and jeans were covered with dust and a couple of cobwebs clung to her auburn hair.

"We came in here to see if we could get to one of the pews

fairly easily. We thought maybe a couple of the men could put it against the wall so people at the sale next week would have a place to sit and rest a bit," Mary said. "But when Patricia pushed the end of that pew out"—Mary pointed toward the pew closest to the door,—"something fell back there behind that last one, like a domino reaction."

"I wanted to make sure I hadn't broken anything," Patricia said with a sigh. "We've really got to get some volunteers together and get in here to clean and organize this room," she said dusting off her hands, then noticing the state of her clothing and swiping at it industriously. "There's no telling what all is in here."

"Were these just stuck back there?" Abby asked, still marveling at the paintings. She bent down and squinted at the brushwork and ran her fingers along the gilt frames.

"Well, they were in a box, and carefully wrapped," Patricia said, "But the box was old and tattered. When it fell it caught on the edge of that box of old hymnals and ripped. I wanted to make sure the contents were okay, and that's when we found these."

"Any idea where they came from? I don't remember ever seeing these. Do you Mary?"

"No, and I would definitely have remembered them. There's something about them. . . ." she let her voice trail off.

"I know what you mean," Patricia said, her voice sounding far away as she gazed at the paintings with the same dreamy look in her eye. She shook her head as if to break the spell and brushed back a few strands of lush red hair that had escaped from her ponytail. She found the cobwebs and startled, picking them out with a few rapid plucks.

"Mary, this is really more your area than mine," Abby said,

squatting down beside the pew to get an even closer look. "You're more into art. You don't recognize the artist?"

"No, not at all," Mary said. "And I definitely would have taken note of an artist who does this kind of work. I am just captivated by these paintings. I know most of the local artists and these are not from any of them. At least not the contemporary ones."

"Maybe there's something in the church records about where they came from," Abby offered, turning to Patricia.

"Yes, I thought of that. I'll definitely look into it. I'll have Janet help me. She knows the records better than I do, of course. But they've been back there a good long time judging by the amount of dust and grime on the box."

"Good idea to get Janet on this," Abby said. "She has a handle on most everything that goes on around here. She's been church secretary for a long time. Though maybe not as long as these have been around." She rose and dusted off her own hands. "Well, good luck with it. Thanks for asking me over to look at them."

"That's it?" Mary asked. "You're not going to help us?"

"Help you what?" Abby asked.

"Help us find out about them," Mary answered, exasperation creeping into her voice.

"Well, as I said, Mary, this is more your area of expertise than mine. I mean, I'll be glad to help search through the newspaper records or the library or whatever. . . ."

"Look at the paintings again," Mary commanded softly.

Abby raised her eyebrows, but then bent down and examined each painting more carefully. Each one featured an angel in some earthly environ. The posture of each was different as was the wonderfully detailed background. Abby squinted as she passed along the line, studying each painting. Then it came to her. Each painting featured one species of bird and one only.

"That's significant, don't you think?" Mary asked.

"Could be," Abby allowed. "I have to admit I don't have much bird symbolism on the tip of my tongue. My work, as you well know, is more scientifically centered on the biological bird, not the symbolic one. But I can certainly do some research and see what the lore is about each of these species. Maybe *that's* why these painting seem so powerful to me. Even though I wasn't really consciously aware of the birds, I must have sensed them somehow."

"That could be," Patricia said, "But they affected Mary and me the same way, and while I think we both like birds," she said, raising her eyebrows to Mary, who nodded, "we're not into them the way you are," Patricia continued. "I think there's just something inherently mesmerizing about these paintings. I can't wait to show them to James."

"Where is Rev. James?" Abby asked. "Maybe he'll know something about where they came from."

"I've already called him," Patricia said, holding up her cell phone. "He was on his way to the Medical Center to visit a church member. James didn't know a thing about the paintings. He's eager to see them when he gets back."

"Well, one thing's for certain," Abby said, drawing her notebook from her vest. "They don't belong in here gathering dust."

"Indeed," Patricia said. "And if I have anything to say about it, they won't be for much longer."

Abby went down the row. She pointed at each painting with her pen and wrote down the species of bird featured. "I'll research that part of it for you and let you know what I find out."

"Great," Mary said. "I told Patricia, if anybody can get to the bottom of this, it's you, Abby. As you've proven time and again, if there's a mystery to be solved, you're just the one to call."

"I'm afraid my reputation in that area is highly overrated," Abby said. "It's just an occupational hazard. For a scientist, an unanswered question presents a challenge, especially when it concerns your own area of expertise."

"That's why I knew we had you," Mary said, reaching over to grab Abby's wrist. She turned her attention back to the paintings. "These beautiful angels and all the little birds. What are they trying to tell us?"

CHAPTER ❦ FOUR

REVEREND JAMES' SONOROUS voice rose from the front of the church. Even when he was making simple announcements, his warm smile and infectious manner gave each small bit of information a special significance.

"First, let me urge everyone to stay for the potluck over in the hall in just a few minutes," he said. He held up his hands and wiggled them in the air. "We're going to have some fun. Good food, the singing of all our favorite carols *and* the children will bring their gifts for the angel tree. That's always so beautiful to see," he said, raising his arms up high. "Each of the children has taken an angel tag from the tree and agreed to make some sacrifice so that a less fortunate child can have a good Christmas. And they've done an outstanding job. Wait until you see how eager our young people are to share. It's a beautiful thing."

Next, with the same enthusiasm and pride, he reminded everyone about the holiday craft fair that would begin on Monday. "The whole community has come together for this one," the Reverend James said. "We've gotten contributions from all over the island. The proceeds from this will go to a fund for repairs to the church and for holiday gift baskets for those in need this Christmas. So come over and do some Christmas shopping next week. You can find some outstanding gifts for your friends and family, and help out a wonderful cause at the same time."

Everyone was beginning to stir in the pews, anticipating the final hymn as Reverend James turned and started to exit the pulpit. But instead of taking his place for the recessional, he walked over to the choir loft and retrieved something. He walked to the center aisle and propped a large frame on the floor by his leg, the back of the picture toward the congregation.

He related the story of how Mary and Patricia had found the paintings in the storeroom. "We've got a mystery on our hands here, folks. And we'd appreciate it if anyone who knows anything about these beautiful angels would share the information with Patricia or with Abby. We'll have the paintings over at the potluck so everyone can get a good look at them," he said as he lifted the one he had chosen and turned it around. "Here's a preview of one of them, and each and every one is just as beautiful as this one."

There was the low rumble of conversation as people craned their necks to see the angel. It was the one featuring the dove. Abby noticed a transfixed look come upon faces of the people near her. They smiled and turned to one another, talking in low voices.

When services were over, Abby helped Patricia arrange the paintings on the pew the two of them had wrestled out of the storage room the previous day.

Patricia had carefully dusted the surface of the paintings

and the frames, and that, coupled with the brighter lighting in the hall, allowed Abby to see an even more ethereal quality in the works. And there was something else, too, a familiarity that stayed just beyond Abby's mental grasp.

Laura Keranovic was the first to come over for a closer look. As Abby had done the previous day, Laura got down on eye level with them and moved along the line, studying each for what seemed like a long time. Finally she stood.

"Well, I have no idea who painted these," she said. "But they are exquisite. Truly remarkable."

"That's quite a review, especially coming from a wonderful painter like you," Abby said. "We all admire your work so much. If you say they're special, that really means something."

"This artist has such an interesting style," Laura went on. "It's naïve and yet knowing at the same time. Do you know what I mean?"

Abby tilted her head. "I would never have thought to put it that way, but I think I see what you're saying."

"The attention to detail is really amazing," Laura continued, gesturing with one dainty finger along a section of the first painting's background. "But at the same time, the depictions of the angels are so very simple and direct. As if the artist is saying, 'Look, there are angels right here in front of you, if you'll only allow yourself to see.' I like that. That's what I believe too."

Abby squeezed Laura's small shoulders. The tiny woman was now almost fully recovered from the serious illness that had plagued her for many months. As always, the people of the island had rallied around her and her little family, and had all chipped in to help them through their tough time.

"I know there are angels, Abby," she said, leaning her head

against Abby's. "And there are lots of them right here on Sparrow Island."

"You won't get an argument from me." Abby said.

Others came by to admire the paintings and several made suggestions to Abby about their possible origin. An older gentleman thought maybe he remembered his father talking about a former pastor bringing back some art from a trip to the Holy Land. Abby assured him she'd look into that even though she didn't think it likely, since the birds featured in the paintings were all native to the San Juans.

A middle-aged woman told Abby her mother had mentioned angel paintings that used to hang in the vestibule of the church when she was a small girl. Sadly, her mother had passed away and the woman couldn't remember any details, but she remembered it because her mother had said she'd always been sad that they had been taken down.

"Now I can see why, if these are the same ones," the woman said as she stared at the row of paintings. "These are just fantastic."

"I think so too," Abby said. "I'm no art expert, but they do seem to speak to people."

Someone nudged her elbow and Abby turned to see Rick DeBow standing behind her. "Hi Abby," he said, standing awkwardly up on his tiptoes.

"Hey, Rick. What's up?" Abby asked, wondering why he was standing in such a weird position. "Got somebody who wants to say hello," he said, stepping aside to reveal his daughter Serena who had been hiding behind him.

"Serena!" Abby cried, wrapping the young woman in her arms. "I didn't know you were coming for Christmas. How wonderful to see you! How are you? How long will you be here? How are your classes going?" Serena was working on her Master's degree in dendrology and Abby considered her somewhat of a kindred spirit.

Serena laughed. "One question at a time, Abby. First off, it's wonderful to see you too. And I didn't know I was coming for Christmas either, not until a few days ago."

"I thought you were working on your thesis over the holidays?" Abby said.

"Well, that leads me to your other question. I'm supposed to be on my way to Costa Rica right now for a research project for my thesis, but the forestry station we were supposed to work out of got flooded and they had to evacuate the area, so the project got canceled. So that's when I decided to come up and visit Dad for a few days. Then I've got to get to work trying to line up another project—fast."

"Oh, I'm sorry to hear that," Abby said. "But the upside of it is that you get to spend the holidays here." Abby patted her on the arm. "Try not to worry. Something will turn up, Serena. You'd be a valuable asset to any project. I'll make some calls Monday morning. As you well know, trees are not my area of study, but I can make an inquiry on the conservancy Internet loop at least."

"Thanks, Abby. I'd appreciate that," Serena said. "I'll be beating the bushes—oops, guess that's a bad way for me to put it, considering my specialty." She laughed. "I'm not panicky yet, but I'd sure feel better if I had something arranged. I have my thesis almost written, and I need this project to quantify some of my theories. I'd really like to graduate on time."

"Yeah," Rick said, "that's a concern. But like you say, Abby,

I can't be too sorry this happened. From a selfish point of view, it means I get to have Serena with me for Christmas. I'm just gonna trust the rest will work out."

"Dad twisted my arm a little," Serena said, giving him a sly glance. "Not that I didn't want to see everyone," she added quickly. "But I felt like I needed to stay put and start making calls right away. He convinced me though."

"I told her the phones work just as well from here and that she can even set up a little office in the spare bedroom at the house," Rick said. "This is the best Christmas present I could hope for." He reached over and ruffled the back of Serena's short hair.

Abby's attention was caught by a movement behind Serena and she looked up to see Tony Malachy standing there. "Tony," she said. "Come on over here, there's some people I'd like you to meet."

"Hey Tony," Rick said, turning toward him. "Good to see you again."

"Well," Abby said, "I guess I don't have to introduce you after all."

"Yes and no," Tony said. "I've met Rick, but I haven't had the pleasure," he said, putting out his hand to Serena. "But I'm assuming you're the daughter Rick was bragging about yesterday. He was awfully anxious for you to get here. I'm Tony Malachy."

Serena put out her small hand in return. "You're the one who helped Dad with the light emergency over at The Bird Nest yesterday." She said. "Nice to meet you."

"Yep," Rick said. "This is the guy that bailed me out. Poor Terza was in quite a stew, and without Tony's help I'd never have gotten it all sorted out." He turned to Abby. "You've seen that Martin and Terza have gone all-out for the decorating contest this year? They won last year in the Best Traditional category, but this year they're determined to take the top prize."

"Yes, I've seen how gorgeous the house is. They'd get my vote," Abby said

"Yeah, well, we had a little blackout yesterday. A tree limb went down on that big western hemlock tree out in the backyard. It brushed up against the house and on the way down managed to grab hold of every string of lights just like a grappling hook. I've never seen such a scramble of wires. Course, it broke some of the lines and did in a lot of the bulbs. I had to untangle all the wiring and splice in some new line, and I'd about worn myself out climbing up and down two ladders trying to trace which wire was which. I didn't want to have to take them all down and start all over again. It took me a week to put them up in the first place."

"Tracing those wires was definitely a two-man job," Tony agreed. "But it got done and now it's all magical again. Just like the rest of the island."

"So is this your first time here?" Serena asked.

"Yes," Tony answered, "but I hope not my last. I'd heard about the island all my life and I just finally had to see for myself."

"It took me a while to get Serena up here." Rick said.

"But now he's having trouble keeping me away," Serena interjected quickly. "I fell in love with it. The scenery's beautiful, and of course I'm mad for all the trees. And the people are so warm and welcoming." She looped her arm through Abby's. "Here's a prime example."

Abby smiled and patted Serena's hand. "Who did you hear

about the island from, Tony?" Abby asked, turning her attention back to him.

"Oh, family, friends, a lot of people," Tony said vaguely. He craned to look over Abby's shoulder. "So those are the mystery paintings your Rev. James was talking about. Can I have a closer look?"

"Sure," Abby said, stepping aside. It had not escaped her attention that Tony had just swept aside her question about who had recommended the island to him. Perhaps he simply thought it would be uninteresting to the rest of them, but it sent Abby's antennae up. She always got that feeling when people failed to answer a question directly.

"Wow, these are phenomenal," he said, stepping along the length of the pew and studying each one. "They look really old," he said, almost to himself. His eyes narrowed and he leaned down to examine the canvas, his nose just inches away. "So, no idea who painted them or where they came from?" he asked as he stood up at last.

"Not yet," Abby said. "And yes, I think they must be old. My parents don't remember ever having seen them and my mother would have noticed. She's drawn to anything depicting angels."

"Are your parents island natives?" Tony asked.

"No, but almost," Abby answered. "We all moved here when Mary and I were very small girls. And much as it pains me to say it, that was a long time ago."

"So your folks probably know just about everyone on the island I'll bet," Tony said. "I hope I'll have a chance to meet them."

"Absolutely," Abby said. "In fact, if Serena and Rick will excuse us, we'll go find them now."

Rick and Serena waved them off with promises to catch up to Abby later. Abby made a beeline for her mother, eager to introduce her to Tony. Ellen Stanton was one of the most perceptive people on the planet and a wonderful judge of character. Abby wanted to see how she reacted to Tony.

She spotted her mother helping one of the little boys load his plate with a mound of macaroni and cheese. He was wearing a suit and a little red bowtie and his hair had been tamed into submission with some sort of gel. He looked up at Ellen Stanton and revealed a gap-toothed grin. As they got closer, Abby heard her mother say, "Now don't forget to leave some room on that plate for a nice big cookie or a slice of cake."

"Soft touch," Abby teased as the little boy moved toward one of the tables that had been set up for the children. He held his plate with both hands and took halting little steps so as not to dump everything off onto his dress-up clothes.

"You'd be charmed too," Ellen said, wrinkling her nose. "Isn't he the cutest thing?"

Abby had to agree. She pulled Tony up beside her and resolved to use her very best observation skills to tune into any nuances that might be telling in the social niceties between her mother and Tony.

"Tony," her mother said after Abby had made the introductions. "Mary and Abby told me what a wonderful time you all had baking together the other night. It's so nice to meet you."

"Pleasure's all mine, Mrs. Stanton," Tony said.

The conversation repeated much as it had when Abby had introduced Tony to Serena. Abby noted that when her mother asked the obvious question about who had told him so much about the island, Tony again made a vague comment that deflected the question.

"Oh, sometimes it seems like I'm the only one around who hasn't been to Sparrow Island. Everyone who comes here just loves it and can't wait to talk about it."

Within minutes Tony had her mother engaged in an animated conversation about the history of the island. Abby stood there listening intently, but it all seemed perfectly natural. When Tony asked when the lighthouse was built, Ellen said, "You know, I can't answer that, but I know who can. Let me take you and introduce you to Opal Collins. She knows quite a lot about Wayfarer Point Lighthouse."

Ellen turned to Abby. "Dear, you'd better go back over and mingle with the folks looking at the paintings. Somebody might be able to tell you something. I'll introduce Tony around."

Tony gave Abby a radiant smile, then turned back to her mother. "I'd like that, Mrs. Stanton. I'd really like that."

Abby returned to her post and listened to another round of speculation from various people about where the paintings might have originated. Frank Holloway looked at them, making a humming sound as he passed down the row.

Finally he approached Abby shyly. "You know, I can't be sure, and maybe I'm just wanting to make it so, but I believe I recognize the background in a couple of these. I think whoever did them must have been from here or at least have known the island well."

"Really?" Abby asked. "Why don't you show me?"

"Well, this one here, it looks to me like the view from Arrowhead Hill out toward Paradise Cove, looking southeast. This would have been long before The Nature Museum and the conservatory went in. It was a wilder looking place back then."

Abby regarded the painting, "Yes, yes, I see what you mean," she said. "I remember going out there when I was young, and

I think that's similar to the view I remember. 'Course my memory's a little fuzzy. That's a long time back," she said.

Frank smiled. "Not as long for you as for me," he said. "And as I say, I may be just wanting to see something familiar, but honestly . . ." he said, his voice trailing off as he stared at another of the paintings. He put his fist to his face and nibbled on his knuckle as he disappeared into thought again. "There's something so familiar about the face of the angels too," he said, at last. "I can't tell you what it is, but *something*."

"You're not the first to say that," Abby told him. "It's obvious that the artist used the same person as the model for all of them. I suppose it's possible he or she just made it up, but I doubt it was entirely out of the imagination. But whichever the case, the angel looks the same in each. I mean obviously, except for the way it's posed in each painting. And several people say it looks like someone they ought to know. But no one can quite think of who it might be."

"Well, I'll sure be interested to hear what you find out, Abby," Frank said before ambling over to join the carolers. "We're depending on you to solve another mystery for us, I guess," he said as he looked back over his shoulder.

Abby got something to eat, then watched as the children marched in with their gifts for the angel tree, singing in their reedy little voices, *Joy to the World, the Lord is come.*

The little boy who had captured her mother's heart had sucked in as much air as his tiny lungs would hold and was singing with everything he had in him. One lick of hair had rebelled against the gel and was sticking straight up in front. As he placed his beautifully wrapped present under the tree, he turned to his mother and gave her a very enthusiastic thumbs-up, pumping his hand in the air a couple of times. She put her hand over her eyes momentarily as people around her stifled a laugh, but then she smiled at him and blew him a kiss off her fingertips.

Abby worked her way back around the room and found Serena, Rick and Tony laughing and talking with Mary.

"What am I missing out on over here?" Abby asked as she approached them. "You all are having fun without me."

"I was just telling Rick that I'm more than a little jealous that he gets to have Serena here with him for Christmas and that he'll have to share her with us," Mary said.

Her voice was light, but Abby knew that there was real sadness behind it.

"Tony, I assume Mother took good care of you," Abby said.

"You better believe it," Tony said, "I think she introduced me to half the population of the island. Now if I can only remember all their names. You two have a remarkable mom."

"We sure think so. She's been a wonderful example to us in so many ways. Not the least of which is the way she looks after her friends," Mary said before turning to Abby. "Speaking of which, I've already made up a plate for Goldie Landon and put it in the refrigerator in the kitchen. We mustn't forget to take it over to her when we leave."

"Is Goldie sick?" Rick asked. "I can't believe she'd miss this," he nodded toward the activity and merriment going on in the room.

"She's been under the weather," Abby said. "I think she's feeling better, but she didn't want to risk carrying some bug to others, so she stayed home today."

"Goldie?" Tony said. "That's a name you don't hear much anymore."

"No, I guess not," Mary said. "But in her day I think it was pretty common."

"So, is she an elderly lady?" Tony asked. "Those flu bugs can be rough on the elderly. Does she have someone to take care of her?"

"Well, first off," Mary said with a laugh, "never let Goldie hear you call her elderly. She's a woman of a certain age, as they say, but she is one tough cookie. She lives by herself. But she's no frail little old lady. She raises flowers in a greenhouse and lifts and totes all day long and is usually healthy as a horse. She thinks she picked up this bug when she went over to the mainland to pick up some cuttings last week."

"That's too bad," Rick said. "I hope she'll be okay and able to get out to some of the other Christmas activities."

"Yes," Tony said. "I hope so too. She sounds like an interesting lady. I'd like to meet her."

"I'm sure she'll be fit as a fiddle by Christmas," Mary said.

Tony said his good-byes and left to go back to The Bird Nest saying he'd promised Terza he'd help her with the evening meal since Martin, too, was a bit under the weather.

"He helps out any more around that place, Terza and Martin are going to have to pay *him* to stay there," Rick said after Tony had gone.

"He seems really nice," Serena said. "The way you described him, Dad, I thought he'd be kind of loud and boisterous because you talked about how friendly he was. But he's not that at all. He's quiet, but there's just something about him that's so familiar, like a good friend from high school you haven't seen in a while, or your favorite cousin or something." She looked up to find the rest of them staring at her.

"Yes," Mary said. "That's a good way to put it Serena. He seems like someone you already know and like."

Abby stared at the doorway Tony had just gone through. He was either a remarkable young man, or they were all being bamboozled and he had an ulterior motive for his keen interest in people. Particularly, Abby noted, the older women on the island.

Despite her determination to open her heart to this young man, she couldn't keep the red flags from popping up every time she talked to him. She sighed. She would most certainly give Tony hospitality, but her trust was another thing all together. That had to be earned.

CHAPTER ❦ FIVE

TONY GAZED OUT THE window of his room at The Bird Nest, down onto the quaint little town of Green Harbor. It was just coming alive with the bustle of a new week beginning. He still found it hard to believe how friendly everyone had been. It was just as he'd always heard. But he hadn't really believed it could be this way. Not in the real world.

He was very pleased with the progress he'd made so far. He looked at the list he'd left on the antique desk in the corner of his room. He'd met six of the women already, and he'd found out information about another four of them. Plus he'd learned of three more he'd never heard of before he came here. He'd added those to his list as well.

But the hottest lead was those paintings. He somehow sensed they might be the key to everything. He hoped Abby Stanton would get to the bottom of that mystery quickly. And he hoped that when she did find out something, she'd be in a sharing mood.

ABBY ARRIVED at the Sparrow Island Museum and Conservatory bright and early on Monday morning. There was still much to do before the open house.

Wilma Washburn was at her desk. Abby gave her a quick wave before dashing into her own office. She powered up her computer and while it was whirring to life she raised the shades to let in whatever natural light her windows could garner on this overcast day.

As she unloaded her bag, she frowned at the small notebook that held her to-do list. She'd gotten so sidetracked by Mary and Patricia's discovery of the paintings on Saturday that she hadn't earned a single checkmark. She would go into Green Harbor at lunchtime and knock a couple of items off, she decided. It wouldn't take that long.

She spent the next half hour on the business of the day, emptying her e-mail box and opening her mail. She double-checked the list of invitations that had gone out for the open house to make sure they hadn't omitted anyone. Everyone on the island was invited, of course. She and Hugo had done that via a blanket invitation in newspaper advertisements and flyers posted at all the businesses and services. But personal invitations had gone out to donors and professional associates on the other San Juan Islands and on the mainland.

Abby checked the RSVPs against the invitations and saw that six people had not replied. With the mail services so over-loaded with Christmas cards and packages she feared the invitations might not have reached their destinations, so she called each one personally. She learned that three planned to attend and had simply failed to return their cards. But, as Abby feared, the last three had not received the invitations and were happy to get Abby's call.

The last on the list was Will Unger, a freelance wildlife illustrator who visited the island often and who had donated several prints of his illustrations to the museum.

"I'm not sure if I can get out for the open house, Abby," he said. "But I'll sure try. You know Madeleine and I would both love to see everyone. And the kids would love it. But, I'll have to check in with her to see what's on the family docket. I'll let you know."

"That's not necessary, Will," Abby said. "I just wanted to make sure you knew about it. I'm sorry the invitation didn't reach you. We'd love to see you all if you can come. If not, we'll hope to see you again sometime soon."

"I tell you what, we'll do our best," Will said. "It's been a while since I've seen a Sparrow Island Christmas. And you all certainly know how to do it up in grand style. Everyone knows that!"

They chatted a bit longer and before hanging up, Abby told him once again she hoped to see him and his family at the open house. As she put the phone into the cradle, she stared at it for a good long while, lost in thought.

Will was from Spokane, the same place Tony was from. And he'd used almost the same turn of phrase Tony had used when referring to how he learned of Sparrow Island. What had Will said—everybody knows about a Sparrow Island Christmas? It didn't sound cagey at all coming from him. Yet her antenna had gone up when Tony had said virtually the same thing.

Why? Abby examined her conscience. Could it be that she was mistrustful of Tony simply because of his age? She'd never believed she had that bias in her, but maybe it was there in her subconscious somewhere awaiting a chance for treachery.

What were the facts? What did any of them really know

about Tony? Abby searched her memory, trying to remember each conversation. What did Tony do for a living? That's usually one of the first things you find out when you meet someone new. Had she failed to ask the question, or had he slid past it the way he had when asked about who'd recommended the island to him? Abby flipped her notebook to a blank page and started a list. Tony was here as a gift from someone. Who? No idea. He hadn't said specifically. Did he have a family? No clue. He'd mentioned no one by name, though he'd alluded to his grandmother. Nothing about what he did for a living. She wrote down that he was from Spokane, but then added a big fat question mark after it. Even that wasn't for certain.

He knew so much about them and they knew so little about him. But on the other hand, what had he done to deserve her wariness? Nothing. In fact just the opposite was the case. Everywhere Tony went, good feelings and happy outcomes seemed to sprout up like mushrooms from the fecund forest floor.

Not for the first time since Tony Malachy's arrival on the island Abby felt herself caught in an internal war. She felt, on the one hand that she was an optimistic and open person. She expected the best of people and she made friends easily. Moreover, she *kept* her friendships once they'd been established, even the long distance ones. She was a dedicated letter writer, though she'd succumbed more and more to the immediacy of e-mail in recent times. And her phone bills certainly reflected her dedication to the friends she'd left behind in New York.

But she was also a scientist. Had been for a lot of years now. And during all her years of doing fieldwork and working in the laboratory at Cornell, she had trained herself in the disciplines of her work. Inquiry, testing and verification were hardwired into her brain. Anything that stood out from the norm was going to get her attention. And Tony Malachy definitely stood out from the norm. But the fact was that his abnormality was *niceness*.

Abby went to her window and stared longingly out at the conservatory. How she'd love to be out on one of the trails right now. Then she closed her eyes, quieted her mind and said a fervent prayer for guidance and wisdom.

Abby thought back to her conversation with Mary the previous day as they were driving out to take Goldie her meal from the potluck. It made her a little ashamed to remember it.

Abby had asked Mary whether she thought Tony's interest in Goldie was a bit odd. Mary had given her a look Abby knew all too well. The big sister look. Abby had been on the receiving end of it all her life. It was part bemusement and part exasperation.

"I'm serious, Mary," she'd said, firmly. "You don't think it's unusual that he was that interested in Goldie's age and circumstances, and even her name! That doesn't seem strange to you?"

"Abby," Mary had replied evenly, now bringing out the big sister tone as well. "Think about it. If you heard about a woman of Goldie's age living way out here all by herself with nothing for companionship but her flowers and plants most of the time, wouldn't you find that interesting? Wouldn't anyone? Goldie *is* a character, and I mean that in the most affectionate way."

"I guess," Abby had allowed, feeling chastised. But as the familiar scenery of the island rolled by outside her window, she thought back to all of Tony's inquiries about people on the island. So many questions. Was it really just friendly curiosity?

The phone on Abby's desk rang, snapping her back to the present. She fielded the call from the caterer for the open house, then glanced at her watch. She was shocked to see that it was almost lunchtime. Where had the morning gone? She leafed through her Rolodex—one more task to accomplish before she could head into Green Harbor.

As promised, she'd make some calls on Serena's behalf. Forestry was outside her area of expertise, but she had a few contacts in the field and Serena needed all the help she could get.

A tap at the door made Abby look up and she was surprised to see Wilma Washburn standing there when the door swung open. In all the time Abby had been at the museum, she couldn't remember a time when Wilma had come back to her office. If she needed to tell Abby something she usually did it by interoffice phone.

"Am I interrupting?" Wilma asked.

"No, Wilma, come on in," Abby said, trying to keep the question out of her voice. "I was just looking up some numbers to make a couple of calls before I break for lunch. What's up?"

"Oh, I just wanted to see how you were doing." Wilma said. "I was thinking about our conversation last week about how stressed out we both were about getting Christmas things done."

"Well, funny you should say that," Abby said. "I didn't make much progress this weekend, so I'm going to dash into Green Harbor in a few minutes and see if I can't get some shopping done on my lunch hour. How about you?"

"I'm great," Wilma said, taking a step forward. "Really, great. I guess that's sort of what I wanted to share with you. I've still got a list as long as your arm, but I've got a new attitude about it. It just came to me all of a sudden at dinner the other night when Tony came to eat with us. I had my whole family there, except Artie. I was hoping he could come, but he was on duty. We had just a simple meal, and Tony asked all kinds of questions about the island. He kept telling us how lucky we are to live here and to have family around. And it came to me that he was so right. This is what it's all about, just sharing our lives, not all the craziness. He's such an insightful young man."

"Yes, that seems to be everyone's reaction to him," Abby said, determined to keep her doubts to herself. "I must tell you, I was a little surprised when you invited him for supper. I mean, since it came right on the heels of us talking about feeling overwhelmed and all. That was really nice of you."

"You're not the only one who was surprised," Wilma said. "I surprised myself. But he was just so interested in knowing more about the island and about tribal life that I just got carried away."

"But you had a good time?" Abby asked.

"Oh, we had a wonderful time. It was so relaxing. It made me realize that right here on Sparrow Island you can find everything that Christmas is all about practically every day of the year. So what if I don't get the baking all done or the wrappings all perfect? We're all together and happy and healthy and we have so much to be grateful for."

"I can't argue with that," Abby said.

"Anyway," Wilma said, stepping backward toward the door. "You go into town to shop, but take some time to enjoy the decorations and being out in the fresh air and, well, all of it," she said, wagging a maternal finger at Abby before trundling back to the doorway. "That's what I wanted to tell you."

"I'll do that, Wilma," Abby said, trying to keep the stunned expression off her face. "Thanks for the reminder," she added as Wilma closed the door with a soft thud.

Abby sat, trying to take everything in. *Who was that woman and what did she do with the real Wilma?* she thought. This was the most effusive Abby had ever known her to be. And while Abby was very fond of Wilma, *chatty* and *cheerful* were words she would never have used to describe her before today.

She was positively jubilant. Would wonders never cease? Abby smiled. If Tony Malachy was responsible for this remarkable transformation, he was a special guy indeed.

ON THE DRIVE into Green Harbor, Wilma's words came back to Abby. She would, she vowed to herself, enjoy this outing. She thought back to when she was a child and recalled all the joy she'd felt in making or purchasing gifts for her parents and Mary, or for her friends. She'd been equally excited about seeing their reactions when they opened her gift to them as she was about opening her own.

She'd once bought her mother a china teacup and saucer at a discount store when her father had taken her and Mary to Seattle to Christmas shop when they were little. She had thought that cup and saucer set was the most beautiful thing she'd ever seen, and *very* classy—like something a titled Lady might use at an English tea party. And she was sure her mother would find it elegant. The cup had a tulip shape with a tiny foot on the bottom that fit into the dimple of the saucer. There was a rosebud on the side of the cup and it had a dainty multi-angled handle. Both the cup and the saucer had a gold painted rim.

Her mother had beamed with pleasure when she'd opened

it, and as Abby had hoped she'd insisted on using it for her coffee on Christmas morning.

It wasn't until much later in life that Abby came to realize it was a cheap set of souvenir bric-a-brac of the kind you'd find in any five-and-dime store or tourist trap shop.

Her mother still had the set and kept it in a place of honor alongside her own mother's fine china in the dining room cabinet at Stanton Farm. As an adult, Abby had once given her mother her blessing to get rid of it.

"I'd never dream of such a thing," her mother had informed her. "And you should know better than to suggest it. Your desire to please me transformed that little cup into the most priceless porcelain in the world on that Christmas morning. And every time I've looked at it over all the years you were away, it's made me feel happy and close to you. I'll cherish it forever."

Suddenly Abby was excited about her shopping again, no longer thinking of it as a chore, but as a treat. Wilma's new attitude was contagious.

Her first stop was at In Stitches to buy yarn and a new knitting bag for Mary. She browsed, trying to select colors that would please Mary. Their tastes were as opposite as their personalities. Mary preferred bright colors and lots of shine and sparkle, while Abby went for naturals and muted shades.

The rows of colored yarns, threads and flosses were pleasing to the eye and Abby was enjoying both the sight and the tactile feel of each as she made her choices.

As she moved from one rack to another she couldn't help but overhear some of the conversation of the Busy Bee Quilters who were there finishing up the quilt they'd made to be raffled off during the craft fair.

Abby's ears perked up when she heard Beverly Hodges say, "My mother-in-law will never be convinced it's anything other than a miracle. She swears she was driving by the square on her way home last night and she saw an angel. Out by the clock. And you all heard the clock is running again, right? After all these years."

"I heard that. Isn't that the strangest thing?" one of the other quilters said.

"Maybe the town decided to finally have it fixed, I don't know," Beverly said. "But as far as my poor mother-in-law is concerned, she's put two and two together and I'm afraid maybe she's gotten six. There was a light drizzle and it was after dark, so who knows what she saw. I hate to even think about it, but maybe it's time for Tom and me to talk to her about not driving at night anymore."

Abby frowned. Corrine Hodges was getting up in age, but she seemed perfectly competent. And as far as Abby knew she was a pragmatic woman, not at all given to flights of fantasy. What *had* she seen out in the park?

Corrine had been one of the people who had looked longest and hardest at the angel paintings yesterday. Maybe she'd just had angels on her mind when she saw whoever—or whatever—it was she saw later that night.

Abby resisted the urge to go over and nose in and start asking questions. She didn't want to get sidetracked again like she had on Saturday. And anyway, Corrine was a good friend of her mother's and Abby felt sure she'd be hearing more about this episode later.

Abby left In Stitches with a large bag dangling from each hand. She'd earned a checkmark and she felt really good about the choices she'd made for Mary. She couldn't wait to have her open the package on Christmas Day. And she'd have the added joy of watching Mary in the weeks to come as she turned the skeins of yarn into a sweater or an afghan.

Abby came out of the store and looked down the street. She glanced at her watch and calculated. She had a granola bar in her pocket that could pass for lunch. That would leave enough time to do one more errand. She could stop in at *The Birdcall* and have a quick look at the records to see if she could find any information about the paintings. Or she could continue with her shopping.

Much as she wanted another checkmark on her list, the enticement of finding out something about the paintings won out. She put the bags into her car and stepped the short distance down to the newspaper office.

William Jansen, the *Birdcall's* owner and editor-in-chief was sitting at a desk in the front office punching furiously at the keys of his computer. His usual scowl was stitched across his forehead and his lips were moving as he typed.

"Hey, William," Abby called, "any hot news today?"

"Guess you'll have to buy the paper to find out," William said, gruffly.

"You know we always do, William. We read it from front to back, every single week," Abby answered. She wasn't fooled by William's brusque manner. She knew he was a kind man deep down. But he wanted to project the image of an old-time, tough newsman. It was important to him, and Abby always tried her best to make him feel important.

"You're a concerned citizen, Abby. You stay informed. Good for you," William said. "What can I do for you today? You got any tips for me?"

Abby told him about the paintings. "I was wondering if I

could look at your archives. You know, far back," she said, brushing her hand over her shoulder. "See if there's any mention of paintings being donated to the church. Or maybe news of one of the previous pastor's acquiring them. Anything at all that would give me a place to start."

William stood listening closely, his bushy eyebrows working up and down and his mustache twitching.

"You say you found them in the church somewhere?" he asked, whipping out his notebook with a flourish.

"Yes, in the storage room," Abby told him. "I didn't find them. Mary and Patricia Hale did. There are seven of them. They're really beautiful."

William proceeded to do a thorough interview on the subject before telling Abby, "You're welcome to go through the records, but as you well know, this wasn't much of a newspaper before I came along. And Elmira Underwood, God bless her, didn't so much report the news as just the gossip and rumors. And she had a strange sense of what was newsworthy, I can tell you."

"Yes, I do know that, William," Abby said. "I remember some of the stories in the old papers. We're fortunate to have a real newspaper like *The Birdcall* on the island now and to have you at the helm. But maybe there's a chance I could find out *something*."

"Do you have any idea about when the paintings were done or when the church came into possession of them?" William asked as he came around the desk and motioned for Abby to follow him toward a back room.

"No," Abby said. "No idea at all. That's what I'm looking for. Some little bit of information to get me started on the search."

"Well, there's good news and bad news," William said. "The good news is a lot of the back issues have been put on microfiche. The bad news is, they haven't been indexed." He swung a door open wide and bowed low and gave Abby a ladies-first sweep of his hand and she stepped over the threshold into what looked like utter chaos.

"Oh my," Abby said, doing a slow survey of the small room. Three large file cabinets were pushed against the walls and tattered boxes were stacked haphazardly on shelves, tables and on the floor.

"Exactly," William said, nodding slowly. "These are all Elmira's reporter's notes. I've had a couple of high school students in here trying to make some sense out of it, but it's still just one big mess. Elmira wasn't big on a filing system either. All that trouble to put everything on microfiche, but no index—typical Elmira. The students are constructing one. What they've got so far is here," he said, pointing to a notebook open on the table. That's where I'd start. But they're moving backward chronologically, so if you say the paintings are old, they probably haven't gotten that far yet."

"Is there any order at all to the notes?" Abby asked, letting out a sigh.

"Well, it *is* chronological—sort of. At least within each box. That much I can say," William answered. "Beyond that, you're on your own."

Abby thought of everything she had yet to do for the open house and made a clucking sound with her tongue. "I may have to come back when I have more time, William. But if it's okay with you, I'll spend a few minutes trying to get my bearings and figure out how to go about the search when I do get the time," she said.

"Help yourself," William said. "Just make sure you leave everything in order when you're done," he said firmly.

"Order?" Abby said, her voice rising. "How would you *know*?"

William gave a dry cackle as he went back to his desk to jab at his keyboard some more.

After fifteen minutes Abby had learned that Mrs. Underwood was very diligent about dates, that she didn't concern herself too much with research and that she had a strange fascination for abnormalities in garden vegetables and baked goods that caused them to resemble famous people. From Humphrey Bogart's face in a crookneck squash to President Eisenhower in a dinner roll, Elmira had hauled her trusty old Graflex camera out to photograph it and print it in the newspaper.

Elmira kept notes on napkins, Sunday school programs, grocery receipts and sugar sacks. And she filed them all dutifully. It made for some really messy files, but Abby was heartened to see that she'd kept them all. Her notes were cryptic, but given some time, Abby thought maybe she could figure out her pattern. And if the paintings originated here on Sparrow Island and had been made public, Mrs. Underwood would likely have known about it and reported it. If only she had a date to get her started, things would be infinitely easier. She decided to examine the paintings more closely.

Abby exhaled a breath, blowing an errant strand of hair out of her face. She dusted off her hands and made sure she'd left the files she'd looked at just as she'd found them.

"William, I may be back later to look some more if that's okay with you," she said, when she was back out in the main office. "But I need to get back to work now. We've got the

Christmas open house this week, you know. You're coming, aren't you?"

"Oh, you bet," William answered. "I'll be covering it. Come back whenever you want to look in the *morgue*," he said, emphasizing the last word. "That's what we call it on the newspaper you know, not the archives."

"I stand corrected," Abby said with a little bow. "Though that sounds a little creepy."

William laughed his dry laugh again. "Say, I'd like to get going on that story about those paintings. Okay if I drop by the church and take some photos?" he asked, hoisting the camera that had been sitting on the corner of his desk.

"Well, that permission isn't mine to give," Abby said hesitantly. "But I doubt Rev. James would have any objections. Especially if it helps us find out something about where they came from or who painted them."

"I'll call over there now and see if I can get the photos this afternoon," William said, lifting the phone receiver. "Maybe I can get it into this week's edition."

"Thanks, William," Abby said, heading for the door.

"Oh," William called, holding up a hand, "and I'll ask my high school kids to keep an eye out for any mention of this while they're sorting records. Who knows, if these paintings are as extraordinary as you say, maybe Elmira stopped looking for Elvis in a zucchini long enough to do a story on them."

CHAPTER ❦ SIX

Mary had gotten up early and had a quick, no fuss breakfast with Abby. Since Abby had come back to Sparrow Island they had made a special effort to start the week off together. That's when they coordinated their calendars and encouraged one another toward the goals they set for the days ahead. Then they sometimes did a Bible reading together and said a prayer asking for a safe and productive week.

And there was plenty of activity on this week's calendar. The museum open house, the craft sale, the basket project with the children from Little Flock, getting last-minute orders filled for Island Blooms, food to prepare, gift wrapping still to be done, last-minute shopping. The list was long. Mary was feeling a bit overwhelmed by it all until Abby brought out her Bible.

She had chosen the reading of the parable of the growing seed. "This is what the kingdom of God is like. A man scatters seed on the ground. Night and day, whether he sleeps or gets up, the seed sprouts and grows, though he does not know how" (Mark 4:26–27).

This was one of Abby's favorite readings and Mary felt blessed to have her share it. One never knew what small seed of kindness or example during any typical day might serve as an inspiration for others. This was important to remember, especially when times were hectic.

After Abby left for the museum, Mary first thought to go to Little Flock to help set up the craft sale, which was due to open for business at 10:00 AM sharp. But then she realized there wasn't a lot she could do that would be helpful. The boxes were awkward for her to carry in the chair, and she couldn't easily reach to unpack things from the ones on the floor.

There was really no need for her to be there just yet. She'd signed up for the noon to four shift today to collect money, so she wasn't needed until then.

It was situations like this that still made Mary frustrated with her physical limitations. She consoled herself by thinking of all the preliminary things she'd done to get ready for the sale. She'd opened up her home to do collection and pricing. She and Abby had hauled a lot of boxes to the church. Plus she and Patricia had drawn up that diagram for how the tables should be arranged and what would go on each. She'd handed that over to Patricia yesterday and there were plenty of volunteers signed up to help with the setup.

But she felt restless at home. She hadn't wanted to let on to Abby about how down she really was about not seeing the children over the holidays. Intellectually, she knew the circumstances made it impractical for them to make the trip. But her heart had its own agenda. She looked around at her living room. She and Abby had spent a wonderful Saturday afternoon decorating it and it looked beautiful. But it seemed so empty.

Nancy had all but begged her to come there for the holidays, but Mary just couldn't see spending Christmas amidst the palm trees and balmy breezes of Tampa. She didn't like to be away from Sparrow Island for very long at any time of year, but especially at Christmastime.

As for Zack, it was ridiculous for him to spend the money to come out here for such a short stay. And, Abby's teasing aside, Mary had been secretly thrilled when she'd learned that he'd be spending Christmas with Lily. Whether they could see it or not, it was clear to Mary that the two cared very deeply for one another. She saw it in the looks that passed between them and the way one lit up when the other came into the room. It was just the way she and Jacob had looked at one another all those years ago.

Though she didn't exactly believe in love at first sight, when she and Jacob had first met, there had definitely been a spark. She could still remember exactly that low buzz of electricity in the air when they'd first talked and gotten to know one another. She'd been with her parents and Abby. They'd all been aboard the ferry on their way to the mainland to send Abby off to college at Cornell.

Jacob, tall, fit, handsome and somewhat shy, had just finished a visit with his parents who vacationed each summer on Sparrow Island and was heading back to the mainland too.

Mary and Abby had been talking excitedly with their mother about Abby's college courses. Their father had wandered off to visit with a couple of friends he'd seen when they'd boarded the ferry.

Mary and her mother had spent the time double- and triple-checking Abby's supply list and her travel itinerary and trying hard to keep from being teary-eyed at the thought of saying good-bye.

Their father had come back a short time later with Jacob in tow. He introduced him, then told Mary that Jacob was very interested in woodworking and carving, and that he'd started a scrimshaw collection. "Mary here likes all kinds of arts and native crafts," George Stanton had told the young man.

Jacob had sat down to talk, and Mary had felt an immediate attraction to him. He was earnest and serious and, as it turned out, was the perfect balance for Mary's more outgoing personality. At the end of their long discussion on that first day, Jacob had shyly asked if he might write or call Mary.

Mary believed that she had started to love Jacob Reynolds that very day, and she loved him still, even though he had been gone for over a decade. He'd been the victim of a devastatingly fast-acting cancer that had left little time for her to prepare for life without him. All these years later, she still hadn't been able to bring herself to take off her wedding ring.

Her current relationship with Sergeant Henry Cobb of the San Juan Sheriff's Department was different. But it was special in its own way. It was a mature relationship, and both their expectations were tempered by their life experiences and circumstances. She had grown very fond of Henry, more than she liked to admit at times. And she knew he was devoted to her. He proved that over and over.

But still she held back. She often thought things might be different if she wasn't in the chair. She and Henry had only been seeing one another a short time before her accident, and she had tried her hardest to discourage his attentions afterward, feeling it wasn't fair to him to ask him to deal with her limitations. But he had persisted, ultimately convincing her of his sincere regard for her. And Henry certainly seemed to take her physical limitations in stride. He was helpful, but he didn't pander. He encouraged her to do things for herself, and Mary appreciated that.

She hadn't so much fallen in love with Henry as she'd fallen in like with him. At least that's the way it was at first. But their relationship had grown richer and stronger over time. She'd begun to wonder again these days if she was being fair to him. But for different reasons this time. She still felt a loyalty toward Jacob, and she liked the independence of having her own home and her own life apart from Henry. But on the other hand, she couldn't imagine her life without him.

As Rev. James had counseled her when she'd talked with him about her concerns, a relationship at this time of life was bound to be different in nature. After all, she and Henry wouldn't be looking to settle down and raise a family together like she and Jacob had been when they were young and just starting out their adult lives.

That was all behind her now, and it had passed Henry by completely. He had never married, despite the fact that he'd been a handsome young man and had plenty of young women interested in having his attentions. Part of it, Mary supposed, was the job. Law enforcement was difficult for families. Mary knew that full well. She worried about Henry all the time. If she ever doubted how much she cared for him, all she had to do was take her pulse when he was out on a dangerous case.

Henry never pressured Mary. In fact, he'd told her straight out he was content to let her set the pace. She'd never felt that he was unhappy with the way things were. His job was demanding and she thought he liked the fact that she had her own friends and her own interests. But it would be natural for him to want more of a commitment from her. After all, they'd been through a lot together.

Henry had been the first responder to her accident and he'd been the one to wait and pray with her during those first terrible minutes. That had brought them close and they'd grown even closer since. He'd been a tremendous emotional support throughout her rehabilitation and her struggle to learn to live a full life despite her condition. She loved him. There was no doubt about that. It was just hard for her to finally come to accept that she could love someone else without turning her back on Jacob.

She sighed and glanced out her kitchen window. "Finnegan," she said, not looking back at the dog. "What say we go out to see Goldie and see how she's getting along? Make ourselves useful? This house is too, too quiet."

The dog let out a little chuff and came to stand beside Mary's chair, looking out the kitchen window as if to commune with her. Mary reached over to stroke his soft golden fur. It brought her comfort.

"Come on boy," she said, turning her wheelchair toward her room. "Let's go pick out a bright, cheerful sweater for me, and we'll put on your special Christmas cape I made you. And as of now, there's a new rule, no more moping during the holidays."

Finnegan put out his tongue and panted his agreement.

MARY STILL STIFFENED each time she drove past the place where her car had gone off the road on the fateful night of her accident. She clutched the steering wheel of the van until her knuckles turned white and talked to the dog to soothe herself.

"Goldie's going to be happy to see you, boy," she told him. "She always likes a visit from you."

Finnegan let out a noise that was halfway between a growl and a whine, then gave a mighty sneeze.

"Oh, that's nothing to sneeze at, Finnegan," Mary told him with mock solemnity. "I'll let you in on a little secret. Before you came along Goldie didn't even like dogs. But you seem to have that effect on a lot of people. Even me," she added in a whisper.

Mary considered the string of events that had lined up just right to bring Finnegan to her and smiled. Some people would call it a twist of fate or maybe just lucky coincidence. But Mary knew it was God's plan working in her life.

If Zack hadn't gone on the road with the jazz ensemble— and if Lily's brother Jeff, a jazz aficionado, hadn't gone into the club with his service dog, Miles—and if Zack hadn't struck up a conversation with him—and if Jeff hadn't put Zack in touch with Lily to learn more about service dogs—and if Lily hadn't recognized that her charge, Finnegan, would be perfect for Mary—and if Zack, Nancy and Lily hadn't practically coerced Mary into giving Finnegan a try—well, Mary didn't like to think about it. She'd have missed out on so much.

But thanks in large part to the patience and wisdom of her friends and family and to Rev. James' counseling, Mary had opened herself to new possibilities. Finnegan had given her a new lease on life and everyone on the island had fallen in love with him. Even Blossom, who could be quite haughty, had taken to him right away.

Mary supposed the cat was comfortable with her place in the household and hadn't felt threatened by Finnegan. After all, she was a beautiful cat, a white Persian with sparkling blue eyes. And she *knew* she was beautiful. That was evident.

Mary tooted her horn as she pulled up into Goldie's driveway, their traditional arrangement whenever she came to visit. They'd come up with this system because it was difficult to hear inside the greenhouse with the heaters and the fans going and Goldie didn't get a lot of visitors. She and Mary had agreed on this signal so she didn't scare Goldie half to death when she came in on her. She could make out Goldie's form moving around in the greenhouse and was relieved to see that she was out and about. Goldie was a feisty woman, but she was getting up in age and Mary worried about her living out here all by herself.

Goldie came to the door and waved to Mary. "Need any help?" she asked.

"No, I've got it," Mary called back. "Go on about your business, I'll be in there in a few minutes."

This exchange was also part of the traditional arrangement and the familiarity of it made Mary muse on yet another blessing that had come into her life in the guise of a chance meeting aboard the ferry.

She'd first met Goldie one fine spring day several years back when Goldie had been bringing some cuttings back from the mainland to her greenhouse here on the northern part of the island. She and Mary had struck up a conversation during the crossing and discovered their shared interest in flowers. Mary had asked to come out and see the greenhouse, and Goldie had agreed.

Slowly a friendship had started to bloom, along with Goldie's unusual flowers. They'd later formed a business arrangement that benefited them both. Goldie had given Island Blooms the exclusive sales rights to the exotic plants that she grew as a hobby, including several rare varieties of orchids.

But far beyond the business link, their friendship had grown closer and had been a blessing to them both.

Until Mary started coming out to visit, Goldie had become almost a recluse. After years of working clerical jobs in town, she had retired to her family home away from everything and settled into contented solitude with her orchids. But Mary had coaxed her back into church and had slowly enticed her out to social gatherings. Goldie still enjoyed her own company for the most part, but she now took a much more active role in the community.

"Oh, Goldie," Mary said as she wheeled into the greenhouse. "So many pots of Christmas cacti."

"Yes, and so few blooms," Goldie said, using her fingers to knit a strand of white hair back into the braid that ran straight as an arrow down her spine. "I can't understand what's going on with them. I've kept the greenhouse at the precise temperature prescribed to force the blooms and I've nursed the plants along with great care, but they're just being stubborn."

"Well, I guess Mother Nature has her own timetable," Mary said. "And anyway, they're beautiful just as they are."

"That's true," Goldie said, reaching out to run a finger along one of the shoots. "They do have their own kind of primitive beauty. But still, I'd like at least the ones I've promised for the services at the church to be bloomed out by Christmas. And the poinsettias, too. After all, they're called the Christmas star, not the Christmas plant. They're usually foolproof, but they're looking anemic this year also. Maybe I'm losing my green thumb."

"That's impossible," Mary said firmly. "You can get anything to grow. But I came out here to see how you're feeling. You looked a little tired yesterday, but you've got a little pink back in your cheeks today."

"Oh, I'm about back to normal," Goldie said. "How about you, Mary?"

"Oh, I'm fine," Mary said, exhaling a breath she wasn't aware she was holding. "Here, I brought you these," she said, passing a small jar and a cellophane-wrapped loaf of banana bread over to Goldie. "That's a special spiced cider mix in the jar. It's Abby's recipe."

"Do you have time to come in and have a cup?" Goldie asked, searching Mary's face as if something she found there troubled her.

"I don't want to keep you from your work," Mary said, hesitantly. Finnegan countered with a sharp bark and both women laughed.

Goldie assured Mary that she'd done all her chores, and Finnegan fairly pranced as they entered the house. He knew full well that Goldie had taken to keeping his favorite doggie treats and that he'd be given one to enjoy while the women visited.

"ARE YOU SURE you're okay, Mary?" Goldie asked as she pulled two thin slices of the banana bread from her little toaster oven and slathered them with honey-butter.

"Yes, I'm fine, Goldie," Mary assured her. "I guess I'm just a little blue about not being able to see my children this Christmas. I've been trying to tell myself it's okay and making all sorts of resolutions not to mope about it. But the truth is, it hurts. You know, there's just something about Christmas. It's all about family, and while I am very grateful to have Abby with me and Mom and Dad here—" Mary's voice cut off abruptly as it came to her who she was talking to. Goldie had no family left at all. Not a single relation. She looked up at Goldie with a stricken look on her face, ashamed of her insensitivity.

"It's okay," Goldie said, placing two cups of warm cider on the table. "I know what you mean."

"Oh, Goldie, it's not okay," Mary said miserably. "What a thing to say. I just wasn't thinking."

"Really, Mary, it's okay," Goldie said, reaching over to squeeze Mary's hand and training her faded green eyes on Mary's face. "You have every right to miss your children and you *should* be grateful to have your sister here. You don't know how much I wish I still had my sister here with me."

"Goldie," Mary said, tilting her head and giving Goldie a quizzical look. "I didn't even know you had a sister."

Goldie nodded firmly, staring at her cup as she turned it around on her saucer, lost in her own thoughts. "I did—or I do. I've never quite figured out how to answer that. She's still my sister, even though we're separated by death."

"I know exactly what you mean," Mary said, studying a glint of light reflecting from her wedding ring.

"A lot of years have gone by since I lost her," Goldie said, "and still I think about her all the time and wonder what her life might have been like if she'd lived."

"I take it she died young," Mary said.

Goldie nodded again slowly before taking a sip of her cider. "Seventeen," she said, finally. She puckered her lips and took another sip. Mary waited patiently for her to continue.

"It was almost more than my parents could bear," Goldie said at last. "Boating accident. They never did find her body, which was very difficult for all of us."

"I had no idea," Mary said, sucking in a breath. "Oh, Goldie, I'm so sorry."

"Well, like I said"—Goldie lifted her hand to flick a tear from her cheek and gave Mary a wan smile—"it was a long time ago. But, oh Mary, what a beautiful girl Sylvia was. Very talented and just sweeter than you could imagine. I wish you could have known her. Losing her was such a blow. Then, within five years after that, both our parents were gone. Neither of them had brothers or sisters, so there were no aunts and uncles or cousins. I'm the last of the line."

"Are you lonely, Goldie?" Mary asked before she could stop herself. She'd often wondered, but would never have come right out with the question under normal circumstances. But given what she'd just learned, she felt compelled to ask.

"Now and again," Goldie said, tilting her head from one side to the other and pursing her thin lips. "But, honestly, I have to say most of the time I'm content. It's just this time of year, well, it's sad not to have any family." She broke off a piece of banana bread and lifted it toward Mary. "But I count myself lucky now to have close friends to break bread with. And I owe a lot of that good fortune to you. Merry Christmas to you, Mary."

"And to you, my friend," Mary said, breaking off a piece of her own.

After they'd visited a while longer, Mary begged her leave, telling Goldie she had to get to the church to work her shift at the craft fair.

"You'll be at Stanton Farm for Christmas dinner, right?" Mary asked as Goldie saw her to the door of her little house.

"Yes, your good mother has already called to invite me," Goldie said. "I'll be there. And I'll be grateful to be among friends on that special day."

CHAPTER ❧ SEVEN

Abby had been forced to return to the museum for the afternoon with only one earned checkmark on her list, but she'd decided to claim another after calling Bernadette at Beach Bag Books and asking her to reserve a copy of the new biography on World War II General Omar Bradley for her father.

She stopped by after work to pick it up, then drove to the church to see if anyone was still around to let her in to have another look at the paintings.

Patricia Hale was all by herself in the hall. She was standing by one of the tables, keys in hand. "Oh hey, Abby," she said. "Are you looking for Mary? She left about a half hour ago."

"No, I knew she'd already be gone," Abby said. "Actually, I wanted to do a closer examination of the paintings if that's okay with you. But I see you're on your way out. I don't want to keep you."

"No problem, you're welcome to stay and do that. I'll go ahead and lock the door and you can just make sure it latches when you leave. I hope you don't mind if I dash off though," she said, looking at her watch. "I've got to pick Toby up at his friend's house, and I've still got to get home and make dinner. We promised Toby we'd take him over to Pelican court to see the Christmas lights tonight."

"No, please, you go ahead," Abby said. "I won't be long. How'd you do with the craft fair today?"

"Oh, it was fantastic," Patricia said, pulling her lustrous red ponytail out from her jacket collar and shaking it down her back. "I just can't believe how many beautiful things people donated. We took in enough today to totally fund the Christmas baskets for the needy."

"That's excellent," Abby said.

"Oh, and we've got room for your birdhouses now," Patricia said, pointing to a corner table. "So anytime you want to go ahead and bring those over would be fine."

"I'll go over to Rick's and get them right after I finish up here," Abby said, nodding her head toward the paintings. "I'll bring them by in the morning."

After Patricia left, Abby looked down the line of paintings and chose the one with the sparrows. She took it to the check-out table and moved aside the empty cash box and placed the painting on the surface, face down. She examined the back and saw that she had easy access to the brads holding the painting in the frame as the paper backing had completely disinte-grated. She got her multi-tool from her backpack and used the pliers to carefully pull the brads out. She set them aside in a lit-tle pile on the table.

The canvas was in good shape and did not, as Abby feared it might, stick to the inside of the frame when she gently applied pressure and popped it out. She turned it over and started to examine it, inch by inch. She was soon rewarded. Not by a name, or even initials, but by a date at least. In the lower right-hand corner, obscured by the frame, was a small but distinguishable '48 bordered by a right-angled bracket. Nineteen forty-eight.

Now at least Abby had the when, if not the who. That would give her somewhere to start. She looked at the painting again, wondering about the talented hand that had produced it. She couldn't help but think that if she had ever created anything half so beautiful she'd want to claim it with her signature as most artists did.

She gave the painting one more quick scan, but found nothing else that might lead her to the artist's identity.

She looked down the row of paintings and thought again of what Frank Holloway had said about the terrain. Yes, indeed Sparrow Island would have looked much different in 1948. Especially up near the northern part of the island. Abby thought instantly of Goldie. That's who she should ask about the paintings. Some of these locales would be out near her place. She was an island native, and one especially attuned to the island. Abby placed the painting carefully back into the frame and secured it in place. Yes, that's just what she'd do, she thought as she locked up. First chance she had she'd call Goldie.

Abby stood back and gave the series of paintings one last appreciative look. She loved the idea of angels inhabiting Sparrow Island. She knew it was true; there were angels here, though they usually made themselves known in more mundane ways than those depicted in the paintings. They didn't descend from the clouds, but they volunteered their time and talents as the dozens of people working the craft fair had, all to benefit those in need. They took meals to the sick and made the time to listen to those in emotional turmoil. And they befriended strangers—strangers like Tony.

After she locked up, Abby walked down to the dock to her father's fishing boat, which was now enclosed in a cage of PVC pipe. Strings of lights ran around it like strangling vines and neither her father nor Bobby looked happy.

"How's it going?" she asked.

"We've had better days, right Bobby?" her father replied, looking up from where he was cleaning the contacts on a battery pack.

"None of it's working like it's supposed to," the boy said, looking up at Abby, his blue eyes squinting in frustration.

"I think it's the weather. Everything's damp. We keep blowing bulbs and the batteries are corroding. But we'll keep at it, won't we, Bobby?" her father said, forced cheerfulness in his voice.

"Yes, sir," Bobby said with a sigh as he plugged another bulb into the tester.

"Well, good luck," Abby said, thrusting her hands into her coat pockets. "Don't stay out too much longer. It'll be dark soon and it's getting chilly."

Her father gave a half wave and Bobby barely looked up from his task as she walked away. Abby hoped Bobby was not getting too invested in the idea of winning the contest. This had all started out as a lark. The idea of entering her father's humble fishing boat alongside the bigger, sleeker and fancier vessels had been humorous. But it seemed to Abby that both Bobby and her father were getting a little carried away with it. She could understand it from Bobby. The boy had a double dose of enthusiasm about everything he did. But her father was a practical, sensible man—normally. Yet he seemed caught up in the competition too.

Her next stop was Rick DeBow's house. She wished she could walk. The cool air was invigorating and she was enjoying the physical exercise. She even enjoyed the canned Christmas music she heard from time to time coming from different offices and shops. But she made her way reluctantly back to the car. She needed it to transport her birdhouses.

She'd gotten it into her head a while back that she needed a hobby. All Mary's various needlecrafts and scrapbooking and sewing projects had made Abby feel like she was missing out. And, of course, the logical choice was building birdhouses. Anything that could benefit the birds held an automatic attraction. Plus, Abby was drawn to the more physical aspects of woodworking.

Rick had generously let her use his workshop and all his tools and had even given her some tutoring. She'd made quite a number of birdhouses this fall. The first half dozen or so definitely showed her lack of mastery. But with practice and Rick's patient instruction, she'd gotten to be a passable carpenter and she found she truly enjoyed working with wood. Her favorite thing was sanding. She loved the smooth feel and the earthly fragrance of the various woods. The repetitive motion left her mind free to ruminate on other things. She found she prayed well in the workshop. Many prayers, both of thanksgiving and of petition had gone forth from Abby's heart as the birdhouses took shape.

She'd been working over the past few weekends on several small birdhouses she was donating to the craft fair. They were sturdy and well built, if not particularly charming.

As she pulled into the driveway, Rick was heading for his

workshop. He had a cup of steaming coffee in one hand and a wad of bubble wrap in the other.

"Hi, Abby," he called. "I was wondering, since you're taking your birdhouses over to the craft fair, would you mind taking my contribution along too? I was just coming out to package it up."

"Not at all. Long as I can fit it into the car," Abby answered. "What did you make?"

"Oh, it's just a wooden box," Rick said. "It's small."

The two of them converged in front of the garage and Rick handed Abby his coffee cup so he could force open the stubborn side door with a body slam. Abby smiled. She'd learned to muscle her way in like this since Rick had given her building privileges in his workshop. "You'd think a handyman like yourself would have taken care of that by now, wouldn't you?" she asked, her voice teasing.

"Yeah, you know," Rick answered, "the cobbler's kids who go without shoes and all that." He took his coffee cup back and gestured for Abby to enter before him. He flicked on the lights and the space flooded with florescent light.

Abby worked her way around to a back table where her birdhouses sat covered with a drop cloth. "These are not nearly as nice as Mr. Phillips'," she said, "but maybe somebody will want to buy them."

Rick stepped in front of her and motioned for her to stop. "Mr. Phillips' birdhouses are very nice," Rick agreed, "but wait until you see what Laura Keranovic has done with yours."

"She painted them? I didn't think she was going to have time," Abby said, grabbing at the cloth.

Rick stayed her hand. "She wanted it to be a surprise," he said. "I gave them a couple of coats of shellac to protect them outdoors, though I doubt anyone will risk putting them out in the weather." He grabbed the drop cloth and whisked it away, with a theatrical "Ta-dah!"

Abby gasped. Laura had taken her plain, pedestrian birdhouses and turned them into works of art. She'd given them an allover design of color and markings similar to the beautiful Pysanky eggs she always did at Easter. The effect was whimsical and exotic. Abby laughed and clapped her hands. "I may have to buy one of my own birdhouses," she said.

Rick nodded, sipping his coffee. "You both did a great job," he said. "You're getting good at this.

"I had a good teacher," Abby answered. "And a good friend who trusts me with his power tools. Let me see the box you made."

Abby was anticipating a plain wooden box, maybe with a hinged lid like a pirate's chest. But when Rick pulled away the cloth, Abby's first instinct was to reach out and touch it. It was about ten inches square and the entire top was inlaid with an intricate pattern of different woods and colors of stain.

"Rick, this is fabulous," Abby said. "Oh, Mary would just love this, but I've already got her present. I wish I'd seen it sooner."

"Well, I hope Serena likes it, I made her one too."

"She'll love it," Abby assured him. "Where is Serena anyway?" she asked.

"She went on a horseback ride up to Mt. Ortiz with Artie Washburn," Rick said, raising his eyebrows.

"O-oh," Abby said, drawing out the word.

"Yeah." Rick replied flatly. "I have a hunch I'm not the only one she came to the island to see."

"Well, Artie's a great guy," Abby said.

"Yeah, yeah he is," Rick agreed, tilting his head to one side. "And they seem to have a lot of fun together. They both love the outdoors, that's for sure. Anyway, I can't expect her to hang around with her old dad *all* the time."

"Count your blessings. She's here with you. Just enjoy her company whenever you can get it."

"I will," Rick answered. "Once she finds a new thesis project, she'll be off again."

CHAPTER ❧ EIGHT

Would you look at that?" Mary asked, nodding toward the wall calendar as she put out the placemats and prepared to set the table for dinner that evening. "This is the only night between now and Christmas that I don't have some event to go to or evening plans with Henry."

"Makes me tired just to look at it," Abby said, stirring the pot of broccoli-cheese soup to prevent it from scorching, "Not that it doesn't all look like great fun. But I've had a full day today and I'm exhausted."

Abby looked out of the corner of her eye in Mary's direction. She wasn't fibbing, she really was tired, but she'd made the comment to see what she could elicit from Mary. She worried that Mary was overdoing it. Even though she'd made remarkable strides in her recovery, she still hadn't quite caught onto the fact that she needed to pace herself, and she sometimes let exhaustion overtake her.

"Well, I have to admit, I'm pretty tired too," Mary said. "And there's still so much to do. I haven't even got my Christmas cards out. I've never been this late with them. Only six days left until Christmas and I have gifts to wrap yet and I don't have a gift for my secret Santa in the knitting group." She placed the silverware beside Abby's plate and aligned it with precision. "I'd planned to do some more baking tonight, but I just don't think I've got the energy," she said, turning her chair toward the refrigerator to pull out the fruit salads she'd made that morning.

"Mary, why are you doing all this?" Abby asked. "You're making too much work for yourself."

"Oh, I guess I am," Mary admitted, shaking her head until her beautifully coiffed silver hair bounced. "I'm ashamed to admit it, but I fibbed earlier when I said I was at peace with the kids' not being here for Christmas. I've been feeling very sorry for myself about it, up until this morning. But after talking to Goldie, I'm ashamed. I should be thanking my lucky stars for what I've got instead of whining about what I won't have."

"You went out to see Goldie today?" Abby asked, ladling steaming soup into a crockery bowl.

"Yes," Mary answered, wheeling over to the cupboard to get out the water crackers she and Abby both liked with their soup. "I had some time before I had to be over at the church this morning and I wanted to check in on her. I was worried when she looked so pale when we dropped off the potluck platter yesterday. I think she's about back to par. She's working in the greenhouse again. Did you know Goldie had a sister?"

"No, I had no idea," Abby said, placing bowls of soup at each place setting. "Now, when you say she *had* a sister, do I take that to mean she's passed on?"

"Yes, a long time ago," Mary said. "She died very young in

some kind of boating accident as I understand it. Goldie says they never found her body. Can you imagine how hard that must have been?"

"Oh, that's so sad," Abby said. "Poor Goldie."

Mary nodded solemnly. "And it gets worse. Within a few short years of that she lost both her parents. She's got no aunts or uncles. So she's the last in her line. No family left at all. I can't imagine being without family, especially at this time of year."

"Me either," Abby said, pulling out her chair to sit down at the table. She felt fatigue drain away almost instantly as the shared ritual of their evening meal began. Mary said the blessing and Abby centered her thoughts on how grateful she was for hearty food in abundance and all the other blessings of her life here on Sparrow Island.

Mary picked up the teapot and poured water into their cups. "I was thinking, that's one thing I don't quite get about Tony being here on the island," she said. "At least during this season. I understand he's planning to stay through Christmas. I would think he'd want to be home with his family." She put the teapot down and frowned. "If he has family. I don't remember him saying, do you?"

"No, I don't," Abby answered, trying to keep her voice neutral. She didn't want another lecture from Mary about her suspicious nature.

"I know he has a girlfriend," Mary said. "He came to the craft fair today and bought one of Opal's scarves for himself and another he said was for his girlfriend."

"That's nice," Abby said.

"Yes," Mary said, a frown lingering on her forehead. "But you know, it's strange. For all the conversations I've had with that young man, you'd think I'd know more about him. We've talked quite a lot."

"You'd think," Abby said and was careful to leave it at that. What she did not say aloud, but what she had observed, was that Tony usually got more information than he gave from every exchange.

Abby would concede that this could be taken either one of two ways. Maybe he was just interested in people and liked to make them feel good by showing interest and getting them to talk about themselves. But it could also be that he had some other motive for gathering information about people. The question was, what could that motive be?

"I can tell you this for sure," Mary said. "He's a very unusual young man. He's always so helpful, and he must be smart, though come to think of it, I don't know what he does for a living either, do you?"

"Not a clue," Abby said, shaking her head.

"Did you hear he got the clock in the town square park running again?" Mary asked.

"*He* did that?" Abby asked. "That was him?"

Mary nodded. "Went out in the pouring rain the other night to have a look at it after Terza and Martin told him it hadn't run in years and that the town never seemed to get around to having it fixed. Martin said it was a shame too, because he'd always thought a town clock was an important thing. A sort of point of reference for everyone. Terza said Tony just donned a rain parka and borrowed a couple of tools from Martin's toolbox and off he went. Like it just couldn't wait. Half an hour later he was back and the clock was fixed. It's been running like—well like clockwork—ever since," Mary said with a laugh.

"So Tony was Corrine's angel," Abby said softly.

"He was what?" Mary asked.

"Oh," Abby said, looking up. "It's kind of funny. I think Corrine saw him in the park when he was working on the clock. It was raining and kind of dark, and I guess he had that rain slicker on.

"It was probably wet and glistening," Abby said, almost to herself. "And, well, Corrine thought she saw an angel."

"Maybe she did," Mary said, smiling.

Abby and Mary ate in companionable silence for a few minutes. Each was lost in her thoughts with only the muted click of spoons against bowls breaking the silence in the kitchen.

Abby thought of the many holidays she had spent away from home. She'd always had invitations from close friends or co-workers and she'd never been alone. She'd never felt exactly lonely. But her thoughts had always gone back to Sparrow Island and to her family. She'd always felt the pull, the longing to be with them during the holidays.

"I'm so glad you're here, Abby," Mary said suddenly as if reading Abby's mind. Abby looked over and saw that Mary had tears beginning to puddle in her eyes.

"And I'm glad to be here," Abby responded. "I was just thinking that. But now don't go getting all mushy on me or you'll get me started."

"I'll try to contain myself," Mary said, wiping her eyes with the corner of her napkin. "But I do mean it. I'm so glad to have you here with me. Especially at Christmas, but not *just* at Christmas. All year long. Talking to Goldie today, it occurred to me that I don't tell you that enough."

Abby smiled. "I tell you what," she said. "After dinner I'll fix us a nice cup of Earl Grey and a little plate of those ginger cookies and we'll work on our Christmas cards together. Have a little sister time. How does that sound?"

"That sounds wonderful," Mary said. "Just wonderful."

ABBY HAD CHOSEN Christmas cards with a dove bearing an olive branch on the front. People seemed to expect to see some kind of bird on her cards. She tried to oblige and find a different species of bird to feature each Christmas, though she'd had to recycle a few over the years.

"Doves this year?" Mary said. "Those are nice."

"Yes," Abby said, looking at the front of the card, pleased with the illustration. "I used a dove two years ago, but I liked these so much I decided to get them anyway."

Abby wasn't at all surprised to see that Mary had chosen cards featuring angels. Their mother had passed many of her interests on to Mary, especially her passion for angels.

"When I first picked out these cards I thought the illustrations were just glorious," Mary said. "But I have to say, after looking at those paintings for a couple of days, these seem a little—I don't know—diminished."

"Well, they're nice," Abby said, leaning over to see the front of the card Mary was looking at. "But I know what you're saying. There's something so luminous and powerful about the paintings."

Mary nodded. "I found myself looking over at them all this afternoon, and they just made me feel so peaceful. Even after I got home, I've been thinking and thinking about them. I'm, well, I don't want to say obsessed because that makes it sound like a bad feeling. Can we invent a new word and say 'oblessed'?" she asked with a laugh.

"That's a good word for it," Abby said. "Every time I think

of those beautiful angels and their bird companions, this wonderful feeling comes over me. Yes, I definitely feel 'oblessed' too."

"Did you find out anything about the birds the artist chose?" Mary asked.

"Not too much yet, but a little," Abby said. "I think the birds were chosen very deliberately."

"I like the birds, but it's the angels themselves that speak to me," Mary said. "Specifically the face. There's something so familiar about that face. It's like having a name right on the tip of your tongue and then having it slip away."

"I've thought that too," Abby said. "Do you think maybe it's someone famous? Maybe someone we've seen on television or in the movies? Or maybe even someone we know in real life?"

"I don't know," Mary said, frowning. She squeezed her eyes shut. "Oh, it's so frustrating."

"Just try to forget about it and work on your cards. It's usually when your mind is busy with something else that it relaxes and lets you remember things."

"True," Mary said, drawing in a deep breath and flipping open her address book. "In all the hubbub I'd forgotten how much I enjoy sending out Christmas cards."

Abby told Mary about going by to examine the painting and finding the date.

"Oh my," Mary said, "so they could conceivably have been in that storage room for a very long time."

"Probably got moved in there when it was built— transferred from that old outbuilding that used to be behind the parsonage. I barely remember it, but it seems to me they were getting ready to tear it down when it caught fire and burned."

Mary sealed an envelope for her card and placed it on the stack.

"I was thinking of how different Sparrow Island would have been in the 1940s," Mary said. "Think about it. That would have been just a few short years after World War II. About the same time we moved here."

"Yes, I guess pretty close," Mary said. "Course, we were so young, I don't have many memories of those earliest years."

"No," Abby said. "But after we got to be school age I remember quite a bit. The island was definitely different then. That was before we got discovered and the tourists started flocking here."

"Yes, I remember too," Mary said. "I'm afraid we took the beauty of the island for granted sometimes."

"You know who I keep thinking of?" Abby said, and rushed on without waiting for an answer. "Goldie. She loves this island as much as anyone I know. And the angel paintings portray Sparrow Island so lovingly. I somehow just keep thinking of them together. I'm going to ask her to look at the paintings with me first chance I get. She's the right age to have been aware of them when they were done. Maybe she can tell me something about them."

"You're right," Mary said. "And Goldie appreciates art too. She has a couple of very nice pen and ink drawings that I've always admired hanging in her living room."

"As soon as the open house is over with, I'll see if she'll come into town and look at them with me."

Abby was relieved to see Mary looking happy as she worked

on her cards. She thought of poor Goldie and how painful it must have been for her to lose a sister. Abby could still remember the icy clutches of fear that had taken hold of her when she'd gotten the call about Mary's accident. The very thought of losing her sister had been almost more than Abby could bear. And Goldie had lost everyone dear to her in such a very short period of time.

An errant thought about Tony crept into Abby's musings. He'd been very curious about Goldie. And he'd been unusually friendly with Opal Collins and with several other older women. While Abby knew almost all of them to be competent, intelligent women, maybe Tony thought otherwise. Weren't older women often a con man's preferred target? And weren't con men often likeable, friendly guys who were solicitous and helpful?

Well, if Tony was up to something nefarious and he'd set his sights on Goldie, he'd likely get a nasty surprise. She might look vulnerable. She was small and seemingly fragile, but she was no shrinking violet. Goldie had survived very nicely out in her isolated house for a lot of years now. She was accustomed to looking after herself.

"What's so funny?" Mary asked.

Abby hadn't realized she was smiling foolishly. "Oh, I was just thinking of how wonderful it is to be back on the island with all the crazy, loveable characters we have around here," she said and quickly changed the subject. "Did I tell you about Dad and Bobby and how they're getting along with plans for the boat?"

"No, how's that going?" Mary asked.

"Well, let's put it this way, if they decide to put any more lights on that boat, it may sink under the weight of it all. And the rigging," Abby said, rolling her eyes. "They have schematics for space ships less complicated than that. You know this started out as a joke, just something to do for fun. But those two have gotten out of control."

"Oh dear," Mary said, starting to giggle. "Let's hope the whole thing doesn't come down on them during the Parade of Boats. They might be caught in all those strands of wire like fish in a net."

"Not the look they're going for I would think," Abby said. "Though they might win for best themed entry. It is a fishing boat after all."

The two women laughed and talked, and twin stacks of Christmas cards grew up in the center of the table. Angels and birds—contented companions, just like in the paintings.

CHAPTER ❧ NINE

MARY WENT TO BED early and Abby had every intention of doing the same, but when she went up to her room, she saw her laptop on her desk, still open and powered up, and she decided to delve a little deeper into the folklore of the birds.

She read over the notes she had scribbled on the pad beside her computer. Some of what she'd turned up was commonly known, but she'd been surprised by some of the more obscure references.

Almost everyone you'd ask would know the bluebird was associated with happiness. More specifically, Abby had learned, it denoted spiritual joy and contentedness. Abby tried to remember more about the painting with bluebirds, but it was hard to remember the details of each individual painting—except for the dove one. That one stood out because it was different from the others.

For one thing, the dove painting was the only close-up in the bunch. The others featured the angel figure full length and connoted a sense of peacefulness. The poses were fixed and static.

The dove painting was like a snapshot and captured action. The sweet-faced angel's hands were out-thrust, having just released a dove to fly free among the clouds. The dove, as was commonly known, is a symbol of peace and of promise. That certainly fit with the feeling evoked by the painting. But the face on this one just wouldn't let go of Abby. The feeling of familiarity was so strong. Despite the offhanded advice she'd given Mary earlier about just trying to forget it, Abby had tried every trick she could think of to fool her brain into helping her come up with a name. But nothing had worked.

Abby had known that the sparrow was often used to indicate a gentle nature. But she hadn't known it also sometimes symbolized an intellectual person. She wondered if the person who named Sparrow Island had known that. In Abby's experience, this island was populated by lots of gentle souls and keenly intelligent ones as well.

Abby had a fairly clear picture in her mind of the general design of the painting that featured the sparrows. It was the one she'd been looking at when it finally dawned on her that a single species of bird was featured in each one.

The angel in that one was pictured full length. She was suspended in midair, but not amongst the clouds as would have been a more customary angelic motif. She'd been—Abby could only think of it as hovering—above some sort of landform below. The angel was in a forward-leaning aspect. Sparrows had taken the hem of her garments in their beaks and were holding it up in a series of graceful drapes. As Abby recalled, the angel had one arm outstretched over the waters and the land, and the other hand across her heart, with her head bent down, surveying all that lay below. It was a beautiful, serene scene.

Abby yawned and stretched. She shut down her computer and neatened her desk, being careful to stack her notes where she could find them easily the next time she got an opportunity to do more reading on the subject.

She got ready for bed and crawled under the covers, fully expecting her mind to start racing with all the myriad tasks she had yet to do before Christmas, as it had every night for the past week. But she was asleep within minutes. She slept peacefully and dreamt of angels.

MARY WAS HUMMING as she filled Finnegan and Blossom's bowls on Tuesday morning. Abby came tripping down the steps and opened the refrigerator for the orange juice. Within seconds Mary's tune proved infectious and the two of them were soon singing "Angels we have heard on high, sweetly singing o'er the plain," as they fixed a quick breakfast.

"Busy day today?" Abby asked when they'd finished the chorus.

"Yes, quite busy," Mary said. "But I'm looking forward to it. I'm going over to church to help out for a couple of hours on the craft fair. Then I'm going to help the little ones from Patricia's Sunday school class put together the treat buckets they're making for our senior citizens. Oh Abby, those little boys and girls are the cutest little things you've ever seen."

"First and second graders?" Abby asked.

"Yes, such a sweet age. And they're so earnest in wanting these to be pretty and special. Have you seen the little buckets they've made?"

"No," Abby said, picturing sand pails and trying to imagine how they'd managed to make them Christmasy.

"They're juice cans. You know, the tall ones you get in the grocery store that tomato juice comes in? Patricia and I punched holes on either side near the top with a hammer and nail. The kids made little handles from green and red pipe cleaners. Then they made a Santa face for the side and glued on cotton balls for his beard and some red felt for the hat. They're just adorable."

"And what goes in them?" Abby asked.

"All kinds of little treats. Crossword puzzle books, lotions for the ladies, shaving cream for the gents, candy and dried fruit. The kids have brought in things they know their own grandparents like."

"I'd love to come over and help, but you know our open house at the museum is tomorrow and I've got lots of last-minutes things to do."

"Oh, no problem. The buckets are all done, so all we have to do is fill them up. We thought we had a little glitch with the deliveries yesterday, but that all got solved. Thanks to Tony."

"Oh? How so?" Abby asked.

"When he was in buying his scarves yesterday, Patricia got a call from one of the moms who had to cancel helping with the deliveries. Tony was standing right there and overheard. He volunteered to make the deliveries for us. He said it would be a way to see more of the island and help out at the same time."

"That was nice of him," Abby said, trying her best to mean it.

"Tony's really making himself a part of our community life around here. We don't get too many tourists who do that."

"No, no, that's pretty unusual," Abby said evenly, again

trying to keep her welcoming instincts in détente with her long years of training. "But then again, Tony's an unusual young fellow," she said at last.

MARY STARTED OFF for Little Flock in her van, and Abby called Wilma to let her know she'd be in later in the morning. She had a few last-minute errands in town for the open house: picking up the punch bowl, taking a check to the caterer, getting the centerpiece from Mary's shop. But her first stop was to deliver the birdhouses to Little Flock. She'd only been joking when she told Rick she might have to buy back one of them, but the more she looked at them, the more she fell in love with them. She loved the fact that they had been a collaborative effort. Her building, Laura's painting, and Rick's teaching and generous loan of his workshop. She really wanted to hold on to one of them.

Then she had the brilliant idea to buy one of them for her mother for Christmas. If it was at Stanton Farm she'd still get to see it and enjoy it and she could make her mother happy too. She chose her favorite and put it in the backseat of the car, making a mental note to give Patricia or Mary a check to cover it.

She carried the first load into the hall and found several people already milling around. She spotted Mary and took Rick's box and one of the birdhouses over to her to be priced. As she suspected, Mary gave a squeal of delight when she unwrapped the inlaid box from the bubble wrap.

Abby sighed. She and Mary had made a firm agreement about what they would spend on one another's Christmas presents, but Abby could not resist the idea of seeing that look on Mary's face again when she unwrapped the box on Christmas morning.

She gave a small gulp as she saw the tag bearing the price Mary and Patricia agreed on, but it would be worth it. And the money would go to a good cause.

"Patricia, could I talk to you a minute?" she called, "It's about the paintings." She moved away, out of Mary's earshot.

When Patricia came over Abby said. "I really do want to tell you something about the paintings, but this was also a trick to get you away from Mary. Could you set aside that box for me? I want to get it for her, but I want it to be a surprise."

"Oh, that'll be a great gift. She obviously loves it," Patricia said as the two looked back at Mary who was still admiring the box. "I'll leave it out so people can get a chance to see it, but I'll mark it sold."

"About the paintings, I did want to tell you that William Jansen will probably be contacting you, if he hasn't already, about coming to take some pictures," Abby said. "He'd like to do a story and see if we get any information in response."

"Yes, he came by yesterday, right after you saw him," Patricia said. "He's hoping to get it in this week. And I've been digging around a little too," she said. "I called the former pastor's wife. She's a dear lady. She's in a nursing home down near her daughter in southern California. She's in her nineties now, but she's still sharp as a tack. She did remember hearing about the paintings. It was her understanding that they'd been given as a gift to the church. Unfortunately, she couldn't remember who gave them. But she said she was told they were destroyed in a fire years ago when a little outbuilding that used to be in back of our house went up in flames. That must have been a long time ago because I can't see any hint there was ever even a building out there."

"Yes, I vaguely remember one," Abby said. "But, it's probably a moot point anyway. The paintings obviously weren't in it. But if everyone thought they were destroyed, that might explain why they were still stuck back there in the storage room after all these years. I did find out yesterday that the one with the sparrows was probably done in 1948."

"Really?" Patricia said. "Let me think. I believe that would have been when Rev. Holten was here. Is that right?"

Abby tapped her finger on her chin. "Yes, I think you're right."

"Yes," Patricia said, letting out a sigh. "Unfortunately he passed away a few years ago and his wife died a long time before he did. I never even met her."

"Oh well," Abby said. "We'll just have to keep digging."

"Yes," Patricia said, turning her slender body toward the pew that was still serving as an elongated easel for the paintings. She crossed her arms in front of her. "I don't know what it is about these paintings. I just can't get them out of my thoughts. And it's not just the mystery of where they came from or who painted them, though I'd certainly like to know about that. It's the paintings themselves. Those angels just seem to—" she hesitated and looked at Abby shyly. "You'll think I'm being silly, but they just seem to be trying to tell me something. Personally."

"I don't think you're silly at all," Abby said. "I feel the same way. They're very compelling. And familiar somehow."

"Really? You feel that way too? Well, I don't feel so ridiculous now," Patricia said. "You're always so practical and analytical, Abby. If they affect you that way, then I'm not just being overly sentimental."

"It surprises me too," Abby said, "And you're right, I'm not given to sentimentality. Now Mary, she'll tear up over those commercials on television plugging long-distance telephone services. She wears her heart on her sleeve. I'm usually the pragmatic one. But I'm positively enraptured by these," Abby gave a sweeping gesture to take in all the paintings.

A customer caught Patricia's eye, and she excused herself to go ring up a sale. When Mary was occupied with helping someone else, Patricia slipped over and marked the inlaid box sold, giving Abby an exaggerated wink.

Abby went back out to the car to bring in the other birdhouses. Just as she was pulling the box out of the trunk she saw Tony approaching with Miss Opal Collins. He was holding the old woman's elbow as she shuffled along. In his spare hand he carried a large shopping bag.

"Hello, Abby," he said. "If you'll let me get this inside," he said holding up the bag, "I'll come back out and help you."

"Oh, that's okay, I've got it," Abby answered, lifting the box out. "It's not heavy, just bulky."

"I've brought some more scarves and mittens for the sale," Miss Opal said, her voice warbling. She gestured toward the sack in Tony's hand.

"Well, that's great," Abby said. "But didn't you already donate a big box full."

"Well, yes, I did," Miss Opal said, smiling. "But I saw Tony here wearing one of the scarves over at the Springhouse Café yesterday when I was having lunch with Harriet. He told me he'd bought it here and that they were going fast, so I decided I'd better bring over some more. Tony was kind enough to help me get them out of my car."

"Well, you're very generous to give even more of your beautiful work," Abby said, meaning it sincerely. Opal Collins was one of the most talented knitters around. She made her own designs instead of following packaged directions, and they were very pleasing in both color and pattern.

"Well, you know how I love to knit, Abigail," Miss Opal said. "And I'm happy I can make some small contribution with it."

"And it's generous of you, Tony, to help out with the children's pail project. I understand you're going to be doing deliveries for them."

"Yeah, I'm going to be riding around the island anyway. I figured I might as well make it useful."

Back inside Abby gave the box of birdhouses to Patricia, who took them out and placed them on a shelf against the wall reserved for the small woodworking projects. Abby was happy to see that, thanks to Laura, they held their own alongside Mr. Phillips' elaborate creations.

Each of his houses was made to emulate a human dwelling. One was a Victorian, complete with the fancy woodwork ornamentation. Another was a log cabin with a little rocking chair on the front porch. Still another was a Tudor style house surrounded by a broad formal lawn—actually outdoor carpeting—for the birds to frolic on.

Abby turned when she heard someone call her name and saw Serena coming across the room toward her. She looked rosy-cheeked and bright-eyed.

"Serena, I hear you went riding yesterday. How was it?"

"Wonderful," she said breathlessly. "The view up there is amazing. And it was so nice to get out in the fresh air."

"And in such good company?" Abby said, raising her eyebrows.

"Well, yes, there's that," Serena said, smiling sweetly. "Artie's a really cool guy. He's cute too, don't you think?"

"Yes, though I'm not sure a stolid law enforcement officer would take to the idea of being called cute," Abby said with a laugh.

"No, probably not," Serena agreed. "But he is." She looked around the hall. "I'm here looking for a gift for my sister. I wanted to get her something from Sparrow Island."

"Well there are plenty of nice things to choose from," Abby said.

Serena looked past Abby's shoulder. "Hi, Tony," she said. Abby turned and saw Tony guiding Miss Opal toward them. The older woman's steps were shuffling, but she was quick.

"Serena dear, I heard you were in town and Tony here has told me about your little problem with your studies," she said, her voice like the rustle of dry leaves.

"I hope it's okay," Tony said, shrugging one shoulder. "I heard you telling Abby the other day about your project falling through."

"That's a shame," Miss Opal plowed on. "I tell you what. I've got a nephew who works at a forestry research station of some sort up in Vancouver. I'll give him a call and ask him if they have anything for you."

"Thank you, Miss Opal," Serena said, politely. "I appreciate that."

They chatted a few more minutes and Tony escorted Miss Opal to the door.

"Well, see there, you've just got everyone working on your behalf," Abby said to Serena.

"Yes, it's very sweet," Serena said. "But if the Vancouver station had anything available I'd have heard about it or somebody I've contacted would have. I don't think it'll lead anywhere, but I do appreciate the sentiment. She's a kind lady.

That's what I love so much about this island. People look after one another. And it looks like Tony's gotten right into the spirit of it too."

"Yes, it sure looks that way," Abby said slowly, still staring at the doorway Tony had just steered Miss Opal through.

WHEN ABBY ARRIVED at the museum she found Hugo in the lobby talking with a small group of children from Little Flock's Skills and Crafts program. They'd each brought a handmade Christmas ornament to hang on the museum's lobby tree.

Hugo was a counselor in the program and he had encouraged the children to make ornaments for the tree that reflected some aspect of life on Sparrow Island. Abby had been continually amazed at the ingenuity and the variety of the ornaments that had started appearing almost from the moment the tree had been set up. Some of the children had used natural materials like wood or dried flowers. Others had drawn small pictures of different birds or the Orca whales or other wildlife and embellished them with gobs of glitter and ropes of ribbon.

One little boy had made a small papier-mâché pig and put a tiny wreath around his neck. Abby had been a little puzzled by that one until Hugo had passed on the boy's explanation. He had been disturbed to learn in his local history class at school that a war had begun right here in the islands over the ownership of a pig. He reasoned that a Christmas pig could be a new symbol for peace.

Abby doubted it would be replacing the dove anytime soon, at least with the general public. But she knew she'd think of this little boy's hopes for mankind every time she saw a pig for the foreseeable future. And that she'd be heartened by it.

Hugo took a rectangular ornament from a little girl who

looked to be about eight. The ornament was a silhouette drawing of a bird made on a block of blond wood. It had been trimmed with a small cluster of red berries in one corner and had a red ribbon attached for hanging. It was beautiful in its simplicity.

"Would you like me to hang this up high on the tree for you?" Hugo asked.

The little girl nodded and blushed, looking down at her shoes.

"Why'd you draw an old crow, Vanessa?" one of the little boys asked. "They're not pretty birds. And anyway, everybody knows they're bad luck."

A look of distress came over the little girl's face and Abby was afraid she might start to cry. "It's a magpie," she said softly.

"Well, now, let's see what we can find out about this," Hugo said, his deep voice reassuring. "We happen to have the Bird Lady right here. Dr. Stanton, could you step over here and tell us what you know about the magpie?"

He looked at Abby with beseeching eyes, counting on her to bail him out of this one.

"Well, first of all, this is a beautiful ornament, Vanessa," Abby said. "And I think the magpie was a great choice. You want to know why?"

The little girl nodded slowly.

"Magpies," Abby said. "Are *very* smart. Some scientists think they're one of the very smartest birds. They have a pretty strong sense of smell and they use their beaks to turn over rocks—even some pretty heavy ones sometimes—to look for food. This is very unusual for a bird."

Abby sneaked a peek at the little girl who was now smiling uneasily. "And you know," Abby said. "In China, magpies are considered good luck. Their cry—you know you've all heard it *mag, mag, mag?*"

The kids all nodded.

"Well, in China they think that's the announcement of good news. That the bird brings happiness and good fortune."

"That's what my Mom said," Vanessa said quietly.

"Well, your Mom was right," Abby assured her.

"Thank you, Dr. Stanton," Hugo said, giving Abby a grateful glance. "Now let's all finish getting our ornaments on the tree."

ABBY COULD STILL HEAR the children chattering as she closed her office door. She took off her jacket and hung it on the back of her chair and powered up her computer. She'd have to resist the temptation to do more research on folklore, although what she'd learned yesterday about the magpie had certainly just come in handy. If this had happened a week ago, she'd never have remembered that the bird was considered good luck in China. And she would have missed seeing that beautiful smile come over little Vanessa's face.

"Good timing," she mumbled, smiling to herself.

She busied herself with making three new laminated educational placards for various exhibits in the museum. The ones that were up already had become bent and shopworn where people had leaned over the railings. It was important to Abby that the museum be in tip-top shape for the open house.

She and Hugo both wanted to show it off to the donors. But more than that, it was important to Abby that this place that celebrated the islands—her islands—be at its festive best as a sort of gift to all the island residents. She'd invested so much of herself here since she'd become Associate Curator, it felt like she was inviting people into her home.

When she had the placards finished, she went out into the museum's main room to put them up. As she was placing the last one at the Wonderful World of Wings exhibit she saw Hugo escorting the children toward the door. He'd given them a quick look at the recent updates to the Native American display.

"Thank you all for the beautiful ornaments," she called to the children. "You did Sparrow Island proud."

After the children had gone and Hugo had disappeared into his office, Abby went to work with a bottle of cleaner and a polishing cloth. She wiped every surface until it gleamed, being careful to stay out of the way of the few patrons who were in the museum.

She enlisted Wilma's help and the two of them got two folding tables out of the workroom and set them up in the center of the main room. "Okay," Abby said, moving one table an inch so that it was perfectly aligned with the other. "The food will go here and the beverages will go on this one," she pointed to the tables and talked it through, as much for herself as for Wilma.

"Is there an outlet for the coffee urn?" Wilma asked.

"Yes," Abby answered. "Right back here. There's one in the floor. Hugo was really thinking ahead when he helped draw up the specs for this place. Someday there will be another exhibit right here," she said moving her hands in a grand motion as if something were, at that very moment, growing up out of the museum's floor.

"Well, for now, let's be satisfied there's an outlet there," Wilma said before going back to her desk in the front.

Abby got the tablecloths she'd borrowed from Mary's house and smoothed them over the tables, checking that they fell evenly. It occurred to her that Mary must be rubbing off on her. She didn't normally fuss over things like this. She'd never been particularly house-proud about her place back in New York. But she had to admit it gave her a great sense of satisfaction to have the museum looking so beautiful and inviting.

She gave the tablecloth one last smoothing wipe and started back to her office. She stopped short and snapped her fingers. She'd pledged to bring a tray of cookies for the open house—one more thing to get done today.

"Nope," she said, and then realized she'd spoken aloud. She looked around to make sure no one had heard her and then went on to her office. She was not going to get caught up in holiday stress again. If she didn't get out of here in time to make cookies tonight she'd go by St. Christopher's Church on the way home. She'd seen a sign up in the window of *The Birdcall* announcing a bake sale.

She pulled her chair up to the computer and scrolled through her new e-mail. There was nothing from any of the inquiries she'd sent out on Serena's behalf. Like Miss Opal, Abby had been well meaning, but ineffectual.

The more Abby thought about that morning's exchange, the stranger it seemed. Just how would Serena's plight have come up in the conversation Tony was having with Miss Opal? And moreover, why would it have come up?

But in fairness, there could have been a perfectly plausible explanation. Maybe Miss Opal hadn't recognized Serena from across the room and had asked Tony who she was. Miss Opal knew Serena, but her eyesight wasn't what it once was. And it was sweet of Tony to be concerned about other people's problems. In fact, it was admirable. So why was it so hard for Abby to accept that he was just what he seemed—an uncommonly good person?

The phone jangled, startling Abby out of her reverie. She snatched up the receiver and heard Mary's breathless voice on the other end. "Oh, Abby, thank goodness you're there," she said.

"Mary, are you okay?" Abby asked, standing up abruptly and almost pulling the phone from the desktop.

"Yes, yes, I'm fine Abby. It's Janet's mother. Emma's taken a nasty fall, and they don't know how badly she's hurt. Janet's on her way to the Medical Center now. Patricia's gone on an errand. I'm the only one here working at the craft fair, so I can't leave. Would it be possible for you to go over to the Medical Center? Janet can't find Doug and he doesn't carry a cell phone. I'm sure it would help her to have someone with her. She's just frantic."

"Yes, of course," Abby said, grabbing her jacket off the back of her chair and starting to put it on even as they were still talking. "I'll go over right now and I'll call you as soon as I find out anything," she said, hanging up the receiver and grabbing her bag. She stopped in quickly to tell Hugo where she was going, then sprinted out the door.

Emma Stoltz was in good condition for a woman her age, but Janet had just been saying the last time she and Abby had lunched together that Emma was starting to have a little trouble getting around. Janet had been trying to talk her into getting one of those medic alert pendants to wear when she and Doug weren't home in case of an emergency. But Emma had resisted, insisting those were for old people, not her.

Abby drove as fast as caution would allow and pulled into

the lot at the Medical Center right alongside Janet's car. She grabbed her bag out of the back and trotted inside. Mary Ellen Walters, a friend from Little Flock was staffing the front desk. "It's supposed to be only family back there, but I think Janet needs you," she told Abby. "Go on back."

As Abby rushed past the waiting area, which was really only a bench against the hall wall, she saw Tony Malachy sitting there. She slowed and was just about to ask him what he was doing there when Janet peeked out from behind a doorway and came rushing at her, grabbing Abby up in a hug and holding on tight.

"Where's Emma?" Abby demanded, her voice breaking.

Janet pulled away and wiped at her eyes with her fingertips. "She's in here," she said, her voice high and reedy. "She's fine— at least she's going to be fine. But she really gave us a scare."

She pulled Abby in around the doorway. Emma was sitting up in bed. She winced as the nurse put a butterfly bandage on a cut on her forehead.

"Hello, Abby," Emma said weakly. "My heavens, haven't I started a fuss?"

"You certainly have, Mother," Janet said, trying for a light tone. "What are we going to do with you?"

Emma held up a hand then let it drop to her lap. "Don't worry, dear. I've learned my lesson. No more basement steps for me."

"Whatever made you decide to go down there in the first place?" Janet asked, her voice tender.

"I got to thinking about some Christmas candlesticks I had years ago and how lovely they'd look with your new tablecloth. I know they're somewhere in those boxes in the basement and I thought I'd try to find them."

"Did you feel faint, Mrs. Stoltz?" the nurse asked, placing her fingertips on Emma's wrist and consulting her watch. "Or dizzy? Right before you fell?"

"No, not at all," Emma answered. "I just caught my toe on one of the steps and over I went, just like a tumbleweed, all the way to the bottom."

"You were lucky," the nurse said. "Nothing's broken and the doctor says you don't have any internal injuries. You're going to have some nasty bruises and you'll be quite sore for a while, but it could have been a lot worse."

"And it might have been if that wonderful young man hadn't come along when he did," Emma said. "Where is he anyway?"

"He's out in the hallway, Mother," Janet said.

"Could I see him?" Emma asked. "I'd like to thank him properly."

"Would it be okay?" Janet asked the nurse.

"Sure," the nurse said, raising the side rail of the bed until it clicked solidly into place. "Just make it quick. The doctor wants to keep you overnight for observation, Mrs. Stoltz, just as a precaution. I'll be back to move you to a room in just a couple of minutes. Then she needs to rest," she said, addressing the visitors pointedly.

Janet went to the doorway and called Tony in.

"Here's my guardian angel," Emma said as he came into the small examining room. "Come over here, young man, so I can tell you how grateful I am that you saved me."

"I'm glad you're going to be okay, Mrs. Stoltz," Tony said, taking the hand she extended over the top of the railing gently in his. "You had me worried there for a little bit. And I'm afraid I owe you a window repair," Tony said, turning to Janet.

"Nothing compared to what we owe you," Janet told him. She turned to Abby. "We're lucky Tony came along when he did or things could have gone a lot differently. She could have been down at the bottom of those steps all afternoon if he hadn't found her. And the doctors say she was already in danger of dehydration and shock. He got to her just in time."

"How was it you happened to be there?" Abby asked Tony.

"Oh, I was delivering one of the little Christmas pails the kids from your church put together for some of their favorite people around the island," Tony said.

Abby noted that he avoided using a term that referenced age and thought that was especially sensitive, particularly given the circumstances. She liked him for it.

"I'd been there for quite some time by then and was feeling more than a little woozy," Emma said, placing her head back against the pillow.

"I thought I heard someone calling when I rang the doorbell," Tony said, but then I wasn't sure. I was about to walk away when I heard it again. I went around to the back of the house and got down to one of the basement window wells and called out and Mrs. Stoltz answered me. Her voice was weak, but I understood she needed help. I had to break one of Mrs. Heinz' windows to get into the house," he said sheepishly.

"I really mean it," Emma said, her voice growing weaker. "You are my guardian angel. In fact, that's what I thought you were, a real one I mean. I looked up and saw you at the top of those stairs. You had the light from the kitchen window coming from behind you and those beautiful curls of yours were all lit up. I really thought you were an angel."

"Those who know me would assure you that's not the case,

Mrs. Stoltz," Tony said with a laugh. "Just plain old everyday Tony, all too human."

"Well, you'll always be an angel to me, young man," Emma said her voice wavering. "You know, I've always believed angels exist. It's just that sometimes they don't have wings and we just call them friends."

"Well, I'll be honored to be called your friend," Tony said, patting her hand.

"You know all my worries about preparing for the holidays have just evaporated completely," Janet said, leaning over to smooth her mother's hair away from her face and gently kissing the uninjured side of her forehead. "We're going to have a great Christmas this year. And I can't remember when I've felt so much joy—and relief!"

The nurse came back in and shooed them all out. Abby stepped down the hallway a few steps to call Mary while Janet was talking to Tony.

"Thank God for sending Tony when He did," Mary said after Abby had given her the report.

Abby heard the strain in Mary's voice and knew she was thinking back to when she had lain broken and helpless after her accident. God had sent Henry to bring her comfort.

"Yes, Tony was in just the right place at the right time," Abby said. "And Emma's going to be fine. Thank heavens."

CHAPTER ❧ TEN

TONY PULLED ON HIS PARKA and wrapped the scarf Miss Opal had knitted around his neck. It was warm and colorful and he enjoyed wearing it just as he'd enjoyed meeting the sweet old lady who'd made it. He'd thought at first she might be the one. Had kind of hoped she was. She seemed to be very accepting and open. That was a good sign.

But after talking to her for a while, he knew she wasn't right. He'd have to move on. But he wasn't about to give up. There were lots more older women on the island. And when he got some information on those paintings, that might be the breakthrough.

He'd definitely had a stroke of luck when he'd been there when the pastor's young wife had gotten that call from the mom who had to cancel out on her delivery job. He'd picked up a lot of information when he was passing out those little gift buckets. Older people liked to talk and he'd listened and taken in every bit of information.

But then he'd gotten sidetracked by that lady's fall. He was glad she was going to be okay. She was nice. But she had family and friends all around her. He'd seen that clear enough after what happened. So he could definitely check her off the list.

He zipped his jacket and stuffed his hands into his pockets. He went out the door of The Bird Nest, heading for the marina. There was lots of activity down there. Only four days until Christmas and people were busy getting their boats ready for the big parade on Christmas Eve. That would be something to see. He was looking forward to it. And maybe, just maybe, by then he'd have what he'd come for. Four more days until Christmas. He was hoping for a big present.

What he'd been told about this island had certainly proved true. The people here were very open. Very trusting. They'd welcomed him. He hoped when he got it narrowed down to the right senior citizen she'd do the same. He was counting on it.

ABBY BARELY HAD TIME to glance at the newspaper before preparing to rush off to the museum to make sure everything was in place for the open house. But she did see that William had, as promised, run the article about the angel paintings. On the front page, no less. With William's usual flair for the dramatic he had headlined the article "Mystery Paintings Found Hidden in Local Church."

Well, the paintings were a mystery of sorts, but they hadn't been hidden, just stored out of the way and overlooked for a long while. Whatever. If it would help get some information about the origin of the paintings, William was welcome to dish out a little hype.

Mary had already been up and dressed, and was putting Finnegan's harness on him, when Abby got downstairs.

"Where are you off to? I thought you said you were going to sleep in this morning," Abby said. "You know you're expected at the open house tonight, rested and ready to have a good time."

"Oh, don't you worry, I'll be there. Wouldn't miss it," Mary said. "But we'll have to leave a little early. You know we have Henry's work party too, remember? Right now I'm going over to work Patricia's shift at the craft fair so she can fill in at the church office so Janet can go and be with Emma. They've said they'll probably dismiss her this afternoon and Janet can bring her home."

"Wow, that's complicated," Abby said. "Everybody's shifting around."

"Yes," Mary said with a laugh. "We need one of Bobby's charts. How are he and Dad doing with their project anyway?"

"I don't know and I don't dare ask," Abby said. "I'm afraid they'll pull me into this scheme if I show too much interest. I'll check on them tomorrow, after the open house. Now, don't overdo," she said as she put her empty glass from the orange juice into the sink.

"You take your own good advice, Abby," Mary answered. "I plan to come home and get a nap in before tonight."

Abby waved and groaned softly as she headed for the car. A nap before the open house would be heavenly, but there was no way she'd work that in. Not with everything she had to do today.

ABBY AND HUGO ARRIVED in the parking lot at the same time and walked into the museum together. It gave Abby the chance to see things the way their arriving guests would that evening. She cast a critical eye on every detail.

"There's a big bald spot on the tree," she said as they went into the lobby. "Right there in the middle. I'll have to look for another ornament to put on or else move some of them around."

"We can do that later," Hugo said. "Let's check on the food and the sound system first and make sure all the interactive exhibits are in good working order. The last time we had a public event, we blew a fuse and the whole Native American exhibit went dark."

"We don't want that again," Abby agreed, remembering the sight of people leaning over the railings and squinting into the dioramas, trying to make out what they could in the shadowy shapes. It had taken a while to locate and fix the problem, and they'd had some frustrated visitors in the meantime.

The rest of the morning passed in a blur with Abby, Hugo, Wilma and a host of volunteers getting the museum ready for their guests. At mid-afternoon Abby glanced at her watch. "Oh good grief," she said. "I've got to get going. I'll miss my appointment over at Silver Scissors."

"Go," Hugo commanded. "Never let it be said I stood between a lady and her hairdresser," he teased.

"Seriously," he added, "everything's ready, Abby. And it all looks fabulous. Thanks for all your hard work."

"A team effort," Abby said. "Thanks to everyone," she called as she did a few backward steps before turning and rushing to her office to grab her bag. She was thrilled with how everything looked as she walked back out through the museum. Then she noticed the tree in the lobby still had that bare spot in the front.

"No time now, I'll take care of it when I get back," she muttered to herself, glancing at her watch again. She knew

Edmonia Lewis would be booked solid due to all the holiday festivities. If she was late for her appointment, it would make Edmonia run late with everyone else and that would be very inconsiderate.

AS SHE'D EXPECTED the shop was buzzing when she arrived. "Oh Abby, you're here," Edmonia said as she looked up from styling Miss Opal Collins' gray bouffant. "I was beginning to think you weren't going to make it."

"Here with forty seconds to spare," Abby said, catching her breath.

"Everything ready for the big evening?" Miss Opal asked.

"Yes. And if I do say so myself, the museum looks fantastic. It ought to be lots of fun."

"I'm certainly looking forward to it," Miss Opal said. "And I've even got a date for it!"

Several heads turned at once in Miss Opal's direction.

"Oh relax," Miss Opal said with a rattling laugh. "It's not really a date, no reason for tongues to start wagging. But that sweet little Tony Malachy is coming over to drive me. I told him I don't much like to drive at night anymore and he offered. He's the nicest young man. Don't you think so, Abby?"

"He strikes everyone that way," Abby said evasively.

"Well, I seem to be the only one on the island who hasn't met him yet," Margaret Blackstock said, handing a small piece of tissue paper up to Marlene, one of Edmonia's stylists. Marlene took the paper and wrapped a section of Margaret's thick black hair in it before winding it onto a permanent rod.

"But let me tell you this," Margaret said, her Brooklyn accent still thick even after all these years as an island transplant, "if a person seems too good to be true, they usually are."

There were murmurs of protest from several of the women and Margaret held up both hands, "I'm just saying . . ." She let her voice trail off and dropped her hands. "What about you, Abby? What do you think of this boy?"

"He's very likeable," Abby answered as she moved into the chair Miss Opal had vacated.

"That didn't answer my question," Margaret pressed in her usual no-nonsense style. "What do you think of him?"

Abby looked around the room and saw all eyes focused on her. "I like him a lot," she said finally, realizing it was the truth. "And everything he's done since he arrived on the island has been thoughtful and kind. They say you know a man by his actions, and everything he's done has been good."

"Heroic even," Miss Opal piped up, admiring her hairdo in the mirror by the door of the shop. "Did you hear what happened with Emma?"

Everyone nodded and began to discuss Tony's rescue of Emma.

Abby thought of her own words. Was she being completely honest, even with herself? She *did* like Tony and she certainly wanted to believe he was just what he seemed. And it was a sad thing indeed when good deeds only made people suspicious.

Something in the conversation snapped Abby out of her own ruminations. "It's really a shame. Poor Janet's having a terrible time of it these days," Margaret was saying. "What a string of bad luck."

"What do you mean?" Abby asked. "Is Emma okay?"

"Oh, she's fine—or will be," Margaret said, turning toward Abby and forcing Marlene to twist her hands to keep from losing the section of hair she'd just parted off. "You didn't hear?"

"Hear what?" Abby asked, looking at Margaret in the mirror

that ran the length of the salon. She resisted the temptation to turn around and got an approving nod from Edmonia.

"Janet was so rattled when she left the hospital after what happened to Emma yesterday, she drove off with her pocketbook on top of her car," Margaret said. "I've warned her about setting it up there when she unlocks her car, but old habits are hard to break. Anyway, it had the day's collection from the craft fair in it. Janet had it all ready to go to the bank when the call about her mother came in."

"Oh no," Abby said.

"Oh yes," Margaret said firmly. "I went out with her this morning and we walked every inch of that parking lot. And I do mean every inch. We even checked the dumpsters, but there's not a sign of it. Janet's just sick about it."

Abby frowned and glanced at the clock on the beauty shop wall.

"Don't even think about it, Abby," Margaret said sternly. "I know what you're thinking. And I promise, you wouldn't have any better luck than we did. We were *very* thorough. The bag is not there. And Janet and Doug have gone to bring Emma home from the hospital. There's nothing you can do right now, so try to forget it—for now at least—and go get yourself dolled up for the party tonight."

Edmonia picked up a hand mirror from the table and handed it to Abby ceremoniously. She twirled her chair around so she could see the backside of her new do. "And when they compliment your hair, be sure to tell them who styled it," she said.

ABBY HAD TO CONCENTRATE as she crossed the parking lot. It had been a while since she'd worn high heels and she had to adjust her gait. Back at the house she and Mary had been like a couple of schoolgirls getting ready for prom. And Abby had to admit, it was fun to get dressed up once in a while.

Hugo, dressed in a well-tailored black suit and wearing a beautiful red silk tie, greeted her with a bow as she came in the door of The Nature Museum. "Abigail, you look lovely," he said.

Abby felt herself actually blush. "You look very nice yourself, Hugo," she said. "Any last-minute tasks?"

"No, everything's all set," he said. "Our guests should start arriving any minute. Wilma's back in the workroom checking on the extra food trays to make sure everything that was supposed to go in the refrigerator got put in there."

"Okay," Abby said. "I'm just going to put my things in my office, then I'll go back out to the front and move the ornaments around to fill in the bare spot on the tree. Then I think we're all set. Merry Christmas, Hugo."

"And a very merry one to you, too, Abby," he said, leaning over to give her a kiss on the cheek.

Abby felt her face go pink again and scolded herself as she walked away. For heaven's sake, she had passed fifty. Shouldn't she be beyond girlish blushing by now?

Just as she reached the front door, she saw two figures making their way up the steps. She recognized Miss Opal's bouffant silhouette long before she could see the faces in the light.

Abby went to meet them, swinging the door open so that Tony could escort the older woman through.

They exchanged compliments and Tony looked down at his khaki pants and plain brown oxfords. "I'm afraid this was the best I could do," he said. "I didn't exactly come prepared for a dress-up event. Suits don't travel too well in a rucksack."

"You look fine," Abby assured him. "There will be people

here in all manner of dress. I'm just using it as an excuse to get dressed up for once."

"Well, to make up for my appearance, I've brought you a little gift," he said. He reached into his shirt pocket and brought out a small irregular shaped object clumsily wrapped in tissue paper and tied with a loopy red bow. "I heard about the project you were doing with the kids for the tree and I wanted to make my own contribution. I'm learning about the San Juans too. Go ahead, open it."

Abby did as instructed and found a clamshell. It was relatively flat and on the lustrous inside someone had painted a dove with an olive branch in its beak. A hole had been drilled in the top to allow a ribbon to pass through. The painting was simple but pleasing and the natural coloring of the shell added a shimmery background.

"Who did this?" Abby asked thinking of how much it resembled the dove in the angel paintings.

"Tony did it himself," Miss Opal answered. "Isn't he talented?"

"I don't know about that," Tony said. "I'm just a hobby painter, but I wanted to make something for the tree," he pointed behind Abby.

"You won't believe me when I tell you this, but I was just coming out here to move some ornaments around to fill this hole," Abby pointed to the bare spot. "It's as if this tree had a space saved just for you."

"Seems that way," Tony answered.

Abby invited them to go in, have some food and look around. As they walked away she heard Miss Opal say to Tony, "Now, you mustn't let me forget to introduce you to Goldie

Landon like you asked. I'm sure she'll be here if she's feeling up to it."

"Don't worry, I'll remind you," Tony said. "I'd really like to meet her."

Abby tensed, but then shook her head. She pushed the ornament she'd just hung on the tree branch to the side and watched it swing, catching the light. It was a thoughtful gesture for Tony to bring it. And it was very nice of him to volunteer to drive Miss Opal. She'd said it herself, just this afternoon; everything Tony had done since he'd been here had been courteous and helpful. Asking to meet someone was certainly no crime.

The evening was a smashing success. Everyone had a grand time and it all went smooth as clockwork. The refreshments were tasty and all the exhibits worked as they were intended to. Everyone was in a relaxed and festive mood. Abby noticed that Tony seemed to get around to talking to practically everyone there before the evening was over.

Margaret came over early in the evening and touched Abby's arm. "Great party, Hon. I'm going over now to sit with Emma so Janet and Doug can come over for a little while. I had to really wear Janet down to get her to agree to it, but I think it'll be good for them both to get out for a little while. And Emma feels terrible that they were going to miss the party on her account."

"That's really thoughtful of you, Margaret," Abby said. "I don't suppose there's any sign of the craft fair money?"

Margaret put up a hand to stop her. "Tonight we forget our troubles and only talk of happy things. Plenty of time for hand-wringing over that tomorrow," she flapped her hand down to her side and turned to go, then as quickly turned back. "Oh, by the by. I met our young hero, Tony, earlier."

"And?" Abby asked, hoping Margaret's assessment wasn't going to get her own suspicions revved up again.

"And he's cute as a button and one of the nicest young men I've ever met. Shame on me for talking out of my hat before I even met the boy."

Serena arrived with Rick on one arm and Artie Washburn on the other. She looked adorable in a little black dress with a sweetheart neckline that flattered her long neck. She wore a necklace made of three silver chains, each barely thicker than a hair. They caught the light with every breath she took. Abby wasn't sure if the sparkle in her eye was a reflection of the necklace or was caused by Artie's proximity.

Rick stole her away quickly after their arrival to introduce her to some people. Abby couldn't resist the opportunity to tease Artie. "You two are spending quite a bit of time together. Is this getting serious?"

Artie watched Serena from across the room and smiled. "I don't know about serious, but I sure do like her," he said. "She's the only woman I've ever met that likes being outdoors as much as I do. Wish she could stay around longer."

"Yes, I imagine," Abby said.

"Hey, I'm glad to have a chance to talk to you," Artie said jerking his head to one side as a sign for Abby to follow him to the edge of the room away from other people. "This guy my aunt had over to dinner the other night—Tony, I think is his name. What do you know about him?"

"Well, truthfully, not that much," Abby said. "All I can tell you is he seems to be a very nice young man and he's done a lot of nice things for people since he came to the island. That's him right over there," she gestured with a nod of her head. "Would you like me to introduce you?"

"I'm sure I'll meet him before the night's over," Artie said. "I'll tell you why I'm asking. Aunt Wilma, well, that's just not like her to ask a total stranger into her house. I wasn't there. I had duty that night, but as I understand it, she gave him practically her whole life story. The whole family's for that matter. It just worries me a little. What with identity theft and all these days—not to mention the more grisly stuff that goes on—well, you just never know about people's motives." Artie ran his hand up and down his cheek as if checking to see if he needed a shave and stared across the room at Tony.

Abby sighed. "Well, I'll be honest with you, Artie. It worried me at first too."

"You think I should run a check on him?" Artie asked, his body stiffening.

"Oh, I don't know Artie. Should you really do that if he hasn't done anything wrong?"

"No, you're right," he said, letting his shoulders drop. "Still, I'll be interested to meet him," he said, his eyes narrowing as he glanced across the museum floor.

"All I can tell you is that he seems awfully nice and he's gone out of his way to do helpful things for people from the moment he set foot on the island. He seems sincere to me. As to what's going on in his mind and his heart"—she shrugged—"that, I couldn't tell you."

"I'll make it a point to talk to him. If nothing pops out as strange, I can relax and put it down to Aunt Wilma just getting into the Christmas spirit," he said.

Abby circulated and tried to talk to everyone at the party. She laughed and talked so much her voice grew husky. As the evening was winding down, she stationed herself near the door so she could be sure to say good-bye to people as they were leaving.

Artie Washburn left early to go to the sheriff's office party. As he left, he leaned over to whisper in Abby's ear, "I met Tony, and I see what you mean. Nice guy. Sorry about earlier."

Several regular volunteers stayed to help clear away the food and help the caterers pack up. They left one by one until finally only Hugo and Abby were left.

"Well, I'd say the party was a grand success," Hugo said, still looking as crisp and polished as he had at the beginning of the evening. "You must be exhausted, Abby. Can I carry anything to your car for you?"

"No, I've only got my bag," Abby said. "I tell you what, Hugo. You go on. I think I'm going to stay and do a little work in my office."

"Not that I don't appreciate your dedication, but your vacation is supposed to start right now. We're officially closed until after Christmas."

"I know," Abby said. "But I'm still wound up from the party, and Mary won't be home from Henry's office party yet. Plus, I have a few things I'd really like to do on the computer. You know we only have dial-up at Mary's house and it's frustrating when you're used to having a faster line."

"Are you going to be okay here by yourself?" Hugo asked.

"Of course," Abby said. "Hugo, I've worked here alone lots of times. I'll lock up after you. I'll be fine."

And she was—at least for a while. After she'd locked the door behind Hugo she went into her office and switched on her computer. She felt a little ridiculous as she sat in her office chair in her long black dress and embroidered sequined jacket.

But she was soon absorbed in what she was doing and forgot about how she was dressed.

She went to her Web browser and called up her favorite of the sites she'd found on bird symbolism and mythology. She still didn't have her own reference photos of the paintings, but she had the ones William had run in the newspaper. They were grainy and ill defined, but they were at least enough to jog her memory.

The one featuring the hummingbirds had been on her mind throughout the day. The angel in this one was standing on solid ground, barefoot and in the same flowing dress as in the others. A ring of hummingbirds surrounded her. Abby tilted her head to one side, thinking. This was a risky composition. In the wrong hands it could have come across as menacing, but the artist had managed to convey a sense of joy in the angel's face and posture. The figure held both arms out to the side, her palms upturned in a graceful and welcoming invitation. Her head was tilted slightly backward as if she might laugh aloud.

That was it, Abby realized. That's what had been so intriguing to her about this one. How often did you see angels portrayed as laughing or even smiling? Rarely. More often they were somber. But all the angels in these paintings were happy, smiling angels.

Abby typed *hummingbird* into the search engine for the site and waited. As her keys went silent she heard a muffled noise from the main room of the museum. Probably the heat kicking on, she thought. Now that all the people were out of the room, the temperature had probably dropped enough to trip the thermostat.

The screen filled with text and photos and Abby traced her

finger along its surface as she read: "The hummingbird signifies the ability to adapt easily to new circumstances, never wasting time looking back and thinking of what was or might have been." Making the most of now.

Abby smiled. She knew lots of people like that. Mary came instantly to mind. Though Mary occasionally had her down moments, she was living a very full life in the new circumstances the accident had forced on her. And there were lots of other people around the island Abby could think of who fit the same bill—women especially.

Abby heard another thumping sound and stiffened. This was followed immediately by a series of clicks from somewhere in Hugo's office. She sat very still, her hands poised over the keys, and listened. The hair bristled on the nape of her neck and she felt a shiver move up her spine.

She jumped as a whoosh of air passed through the heat vents. The vents rattled and popped as they expanded. Noises she wouldn't have even noticed during the daytime now took on an ominous tone. She put her hand to her heart and could feel it beating fast.

"Stop being silly," she said, but even her own words spooked her, the sibilant *s* sounds seeming to slither into the room. She rose and went out into the museum's main room. She had turned off all the lights except those along the foot rails. The pale up-lights cast shadows on the walls and ceilings. Abby could hear her own breathing and it seemed to catch in her throat and go raspy and jagged.

She headed for the lobby to make certain the door was locked, using all her willpower to keep from running.

The door was, indeed, locked up tight. As Abby turned to go back to her office, the single canister light that was always left on in the lobby shone down, just catching the Christmas tree in the edge of its circle. Hugo had unplugged the lights on the tree when he left, and what with all the natural materials the children had used in the ornaments, only a few caught the spotlight. One in particular caught Abby's eye—the dove that Tony had brought as a gift.

Abby reached out as she had done with Vanessa's magpie earlier and touched the ornament, sending it swinging. As she looked at it, a sense of peace came over her. Here she was on a beautiful Sparrow Island evening and in a place that celebrated everything she loved about her homeland. She'd spent a wonderful evening among friends and family. What did she have to be fretful about?

She reached out and took the ornament off the tree and held it in her hand. She was sure Tony wouldn't mind if she took it home to Mary and hung it on their tree. She wanted to be reminded of this moment of peace and contentment throughout the season.

She put her shoulders back and walked back through the main room. The same shadows that had seemed sinister only moments earlier now seemed cozy and welcoming. She knew every inch of this room, every detail of every display. She kicked off her high heels and padded over to the Wonderful World of Wings. In the shadows she could just make out the silhouette of the dove, suspended from the ceiling by a thin wire. "Peace and promise," she said aloud, then held up the ornament and whispered softly, "Blessed peace."

CHAPTER ❧ ELEVEN

TONY AWOKE SO EXCITED that he was up and dressed long before he could get breakfast at The Bird Nest. He could hear the Chois in the kitchen and smell the wonderful aroma of fresh baked bread. Coffee perking and bacon sizzling were torture to his ravenous appetite. He decided to go out for a walk to try to calm down.

He'd found the one. He was convinced. The one he'd met last night at the museum open house. She fit all his parameters. He ticked them off mentally: she lived alone with no family. From what he could tell she was the right age, though he hadn't asked her that directly. After all, he was a gentleman. But he'd asked enough questions with historical markers to be able to deduce how old she was. She lived in an isolated area and didn't have much contact with people. She was a very independent sort who wouldn't feel the need to solicit other people's opinions about what she did. Perfect. Now all he had to do was zero in. Find a way into her life. Get her story.

He picked up his pace as he walked along the waterfront at the marina. He couldn't remember when he'd been this pumped up and nervous. A lot was riding on this.

"HOW WAS HENRY'S PARTY LAST NIGHT?" Abby asked as she and Mary moved about in the kitchen, making their first leisurely breakfast in a long while.

"It was nice. Very nice," Mary said.

Abby continued beating the eggs she was getting ready to scramble, but turned her gaze to study Mary. There was something in her tone that Abby didn't like.

"Well, that's not exactly a ringing endorsement. Did something happen?" Abby asked.

"What?" Mary asked, looking up distractedly from her task of placing English muffins into the toaster oven.

"Did something bad happen at Henry's party?" Abby repeated.

"Bad?" Mary repeated blankly. "Oh no. Everything was really nice. They made me feel right at home and welcome. It was lovely."

"But?" Abby said, drawing out the word.

"No buts," Mary said, turning her chair abruptly and rolling to the refrigerator. Finnegan was taken by surprise and his nails clicked as he tried to get traction on the kitchen flooring to get to the fridge to open it for her.

"Okay, Mary," Abby said. "If you don't want to talk about it, that's fine,"

"There's nothing to talk about," Mary said, trying to put some conviction in her voice. She turned her chair again with a jerk and the wheel glanced off the leg of a kitchen chair and the orange juice she was carrying to the table sloshed into her lap. "Now look what you've made me do," she said.

Abby set the bowl of eggs down and turned to look at Mary, her arms crossed in front of her.

Mary swiped at the few drops of orange juice, then looked up at Abby miserably. "I'm sorry, Abby. I didn't mean to snap. And what I said was absolutely true. It's just not all of it. All Henry's co-workers and their spouses do make me feel right at home and welcome when I go to these events with him. It's just that the longer Henry and I see one another, the more expectations they seem to have about us."

"Well, that's natural, don't you think?" Abby asked, her voice gentle.

"Yes, I suppose," Mary said. "But it's hard for me. You know I care for Henry. He's a dear, wonderful man, and I can't imagine my life without him."

"And I know for a fact he's crazy about you," Abby said. "So where's the problem here?"

"I guess it just bothers me when people make assumptions about where this relationship might be heading," she said. She looked down at her hands and turned her wedding band slowly around on her finger. "I spent a lot of years thinking of myself as Jacob's wife. All my adult life that's who I was. And if he was still here, that's who I'd still be. I haven't even been able to take off my wedding ring in all these long years."

"I know that, Mary," Abby said softly. "Jacob was a remarkable man, and a devoted husband and father. And he loved you very much. Which is why he'd want you to be happy. He'd want what's best for you. Do you really think he'd want you to be lonely as a way to honor his memory?"

"Of course not," Mary said.

"Well, let me ask you this, Mary," Abby said quietly. "How do you think it makes Henry feel that you still wear your wedding ring? Seems to me that's a pretty clear signal about the limitations you've put on your relationship with him."

"Yes, I suppose it is," Mary said. "Though I haven't meant it to be. I guess I've just always felt that taking it off would be abandoning Jacob's memory."

"Do you still think that?" Abby asked. "Because, I don't need to see Jacob's ring to make me think about him all the time. You can't live in this house and not think about him fifty times a day. He's everywhere," she said, gesturing around the kitchen. "His favorite coffee cup, his books, his collections. Jacob, Jacob, everywhere."

"Yes, I guess he is," Mary said. "It's hard to let go of the past sometimes." She sat quietly for a moment. "I wonder," she started, her voice so soft Abby had to strain to hear her, "if Jacob could get a message to me, what would he say?"

"He'd say he's proud of you and wants you to be happy," Abby said, patting Mary on the shoulder.

As they ate their breakfast, Mary seemed to feel the need to talk about Jacob and about happier times. She reminisced about their wedding day and about Jacob's determination to make it on his own despite his parents' disapproval of his choice of a writing career.

"That's one reason I'm trying so hard to be supportive of Zack's choices," Mary said. "I know how hurtful it was to Jacob that his parents disapproved of him following his dream. I don't want that ever to happen to Zack."

"You've been very supportive of Zack," Abby said, scooping

a thimbleful of Mary's homemade honey butter from the crock and watching it melt as she glided her knife across her warm muffin. "And I know he feels it and appreciates it Mary. He's told me so."

"Well, I try," Mary said. "Of course, I'm sure he knows it's not the life I would choose for him, given my druthers," Mary said. "I don't want him ever to have to give up his music. I know music means so much to him. And he's got to go where the audience is, for now. But there are other ways to keep it in his life. Composing, teaching maybe. He doesn't have to be a performer. And I'd never say this to him, of course, but I am hoping someday he'll settle down and have a family."

"Oh, I don't think that's much of a secret," Abby said. "In your dreams you've got him and Lily married and with three children, living right back here on Sparrow Island."

"Well, a girl can dream, can't she?" Mary said.

After the breakfast dishes were all cleared away Abby picked up the phone and dialed a number. Goldie Landon's voice came on the wire.

"Hi, Goldie," Abby said.

"Abby," Goldie said, "it's good to hear from you. It's the strangest thing. I was just going to call you."

"Listen, Goldie, I was wondering if I could ask you some island history questions. I'm trying to get some information on . . ."

". . . those paintings that were found at the church?" Goldie finished for her. "I want to talk to you about that. I very much want to talk to you about it."

"Okay, what can you tell me about them, Goldie?" Abby asked, reaching for a pad and pen.

"If they're what I think they are, everything," Goldie said.

"But not on the telephone. I'd rather talk about it in person. Can you come out here?"

Abby looked down at her robe and fuzzy bedroom slippers. "Sure, Goldie," she said, spurred on by the intensity in Goldie's voice. "Just give me a few minutes. I'll be out as soon as I can."

WITHIN TWENTY MINUTES they were in Mary's van heading for Goldie's. Once Mary had heard about what Goldie had said, there was no way she was going to be left behind. Last-minute shopping and gift-wrapping would just have to wait. If Goldie held the key to the mystery of those paintings, *everything* else could wait.

Abby felt a twinge when she saw the moped parked by Goldie's greenhouse. A metallic gold helmet hung from the handlebar.

"Well, look at that, Tony's way out here," Mary said. "That boy certainly gets around, doesn't he?"

"Yes, he does," Abby agreed, willing herself to ignore the doubt trying to creep into her thoughts. "Wonder what he's doing out here. He just met Goldie for the first time at the museum last night."

"Maybe he wanted to see the greenhouse. He seems to be interested in everything. And Goldie has some pretty exotic plants."

"Right," Abby said.

Mary gave the horn a couple of quick blasts, pulled up close to the greenhouse and parked. The warning wasn't strictly needed today as Goldie was expecting them, but it was by now a ritual of the friendship and it seemed wrong to omit it.

Goldie came to the door of the greenhouse. She pulled off her heavy canvas gloves and pushed a few strands of gray hair back away from her face. "Good to see you both," she called. "We'll have to talk out here for now if you don't mind. I've got some chores that won't wait."

When they were all out of the van and headed for the greenhouse, Goldie asked, "What in the world is that you've got on Finnegan?" She moved around to get a closer look at the dog, but didn't go near him since he had on his harness and she knew he was working.

"His Christmas cape," Mary said. "Everyone gets to look festive for the holidays."

"That one's really something," Goldie said, looking at the sequins and bangles and appliqués sewn onto the bright red fabric that had temporarily replaced Finnegan's dignified blue working-dog cape. It was bound all the way around with a striped candy-cane edging. "That's even fancier than the one he had on the other day."

"Oh, she's toned it down," Abby said. "She did have bells all along the edges. But Blossom kept going up to Finnegan and batting at them. It was driving the poor dog bonkers. Mary had to at least take those off."

"Well, he looks very Christmasy," Goldie said. "Thank you both for coming all the way out here," she said as she led them into the greenhouse, which smelled redolent with greenery and peat moss. "I don't know that I would have heard anything about those paintings you found, at least not for a while. I don't get the paper. But this young man here," she said, gesturing to the far side of the greenhouse where Tony was watering some plants with a sprinkler wand, "told me about them."

Tony waved then went back to the task at hand.

"So you know something about who painted the angels?" Mary asked.

"You might say I do," Goldie said. "If they're the ones I think they are, I can tell you everything about them. Though I just don't know how they could be the same ones. I thought they were destroyed in a fire years ago."

Abby handed her *The Birdcall* featuring the paintings on the front page.

Goldie sucked in a breath and pressed her gnarled fingers to her lips. She stared at the paper for a few long moments. "My sister Sylvia painted them," she said at last, squeezing her eyes shut. "She was still a teenager at the time. Unusual talent that girl had," she said, her voice growing stronger. "Just remarkable. We all had no idea where that came from. My parents were puzzled about it. They had no artistic talent to speak of, and I can just about draw a stick figure. But Sylvia could draw and paint from the time she could hold a pencil or a brush. Self taught. It was really a gift from God is all we could figure."

"That's astounding," Abby said. "A teenaged girl painted those? I never would have believed that."

"I guess we all talked about her talent being a gift from God so much, she started painting angels. Maybe as payback or something of that sort. Who knows what goes through a young mind. Anyway, she originally planned to do a set of twelve, for the twelve apostles, but she died before she had a chance to see it through."

"How did they come to be at the church?" Abby asked.

"After Sylvia died, my parents gave them to the church as a gift," Goldie said. "That was a lot of years ago," she said, the faraway look returning. "We all thought they burned up in that little outbuilding years back. I tell you, I always mourned that. I'm so happy to know they've been found. Are they damaged?"

"They're beautiful," Abby said. "In wonderful shape. Would you like us to take you into town to see them?"

"Oh no," Goldie said. "Eager as I am, I've got some jealous plants here that need tending. I'll try to make it in tomorrow. And anyway, I've already got a clear picture of them." She tapped her temple. "I can see every one of them right up here, clear as day. It's enough for me to know they've been found."

"You'll see," Abby said. "They're lovely. But I have a question, Goldie. Why didn't Sylvia sign them? I'd certainly want to claim them if I'd had the talent to paint them."

"Oh, I'm sure she did," Goldie said. "She signed everything she did."

"I couldn't find a signature anywhere," Abby said. "I even took one of the paintings out of the frame and gave it a close exam. All I found was a date, 1948."

"Inside an *L*," Goldie prompted.

"An *L*?" Abby said.

"*L* for Landon. That's how Sylvia signed her work. Just with that initial and the date."

Abby shook her head. "I thought it was just a bracket. "But maybe my subconscious knew different. I couldn't stop thinking about you and associating you with these paintings somehow."

"Well, you've got good instincts, Abby," Goldie said. "Sometimes that can take you right where you need to go."

"How are you doing with the plants?" Mary asked.

"I tell you, I'm really getting worried now that the Christmas cacti and even the poinsettias are not going to bloom out in time," Goldie said, frowning. "Tony tells me not to worry," she said gesturing back in his direction. "He thinks they'll make it, but I just don't know."

Abby looked back to where Tony was dutifully watering the plants. He stepped along the row of pots and into a shaft of sunlight angling into the greenhouse. The rays caught his curly blond hair and his fine facial features and Abby had to stifle a gasp. He looked like one of the angels in the paintings. She shook her head. Now she really was losing it. She was seeing angels at every turn.

"Is there anything we can do to help you?" Mary asked, bringing Abby back to reality.

"Yes, please let us help," Abby said. "And I'd really like to hear more about your sister," she added, thinking back to how good it had been for Mary to talk about Jacob earlier this morning.

"Well, if you wouldn't mind helping me wrap these pots in their Christmas foil, we can talk while we work," Goldie said.

Tony finished the watering and joined them. Soon they'd all settled into a rhythm of cutting and wrapping. They left the bows to Mary's more practiced hands.

Goldie began, seeming to tell the story to herself as much as to them. "Sylvia was always an unusually sensitive child. A dreamer. She was small, like me, but not as hearty. She was always obedient and good-natured. At least she was until she was about sixteen."

"What happened then?" Mary asked.

"She started keeping company with a boy from over on Lopez. Jimmy Houghton. He was a little on the wild side. Nothing serious really, certainly not by today's standards. But my parents didn't approve of Sylvia seeing him. He fancied himself some sort of beatnik poet I think, and that appealed to Sylvia's romantic view of life. He really was a nice boy, though. Or at least I thought so after I got to know him a little. He was an only child and he'd been indulged, so he was a little spoiled, but he had a good heart."

"So was it just an infatuation?" Tony asked.

"Well, I thought so at first, but no, it was more than that," Goldie answered, turning a pot and frowning at a brown spot on one of the shoots. She set the pot aside on a table behind her. "I believe they really did love one another very deeply. They were young, but I don't think it was just puppy love, though that's what my parents thought."

"Did your parents try to discourage her from seeing the boy?" Abby asked.

"Not in so many words," Goldie said. "I think they knew forbidding her to see him would only turn them into Romeo and Juliet in Sylvia's eyes," Goldie said with a sad smile. "But they withheld their approval, which to Sylvia was so very important."

"So they didn't like him at all?" Tony asked.

"I don't think they ever really got to know him," Goldie said turning her head to one side as if intrigued by the question. "They didn't like the *idea* of him is more like it, I think. He was two years older than Sylvia—much too old for her in their opinion. And he was getting ready to go off to college that fall. I think they were afraid he'd break her heart."

"What ever happened to him?" Abby asked.

Goldie looked up sharply. "Oh, that's right. You probably don't know," she said, squeezing her eyes shut and taking a deep breath. "He's dead. He and Sylvia got it into their heads to elope. She'd just turned seventeen. I tell you, we couldn't have been more shocked. She left us a note telling us that she loved us all, but that she and Jimmy wanted to be together. Off they went. They tried to take his father's boat across to the mainland, but they didn't make it. It was too small a craft for those waters. The boat was finally located after a few days, capsized. They found Jimmy's remains, but Sylvia never was found."

"Oh, Goldie," Abby said. "I'm so sorry."

"It's okay, Abby," Goldie said. "Really it is. It's nice to be able to remember Sylvia's *life* anyway and share it with someone. And I'm so very thrilled to learn that the paintings have survived. That's the best Christmas gift I could have gotten."

"Everyone is just so affected by them," Abby said. "They're beautiful. And as you might guess, I am doubly enamored with them because of the birds."

Goldie smiled. "Sylvia loved birds," she said. "Mother always said it was because she was so birdlike herself. I've got lots of little drawings and sketches she did of birds if you'd like to see them sometime."

"Oh yes, I'd love to," Abby said. She told Goldie about all the research she'd done on bird symbolism and mythology since she'd first seen the paintings.

"Well, you were certainly on the right track," Goldie said, seemingly pleased. "I guess you understood somehow what Sylvia was trying to say through the series. She studied—really *studied*—that kind of thing. Everything, every single thing in her paintings is there for a reason. She wrote it all down when she was working on them. I think now they call it an artist's statement or some such thing, but she didn't have those kinds of pretentions way back then. She just liked writing it down. There should be a copy of what she wrote about each of the angel paintings at the church or with the paintings somewhere.

I know my parents gave a copy of her notebook to the pastor when they donated the paintings. If not, I may have it up in my attic somewhere. I can look for it."

"I'll ask Patricia if she's found anything like that," Abby said. "She was searching the church records for any hint of where the paintings came from. Speaking of which, I need to call her and let her know what we've found out. She's going to be so excited."

"You can't get a signal out here," Mary said. "You'll have to wait until we get back closer to town."

"You're welcome to use my phone," Goldie said, gesturing toward the house.

"That's okay," Abby said, handing a pot over to Mary to tie the last ribbon bow. "We need to be going anyway. Still lots of Christmas stuff to do."

Abby had to wrestle one last time with her suspicions as she turned to close the door of the greenhouse on the way out. She saw Tony and Goldie in earnest conversation. Goldie's sad smile had returned and Tony was leaned in close talking to her in a low voice.

Goldie was not ordinarily given to demonstrations of affection, even with her closest friends. So Abby was amazed when she saw her reach out to pat Tony gently on the cheek.

CHAPTER ❦ TWELVE

ABBY FELT BOTH INTENSE happiness and equally weighted sadness as they drove back into town. She was delighted to know who had done the paintings and was even more in wonder of the artistry now that she knew they had been created by a person so young. But Sylvia's story was a sad one too.

"Abby, do you see now why I needed to tell you how much I love you and appreciate you after I visited Goldie last time?" Mary asked.

"Yes, I can clearly see why. I feel the urge to tell you again too. Do I say it enough?"

"By word and action," Mary said. "Each and every day, Abby."

"We're lucky," Abby said, thinking of how horrible the loss of a daughter and sister must have been for the Landon family. "Such a tragedy. And you know the parents must have held themselves at least partially responsible."

"I'm sure," Mary said. "From what Goldie's told me about her parents, they were very loving and gentle. And it certainly sounds as if they tried to handle the situation delicately. But when it comes to young people and the affairs of the heart, who knows what will get into their heads?"

"True," Abby said. "I'm glad Tony's there with her," she said, willing sincerity into the words. "He seems to have a way about him. Maybe he can give her some comfort after we've stirred up all these memories."

"Bad memories," said Mary, tilting her head slightly to the side, but keeping her eyes fixed firmly on the road, "but good ones, too, I think. Goldie's a strong woman, Abby. I think it's worth it to her to have to endure the bad memories if she can have the good ones to think about. And I think it's important to her to talk about her sister."

"Like you with Jacob?" Abby asked gently.

"Yes, like me with Jacob," Mary answered. "I enjoy sharing his books with people who never had a chance to know him and read his work. And that must be the way Goldie feels about Sylvia's art. It's as if she's living on through what she did with her life, short as it was."

Abby pulled out her cell phone and saw that she had a signal. She tried Patricia's number, but got her voice mail.

"That's okay, we'll swing by the craft fair and tell her," Mary said.

"Yes, let's do that. I'd like to tell her in person. And I'd like to get another look at the paintings myself, knowing what I do now about them. I think it will help me see them in a whole new light."

"Yes, it'll make them even more poignant, if that's possible," Mary said.

THE MARINA WAS HUMMING with activity as Mary and Abby made a quick stop to check on their father and Bobby and see what kind of progress they'd made with the great light show contraption.

The wind had turned brisk and Mary reached into the bag on the side of her chair to get her gloves. Abby waited as she pulled them on, squinting into the distance to see her father's fishing boat completely covered in a series of tarps. "What in the world!" she exclaimed.

They were both still squinting and frowning in the direction of the boat when they passed Margaret and Joe Blackstock's Bayliner. "Your dad and Bobby are cooking something up over there," Joe said as he wrapped one of his railings with three different strands of colored lights. They're being awfully secretive. Won't let anyone see what they're working on."

"Well, we'll have to check it out," Mary said. "They'll have to show us."

"I wouldn't bank on it," Margaret called from the cabin doorway. "According to Bobby, it's top secret."

Doug Heinz was standing on the dock beside their father's boat, and at first Abby thought he was talking to himself, but then realized her father was behind the tarp carrying on a conversation with him.

"Hi Doug," she said, then turned toward the boat and raised her voice. "Dad, can you pull that thing off so we can talk to you? Mary's here with me too."

"Sorry girls," George said, opening the tarp tent just enough to put his head through. "No peeking. Not until the parade."

"But I've already seen it," Abby protested. "Remember, you showed me your design."

The tarp rustled again and Bobby's head appeared just below their father's. "We changed the design—completely," he said, sticking one thin arm through the opening to gesture a sideways slice through the air.

"Yep," George said. "We were ready to give up, I'm telling you here and now. That young fellow Tony was down here watching us this morning and he said something that got us thinking on an altogether different concept. Now everything's falling into place."

"It's going to be awesome," Bobby said. "But you'll have to wait until the parade to see."

Both heads disappeared behind the tarp.

"Fine," Mary said, raising her voice. "That's the thanks we get for bringing down a thermos of warm cocoa and oatmeal raisin cookies."

Her father's hand shot back through the opening in the tarp and Abby placed the thermos in it. A second later, Bobby's hand retrieved the snack. From inside the tarp came a muffled chorus of "thanks."

"How's Emma doing, Doug?" Abby asked as they all started back up the dock.

"Much improved," Doug said. "She's sore, of course, but she's in good spirits and thankful to have gotten by with no serious injuries. Now if I could just get Janet to stop worrying about that business with her purse."

"No luck, huh?" Mary asked. "I was so hoping it would show up."

"Me too," Doug said. "I just went over this morning and walked the grounds one last time. I didn't really expect to find anything, but I figured it was worth a try. I've told Janet not to beat herself up about it. We'll make good on every cent of it. We may be eating peanut butter and jelly sandwiches for a little while, but we'll make good on it."

"Oh Doug," Mary said. "No one would expect you to do that. It was an accident. It could have happened to anyone under those circumstances."

"That's true," Doug said. "But it happened to Janet. She feels responsible and she wouldn't have it any other way and neither would I. If it will get Janet to stop fretting, it'll be worth every cent. And besides, it's the right thing to do."

AS SHE HAD EXPECTED, Abby found the angel paintings even more compelling now that she knew the story of the young woman who had painted them. Everything that Goldie had told them about her sister came through on those canvases. The romantic view of the world, the love of nature, the keen interest in symbolism and folklore. It was all there. Plus so much more.

Patricia was thrilled to hear that they'd gotten to the bottom of the mystery and that Goldie would be coming in to see the paintings.

"Oh," she said, "I hate to have her see them like this. Maybe I can get someone to help me hang them on that long wall over there once the craft fair has ended tonight."

"I'm no master carpenter, but I can work a hammer," Abby said with a laugh.

"And I can certainly sit back and say 'an inch to the left, no, up a little,'" Mary said, moving her hands around.

"You're hired," Patricia said. "I'll see you both later."

Someone from behind one of the craft tables summoned

Patricia to come and answer a question about Ana's wall hanging. It was the grand prize for the raffle.

"I need to go to the shop for a little while to help Candace with Christmas orders," Mary said. "Would you like me to take you home first or do you want to use the van and come back and pick me up later?"

Suddenly the idea of going home to an empty house was unappealing to Abby. "I think I'll just take the van," she said. "I'll keep my phone on so you can let me know when you're ready. I think I'll go out and see if Mom needs any help getting ready for Christmas."

"Mom's at a luncheon," Mary said. "Remember? Today's the day she and her friends from the Visitors Center were doing their Christmas lunch."

"Oh, I'd forgotten," Abby said. "Well, Dad's surely not going to let me help them. Is there anything I can do at the flower shop?"

"I don't think so. Not today, Abby," Mary said. "All the deliveries have already been done today."

Abby sighed. "Okay. Maybe I'll go on home then. I can get the rest of my wrapping done."

"You know what it is?" Mary asked as they made their way back to Island Blooms where they'd parked the van.

"Know what *what* is?" Abby replied.

"Why you've had this little letdown," Mary said. "You don't want to go home because you've had a little letdown. The mystery of the paintings is solved, and it came too easy for you. You're accustomed to more challenging cases."

"Well, first of all, I don't have cases," Abby said. "I'm an ornithologist, not a detective. And secondly, I am not having a letdown. I just don't feel like being home alone. I want to be out enjoying the hustle and bustle of the season."

"Whatever you say," Mary said, as they got to the door of Island Blooms. Finnegan took a couple of quick steps ahead of Mary's chair and grabbed the leather strap fastened to the turning mechanism on the doorknob and pulled the door open with only a vague gesture from Mary as a command. So practiced was their working partnership that Finnegan seemed to almost read Mary's mind.

"Hey, Candace," Abby said when they were inside. "How's everything going?"

"Hey Abby, Mary," she said looking up from the planter garden she was arranging. "Fine. Busy."

"Need any help with anything?" Abby asked.

"Not unless you've developed a talent for floral arrangement since the last time I saw you," Candace said.

"I can assure you, she hasn't," Mary said. "She just doesn't have a mystery to solve and she's restless."

"Well, all right then, I admit it," Abby said. "Maybe I am suffering from a small case of letdown. I think I'll just go on home now. Call me when you're ready to be picked up."

Abby had her head bent down zipping her jacket as she went out the door. She collided with Serena DeBow on the sidewalk just outside.

"Abby," Serena said. "I've been trying to reach you and here I've run into you—literally."

"Hi, Serena," Abby said. "I've been thinking about you too. How goes the search?"

"It's over," Serena said, beaming. "You'll just never guess." She flapped a hand. "I hate it when people say that. But you *will* never guess so I'm going to tell you. You know Miss Opal said she'd call her nephew. Well, do you know who her nephew *is*? He's only the head of the forestry research station in Vancouver. He told me right up front he was only making the call as a courtesy because his Aunt Opal asked him to and he can't say no to her."

Serena stopped and took a deep breath and Abby rotated her hand to signal her to hurry the story along. She could see that Serena was excited, and she wanted to know the whole story right away.

"But then he started asking me about myself. I told him I was looking for a project to follow for my master's thesis, and I told him what it was about. He asked me to send my résumé, which I also thought at the time was just a courtesy. But he called me this morning and said he was impressed by my résumé and if I was interested he had something for me. Abby, he has the perfect—I mean the perfect—project for me to follow. It's better than the project I originally had set up. It just seems like it was meant to be."

"Oh Serena, that's wonderful," Abby said.

Serena nodded vigorously. "Yeah. Thank goodness for Miss Opal. I was just going into Mary's to order some flowers for her. And I'll have to think of some way to thank Tony too. If he hadn't told Miss Opal about my situation none of this would ever have happened."

"Let me take you to lunch to celebrate," Abby said.

"Oh, I'd love that, Abby," Serena replied hesitantly, "but I'm meeting Artie for lunch. Why don't you come along with us?"

"Oh no," Abby said. "Another time. You two go ahead. I've still got Christmas things to do yet anyway." She reached out her arms to gather Serena into a hug. "Congratulations again. This is wonderful news."

After Serena had gone into Island Blooms, Abby stood on the sidewalk a moment enjoying the slight nip in the air and breathing in the fragrance of evergreen. Wonderful.

She headed for the van, but with every step she took her enthusiasm for going home diminished. Once inside the van she pulled out her cell phone and called Goldie. Chances were good that she'd still be out in the greenhouse, but it was worth a try. Goldie answered on the fourth ring sounding somewhat breathless.

"Goldie, it's Abby. Listen I know this may be an inconvenience and if it is, just say so. Patricia hasn't found anything in the church records anywhere about the paintings, and I was wondering if I could come back out sometime this afternoon and help you look for Sylvia's notebook about them."

"Strange you should call just now, again," Goldie said. "We seem to be on the same wavelength today. Tony has been helping me, and we've brought all of Sylvia's notebooks and things down from the attic. Come on out now if you'd like."

Abby found herself again fighting her internal war about Tony as she was driving back to Goldie's house. She prided herself on being a prudent and sensible person. She tried to use good judgment and she didn't accept things at face value. But where was the line between prudence and chariness? Had she crossed it?

Tony seemed to be everywhere on the island. And he was making friends very quickly. Even with someone as reticent as Goldie. She thought of what she'd overheard Miss Opal say when going into the open house. It sounded as if Tony had specifically asked for an introduction to Goldie. And now, here he was a day later, working in Goldie's greenhouse and doing little chores for her inside her house. Why would a young man choose to spend his time—his vacation time, no less—with these older women? What was he up to? It just didn't seem probable that anyone could be that generous.

Abby wanted to believe that he was just what he seemed. In fact she wanted that very much, she realized. That would be an inspiration. She wanted to believe. If only she could overcome her qualms. Her lips moved as she whispered one of her favorite Psalms. "The Lord is my strength and my shield; my heart trusts in him, and I am helped" (Psalm 28:7).

But the sight before her as she entered Goldie's house rekindled her disquieting thoughts. Goldie and Tony were sitting around the large oak dining table. The lace tablecloth had been neatly folded and put aside on the sideboard along with a silver tea service and a large ceramic bowl that held one of Goldie's more exotic species of orchids.

The tabletop was covered with notebooks, photos and pieces of paper. Tony was methodically organizing it all into piles, examining each item with intense interest. Some of the papers were discolored and looked brittle, and he handled them with great care.

"These are all Sylvia's?" Abby asked, staring at the piles of papers.

"All," Goldie answered. "Lots and lots of sketches. Some diaries and letters and a few old photos."

"Here's a picture of Sylvia," Tony said, almost reverently. He handed the picture to Abby, careful to hold it by its scalloped edge. She took it and stared down at the black and white image of a young girl in a shirtwaist dress. Her hair flowed down over her shoulders in soft curls. Her chin was tilted down toward her chest and she gazed up shyly at the camera. She had the same fine features as Goldie, but appeared more delicate, more fragile.

"She's lovely, Goldie," Abby said.

"And look at her hands," Tony said, pointing to the photo. "Definitely an artist's hands," he said.

Abby had to agree. Sylvia was seated on what looked like a dry stack rock wall with her legs crossed. Her hands were crossed loosely over her knee. Her long fingers were held—even at ease—in an expressive posture.

"I took that picture," Goldie said. "It's the last I have of her. She'd been out behind the house,"—she gestured toward the back of the small house she'd inherited from her parents—"painting, as usual. She was always painting, at least when she had the supplies. This wasn't long after our birthdays. Hers in May and mine in June. She'd gotten a new canvas and paints, and I'd gotten a camera."

"Your last birthday together?" Tony asked and Abby was surprised to see what looked like a pained expression on his face that went beyond sympathy.

"Yes," Goldie answered, her voice as distant as her thoughts.

Tony cleared his throat and went back to sorting papers, and Abby took that opportunity to study him closely. He looked up briefly and gave Goldie a smile, and Abby felt the disquieting feelings trying to sneak up on her again.

"Here's what you came for, I think," he said, handing Abby a notebook with the words Sparrow Island Angels scribbled across the cover in numerous different handwriting styles.

Abby put it down on the table and carefully flipped the pages. She saw sketches and blocks of text and lists of words and long lists of birds. There had to be at least fifty pages.

"You can take it home with you and look it over if you'd like, Abby," Goldie said. "I would like to have it back though. This is all I've got left of Sylvia, except of course for what's in here," she said, placing both blue-veined hands over her heart.

"That's a lot," Tony said.

"I will take it and read it over if you're sure you don't mind, Goldie," Abby said, watching Tony's every small movement as he went back to moving the papers about. "And I'll be very careful with it, you can be sure."

"If I didn't know that, I wouldn't have offered to let you take it in the first place, Abby," Goldie said, handing over the notebook.

"Can I give you a lift back to town, Tony?" Abby asked. "I've got Mary's van. We can stow the moped right in the back. It's getting pretty nippy out there to be riding around on that thing."

"Oh, no thanks, Abby. I'll be fine. I'm just going to hang around here a little while and help Goldie get all this stuff straightened up. Maybe look through some of it with her," he said.

As Abby drove the road back to town a dark cloud was forming to the west, matching her mood. Was it odd for Tony to be showing so much interest in Goldie's family history? It was an interesting story all right. Abby herself had found it completely absorbing. Hadn't she pushed the issue and driven back out to Goldie's because she was so eager to read Sylvia's notebooks about the paintings? But then again, she knew Goldie, so of course she was interested. Tony had only just met the woman. And already he was making himself right at home in her greenhouse and in her home.

And doing what? Abby's warm, human side demanded. Helping Goldie with her work. Helping her get things from the attic and sorting through papers. Listening to her reminisce about her sister. All good things.

Yes—so far, Abby's calculating scientist countered. *But what is his motive? What is his objective?* "What is he up to?" Abby muttered aloud.

She was surprised by the sound of her own voice inside the empty van. Oh great, she thought, if she kept this up soon she'd be able to start her own one-woman debate team.

Lord, give me an open mind and keep my heart from making judgments, she prayed as she went to pick up Mary.

CHAPTER ❧ THIRTEEN

ABBY STARTED INTO THE living room to ask Henry if he'd like a cup of coffee while he waited for Mary to finish getting dressed for their official Christmas date together.

Henry was pulling out all the stops. He'd made reservations at Winifred's, the finest restaurant on the island. He'd brought a box of chocolates and a *New York Times* crossword puzzle book, complaining facetiously to Mary that it was difficult to be dating a florist. Bringing flowers seemed a little silly and coming up with something else she'd like was taxing his imagination.

Abby stopped short in the doorway. Mary was dressed and had already joined Henry in the living room and the two were talking and laughing.

Abby backed away from the doorway and went back into the kitchen. Henry was a really good man and he had been so devoted to Mary. He was all cool efficiency on the outside, as one might expect from an experienced law enforcement officer.

But Abby knew Henry was also a sensitive and caring man. He'd certainly shown himself to be a patient one. And besides that, he was fun to be around. Abby hoped he'd be in Mary's life for a long time.

Sylvia's notebook was sitting on the kitchen table, and Abby, mindful of its value, moved it to the telephone table to protect it from any accidental spills and stains. She was eager to look through it, but she wanted to take her time and really take it all in. She looked at her watch and decided on a quick omelet for dinner. Mary and Henry would probably be on their way soon, and she'd be able to devote the entire evening to the journal.

The mystery of who painted the angels had been solved, but there was still plenty that was mysterious about them. She wanted to know everything that had been in Sylvia's heart when she painted them.

AN HOUR LATER, Abby's thoughts were again of Mary and of her conflicting emotions about Jacob and Henry.

As Abby lit a fire in the fireplace and settled on the sofa with the journal, she looked around, really studying the room. So much of Jacob here. Everywhere reminders of a life he and Mary had built together. A large oak and glass cabinet dominated one corner of the room. Jacob had built the case himself, installing banks of lights to illuminate each delicate piece of his extensive scrimshaw collection.

Abby got up and walked over to the case. It had been a long time since she'd actually looked at the bone and ivory pieces. Each was a beautiful memory of a once vibrant and living thing.

The books on the shelves, several written by Jacob himself, were reminders of Jacob's talents and special interests. Most of the furniture was of the vintage that meant Mary and Jacob would have picked the pieces out together.

Abby stilled herself, standing by the mantelpiece, and said a short prayer of thanksgiving for the life of Jacob Reynolds. She felt blessed for having known him. And she prayed for strength for Mary—and for Henry.

She settled back on the sofa and watched the flames dance in the fireplace for a moment. Blossom came into the room, jumped into her favorite chair and curled into a ball. Abby was happy for her company.

Sylvia's notebook had a hard synthetic leather cover and the material had started to flake off in places, leaving a residue on Abby's hands. She spread the afghan from the back of the sofa across her lap to prevent it from getting on the upholstery and opened the notebook to the first page.

Sylvia's script was still girlish, and like every teenage girl Abby had ever known—herself included—Sylvia tried out different styles of handwriting depending on her mood. First she'd use a forward slant, then upright, then a slightly left-leaning aspect. Big loops, small loops. Severe angles, a more flowing script. Sometimes all the styles were utilized within the same paragraph. It was a poignant reminder of just how young Sylvia had been when she had embarked on this project she called "The Angels of Sparrow Island."

The first few pages set out Sylvia's inspiration and intention for the series. As Abby read the girl's words they resonated so deeply with her she was scarcely able to catch her breath.

Some people don't believe in angels. But I don't have to decide whether I believe or not. They are just here. I live among angels. Right here in this place called Sparrow

Island. It's true the angels I know don't have wings or play harps—well, Mrs. Shaw does play the harp, but she's the exception. My Sparrow Island angels are family and friends who will fly to your aid in a split second if you are ever in need. They will minister to you with a fresh baked pie covered in a perfect lattice crust, with a cord of firewood when your stack is running low, with a tractor and a chain when your car is stuck in the mud, and with a listening ear when your heart is heavy.

Below this introduction Abby recognized a rough sketch for the painting that featured the angel hovering over a landform with the sparrows holding the hem of her diaphanous garments. In this sketch, free of the distractions of detail and color, Abby could clearly see that these were the San Juans as they appeared from a plane approaching from the east, the usual aerial shot featured in geography books and travel brochures. She moved her finger down the page to where Sylvia had continued with her journal.

Do angels have to take a human form, I wonder? Or are they free to take whatever form they wish? I would ask Rev. Hartley about this, but I am afraid he would think I was being impertinent, which is not true at all. By the way, I just learned that word this week—impertinent. I like the way it sounds, but I hope never to be what it means. But I'm getting sidetracked, as usual.

I wonder, too, if angels get assignments—if they get sent down among us humans to try to teach us? This seems to be a popular thing in the movies, and I really like the idea. If they're here, then anybody you meet during any day could be an angel. If more people thought that, maybe they'd be nicer to one another. I like to think we have an angel whose job it is to watch over Sparrow Island, and over all of us who live here. And since it's such a big job, I think she would have taken on apprentices. That's where my family and friends come in. That's going to be my first painting. Sparrows stand for gentleness and humbleness. A good Christian bird—naturally he'd want to keep company with the angels. I can see it clearly in my mind already. I want to make it beautiful.

Abby smiled. Such a fresh, innocent view of life. And Sylvia had certainly done what she'd set out to do. She'd made the painting beautiful. So the sparrow painting was the first in the series. Goldie said she painted them over the course of almost three years, so she must have been about fifteen when this first one was begun.

The following pages detailed the colors Sylvia planned to use and dealt with the inventory of her supplies with such entries as: *Only a tiny dab of titanium white left. Will have to help Mrs. Rowland with weeding her garden again to earn some money for a new tube.*

Then a more detailed drawing, with the colors approximated with colored pencil and notations about the color combinations of the oils she had planned. *A dime of ecru with a dab of forest green worked in.*

Next came Sylvia's more formal statement about the painting, written, Abby presumed, after it was finished. It was an ode to Sparrow Island and to her hopes and prayers for the health and safety of all its residents. And also her thanks for the opportunity to grow up in such a beautiful place.

Again Abby felt a lump in her throat. This seemed to be her night for high emotion. She felt the same way Sylvia did about the island. And she felt blessed to have had the opportunity to return here after having been so long away. She thought of how the people here had welcomed her back with open arms. Even people she hardly knew who'd moved here while she was away and who she'd only seen during her brief visits home. Even people she'd never met at all. They'd all made her feel like she was coming home.

Abby wasn't as naïve as young Sylvia, and she knew there were some glaring exceptions to the rule, but most people on Sparrow Island *were* good, caring people. Abby realized that she had already started taking it for granted even in the short time she'd been living here again. It was good to be reminded.

The next painting Sylvia planned was the one with the hummingbirds. Abby chuckled softly as she read Sylvia's thoughts:

My sister Goldie is an angel. Not a perfect angel—she can be bossy and she's kind of a tomboy. But she's really swell. She's the person I'm closest to in the whole world and she's an angel to me. I can tell Goldie anything and she listens, even when she thinks whatever has come into my head is silly. She teases me sometimes about being a dreamer, but she's never mean about it.

She is so pretty. I feel kind of funny saying that because it is almost vain. I'm not saying it about me, but people all the time say we favor one another. It makes me feel good when people say we look alike.

She is tiny, but she is proportioned just right to her frame, and she has the most beautiful clear skin and a heart-shaped face and naturally curly hair. I am using her as the model for my angels, though I have to just imagine how to make the body look graceful. Goldie can't be still long enough for me to sketch her, and besides, Goldie is not what you would call ladylike. She's more at home in a pair of overalls, digging in the dirt to plant something or other. I have gotten some books of ballet dancers from the library to look at for the poses.

For this painting I am about to start, I am using a hummingbird. At first I picked it just because it reminds me of the way Goldie is, all quick motion and darting here and there. But I looked it up and the hummingbird stands for being able to deal with things as they come—not looking back—and for making the most of what is. And that's my sister all the way. That's one of the things I love best about her. I wish I could do that better. I'm guilty of letting disappointments get me down and thinking all the time about the what-ifs. But not Goldie. Not my hummingbird sister.

Abby smiled as she studied the rough sketch. No *wonder* the angel had looked so familiar. She'd been right there in front of them all this time. And yes, though Goldie's face was now wrinkled with age, Abby could still see what the young Goldie would have looked like. Her hair was completely gray now and the curls were held captive in that sturdy braid, but the heart-shaped face was still beautiful. And she had the hummingbird's penchant for living in the here and how.

So Goldie and Sylvia were another set of sisters who were opposites. Just like her and Mary. Goldie was a tomboy and Sylvia was a sensitive artist. Judging by the one photograph she's seen at Goldie's house, Abby guessed that Sylvia was what the young kids now would call a girly-girl, while her sister was more active and outdoorsy. Again, like her and Mary.

Abby wondered if people were constantly commenting on their differences when these two girls were growing up. They'd certainly done that with her and Mary. Not in a hurtful way— at least most of the time. It was as if people wanted to acknowledge each girl's special gift. Mary was the beauty and the social butterfly. She was artistic and creative. Abby was the smart one, the nature girl, the sensible one. Of course, that didn't mean that each of them didn't envy the other at various times in their lives.

But some things don't change. She and Mary could still claim those roles all these years later. And how wonderful that they'd had all those years. Even though they'd lived thousands of miles apart, they'd always stayed connected. Since Abby had moved back here, they'd grown closer than they'd been since they were little girls. They'd transcended a lot of their differences and come to appreciate each other anew. Goldie and Sylvia hadn't been given that time.

Abby drifted into remembrances of when she and Mary were young. Mary, beautiful and carefree, dressed in stylish clothing in bright colors and with a high, lilting, infectious laugh. The two of them walking home from school, Abby only vaguely aware of what she was wearing, sharing her excitement over that day's experiment in biology, or shushing Mary to point out a Bewick's wren in the tall grasses along the roadway. Mary's clear blue eyes dancing as she shared a secret about which girl in her class had a crush on which boy. The two of them dancing down the roadway and twirling under the spring blue sky. . . .

ABBY AWOKE TO FINNEGAN nudging her cheek with his wet nose. She startled and immediately checked to make sure the notebook was okay. It still lay open on the afghan, the pages unwrinkled. She closed it and sat up slowly, working the crick out of her neck from having fallen asleep slumped onto the armrest.

"You okay?" Mary asked, with a soft laugh. She gave Finnegan the command to move back and started taking off his harness and cape. "Sorry, I just couldn't resist that. You were out like a light. And you were mumbling. Were you dreaming?"

"Yes, yes, I was," Abby said, kneading her neck muscles.

"Nightmare?" Mary said, a note of concern coming into her voice.

"No, just the opposite. Very pleasant dreams," Abby said. "I was dreaming about when you and I were young schoolgirls."

"Lot of water under the bridge since those days," Mary said. She got the cape off Finnegan and said, "Off the clock, boy." He sniffed and headed to the kitchen and his water bowl. Blossom decided she'd better make sure she wasn't missing anything and jumped down to pad along after him.

"Is Henry here?" Abby said, running her fingers through her hair and thinking what a sight she must look, though she couldn't imagine what difference that made. She and Henry had worked on a few search and rescue missions together, and she'd always ended up looking like a bedraggled housecat before all was said and done.

"No, he saw me in, but he left right away. He's on duty early tomorrow."

"Did you have a nice time?" Abby asked, watching Mary's face carefully.

"Oh, it was lovely," she said, and Abby was relieved to hear true joy ringing through her words. "The food was wonderful and Winifred's is decorated so beautifully. And they had a young man there playing the piano. Very talented. Played like an angel."

"That's nice," Abby said. "I'm glad you enjoyed it."

"I did," Mary said. "Very much. At first the music made me sad because it reminded me of Zack. But after a couple of songs it was kind of like having a little of him here with me. I just had to concentrate on how nice it was—to sit and listen to the music—and not worry about what might have been."

"Hummingbird," Abby said with a nod.

"Pardon?" Mary asked.

"You're learning to be more of a hummingbird," Abby told her, tapping the notebook. She told her about what she'd read in Sylvia's journal.

"Of course. Goldie. *That's* who the angel looks like. A young Goldie," Mary said, smiling wonderingly. "Maybe I'm learning from Goldie how to be a hummingbird."

"We can all learn from Sylvia's angels," Abby said, carefully closing the notebook and setting it reverently on the side table. "Let me tell you about the one with the sparrows while I fix us a cup of spiced cider. How does that sound?"

"Sounds nice," Mary said. "Let me just go get into my nightgown and bed jacket so I can be comfy."

Abby got the cider out of the refrigerator and poured two cupfuls into a saucepan, adding a little packet of spices wrapped and tied in netting. Wilma had given her a boxful of these homemade packets as a Christmas gift, and Abby was savoring each aromatic one. She wondered idly if she'd be able to wrangle the recipe from Wilma when the holidays were over. This recipe beat hers hands down.

She thought of what she'd tell Mary about the sparrow painting and about Sylvia's paean to the welcoming spirit of Sparrow Island.

Then Abby thought of Tony and the dark suspicions she couldn't quite seem to keep from creeping into her thoughts whenever she saw him. No, that wasn't exactly right. She always felt perfectly comfortable when she was actually talking to him. It was later that she began to fret about him and what he was really doing here. She certainly wasn't upholding the welcoming spirit of the island. Not with those thoughts in her head.

She took in a great breath of the steam starting to rise from the cider, and her thoughts went back to the fun time they'd had with Tony that night when they were making divinity here in Mary's kitchen. Abby usually trusted her first impressions. She'd liked Tony immediately. Almost everyone did.

She made up her mind to call him first thing in the morning and invite him to breakfast. She would be warm and welcoming. She'd get to know Tony better and maybe discover enough to allay her worries. One didn't necessarily preclude the other, right? Even the sparrows did whatever was necessary to protect their nests.

CHAPTER 🌹 FOURTEEN

ABBY GOT UP JUST AS dawn was breaking on Friday morning and was surprised to find Mary up when she came downstairs. Now that the craft fair was over, she'd told Abby she planned to sleep in this morning so she'd be well rested for the Christmas festivities.

She was in the living room, Finnegan dozing at her feet. She was still in her bedclothes and sat in the gray morning light looking out the window. She stared unblinking, out into the backyard and across the waters.

"Mary, are you okay?" Abby asked.

Mary turned her head slowly and looked at Abby without seeming to see her.

"Mary?" Abby said, pulling a chair up beside her and sitting down. "What's wrong?"

"I saw Jacob," Mary said, her voice soft. "Clear as day, Abby," she said. "He came to me in a dream last night."

"It's okay, Mary," Abby said, taking Mary's hand in hers. "It was just a dream."

"I don't think so, Abby," Mary said. "I think it was more than that."

Abby wasn't sure how to respond, so she just sat quietly, letting Mary take the lead.

After a few moments Mary slowly removed her wedding band from her finger and handed it to Abby. "Jacob says it's time," she said softly.

Abby took the ring in her palm and closed her hand over it. It was warm from being on Mary's finger. "I'll put this in your jewelry box. Safe and sound." She looked at Mary and saw a tiny tear glistening on her cheek. "Are you okay?"

"Yes," Mary said, giving Abby a wan smile. "I'm fine. I'm at peace. It's time."

"What does this mean for you and Henry do you think?" Abby asked.

"I'll have to get used to this first," Mary said. "Only time will tell what comes next for Henry and me."

"Jacob would be proud of you, Mary," Abby said.

"He is," Mary said, nodding slowly.

TONY WAS SURPRISED to hear Abby's voice on the other end of the line. And more surprised still when she invited him to breakfast. He'd had the distinct impression that she didn't like him much. Or at the very least that she was holding back. He'd made an extra effort with her, trying to win her over. People on Sparrow Island seemed to have a lot of respect for her, and it was important to have her think well of him. He'd pulled out all the stops, but she wasn't making it easy. He still felt she was distant and wary.

Breakfast would be a great chance to get to know her better. To find out what made her tick.

It was obvious that Goldie valued Abby's opinions. It was important—critically important—that he not do anything to upset Goldie in any way. He felt like he was getting close. But there were still things to find out. Pieces that needed to fall into place. So much at stake.

THE SPRINGHOUSE CAFÉ was bustling as Abby went in the door and waited for her eyes to adjust. She looked around the tables to see if Tony was already seated. She spied him at a corner table and he waved her over. He stood politely as she approached and greeted her with that magnetic smile of his.

"This was such a pleasant surprise," he said. "Not that breakfast at the Chois' place isn't great, but this is a treat. Thanks for the invitation."

"I'm glad you were able to make it on short notice," Abby said. "Things have been so hectic around here, but now that the open house at the museum is over with and we're closed up for the holidays, I've got some time to play hooky. It seems everyone else on the island has had a chance to get to know you better. I felt like I was missing out."

"Well, I don't know that you're missing much, but I definitely would like to get to know the island's famous Bird Lady better. You're a legend."

Ida Tolliver came and took their order. She started back to the kitchen, then stopped and turned. "Oh Tony, I just wanted to tell you, I talked to Ana like you suggested. She thinks it's a great idea. I can't believe how this has worked out. I'm so excited—I just can't tell you. Thanks." She looked back toward the kitchen where her orders were coming up. She lifted her pencil in Tony's direction. "Tell Abby about it, would you? I've got to get these orders out."

Abby looked questioningly in Tony's direction.

He shrugged. "I guess she's going to be helping Ana out with the wall hangings," he said. "Ana told me how much her business has taken off in the past couple of years. And I can see why. Her designs are so unusual. But the way she was talking, I think having the pressure to work on them all the time is taking its toll on her. Then Ida told me how she helps gather things for Ana sometimes and how she'd love to be able to make something so beautiful and how strapped she is for money. It seemed like it would solve both their problems if Ana would use Ida as an apprentice. Sometimes teaching someone else to do something can make it seem all new to you again. Ida obviously has a good eye for selecting natural things to incorporate into the hangings, so it stands to reason she could learn to make them."

"And you suggested this solution to them?" Abby asked, thinking it was a perfect one and wondering why she hadn't thought of it long ago.

"No, no. Not at all," Tony said. "I just told Ida she should talk to Ana about it. Tell her how she feels and see what Ana thinks of the idea."

"Well, it sounds like she did just that," Abby said, smiling happily. She had known for some time that Ana was feeling stressed about having so many orders for her wall hangings piling up. And she had certainly known that Ida was barely getting by on what she earned as a waitress and that she was very hungry for a creative outlet. This seemed like such an obvious fit for both of them. Why hadn't either of them thought of it before? Or why hadn't any of their friends suggested it?

"So, as I was saying," Tony said. "You really are a legend around here."

"Hardly," Abby said. "The stars of the island are the orcas

and the birds. We're blessed here with astounding numbers and varieties of birds. I'm only known because of my association with them. As you say, I'm The Bird Lady. Are you interested in birds at all, Tony?"

"Interested, yes," Tony answered. "Knowledgeable, no."

"Not much bird-watching where you're from, eh? Where was it you said, Spokane?"

"Not so much interest in nature, period, in urban areas I guess," Tony answered. "Not like here. I just can't get over how great the museum and the conservatory are. How long have you been there as Associate Curator?"

Abby told him a little about Hugo and about his passion for the islands and his vision for the museum. And about how he had hired her when she came back here from Cornell to take care of Mary. Then suddenly it occurred to her that he had diverted her question yet again. "How about you, Tony? Do you have family in . . . Spokane, was it?" she tried again.

"Not too much family left, unfortunately," he said. "I've always envied people with big families. Or any siblings at all for that matter. You and Mary seem really close and you're both right here with your parents. That's so great. I'll bet you still do Sunday dinners together, right?"

"Yes we do. Not every week, but whenever we can," Abby answered. "So I take it you're an only child?"

Tony nodded, rocking slightly in his chair. "Yes, I am. I was. I never know quite how to answer that now that my parents are both gone."

"Oh, I'm sorry, Tony," Abby said.

"It's okay," he said. "They've passed on quite a long time ago. I still miss them though. That's why I say you're lucky to have yours here with you. And to live here."

"It's home," Abby said.

"It's a good place to call home," Tony said, looking up just as Ida delivered their plates. Tony's was piled high with blueberry pancakes and Abby had opted for scrambled eggs and a toasted English muffin with the Springhouse Café's special apple butter.

Tony gave Ida a big smile. "Good luck," he said. "Hope it all works out."

"I hope so too," Ida said, showing them crossed fingers. "And remember what I said." she pointed to Tony, "if you ever get brave enough to pop the question to your girlfriend, you've got to let me know right away so I can start working on a hanging for a wedding gift. But give me some time to get good at it first, okay?"

"So, you have a serious girlfriend?" Abby asked Tony as Ida returned to her duties.

"Getting kind of serious," Tony said, smiling as he cut into his pancakes. "She's special. Comes from a big family. I know it sounds corny, but I know she's the one for me. I'm just not sure I have enough to offer her."

Abby smeared apple butter onto her muffin and watched him, trying to decide if he was just fishing for compliments or if he meant what he said, but he didn't wait for a reply.

"So your parents have been here a long time. They probably know just about everybody on the island. Are your mom and Goldie friends?"

"Well, yes. I'd say they are, but not old friends. Mary was actually the first in the family to get to know Goldie," Abby said.

"Goldie told me she used to keep more to herself," Tony said. "She's an interesting lady."

"That she is," Abby said, watching Tony closely. He concentrated on his pancakes, not looking at Abby.

"She certainly seems taken with you," Abby continued. "I don't know if you quite realize what a big deal it is that she let you help her out with her plants. Or that she invited you into her home. That's a huge amount of trust from Goldie."

"Yes, I think I get that," Tony said. "I really like her a lot and maybe she senses that. Maybe it's because we're both without a family that we're sort of drawn to one another."

"Maybe," Abby said, narrowing her eyes to study him. "So you have no family left at all?"

"Maybe a few distant cousins. I don't know. My family situation was always sort of complicated," he said. "My grandmother died about two months ago, and she was the last one, as far as I know," he said, his voice growing quiet.

"Were you close?" Abby asked.

"Yeah, very," Tony said. He took a sip of juice. "She raised me after my parents died. So it was just her and me for a long time. She was a good lady."

"So, are you going to be with us here on the island for Christmas?" Abby asked.

"Yep. Until a couple of days after if all goes as planned. Then I'm off."

"Back to Spokane?" Abby asked.

Tony nodded. "Or maybe to spend New Year's with my girlfriend and her family in Seattle. I'm not sure about my plans yet. Hey," he said, as if the thought had just occurred to him, "what did you find out from Sylvia's notebook about the paintings? Anything interesting?"

"Quite a bit," Abby said, smiling as she remembered the previous evening spent reading by the fireplace. "She was quite a contemplative young woman. And I was right, the birds do mean something. She planned the whole series around them. I'm glad you reminded me," she said putting down her muffin and reaching into her vest pocket for her little notebook. "I want to call Goldie and ask her permission to make copies of the pages in the notebook. I'd love to have a copy to keep."

"I could help you do that and return the notebook for you. I'm going out there later today. I promised I'd help her out again today in the greenhouse."

"Really?" Abby said. "And she said that was okay?"

Tony shrugged. "Yes. She said it was fine if I had the time. And I've got nothing but. I enjoy the greenhouse. She's got so many crazy plants out there, yet she knows so much about them all."

"And she shares all this with you?" Abby asked, unsuccessful at keeping the skepticism out of her voice.

"Well, she's not exactly what you'd call a chatterbox," Tony said. "It's mostly me asking questions and her giving me one- or two-word answers," he laughed. "But it's working for us."

"*Hmmm,*" Abby said. "Well, thanks for your offer to return the notebook. Please don't be offended when I tell you I really have to do this myself. After giving Goldie my word that I'd take care of it and return it to her, I really feel like I need to do it personally."

"Sure," Tony said. "I'd feel the same way. One thing I was wondering," he said, spearing another bite of pancake, "does Sylvia ever say anything in there about maybe Goldie's being—"

"—the model for the angels?" Abby said, finishing the sentence for him. "Yes, and I can't believe I didn't see it earlier. I knew they looked familiar somehow, but I just couldn't get it," she said, setting her coffee cup down and crossing her hands in front of her as if clearing a screen. "I thought about it so hard I was seeing angels everywhere, and in everybody. I even thought you looked like one of them when I saw you in a shaft of sunlight in the greenhouse yesterday."

"Me?" Tony laughed. "Maybe it's because I was standing so close to Goldie." He speared another wedge of pancake. "And the birds? Did the birds mean what you thought?"

"Yes, she planned the whole series around the birds. I told you, we're very tuned into our feathered friends around here." She told him about the first two paintings in the series, the sparrow and the hummingbird and what Sylvia had written about each.

"So Goldie's the hummingbird?" he asked, when she got to that part of the story. He leaned forward in his chair listening intently, his pancakes abandoned.

"Yes," Abby answered, frowning. "I guess you could say that. She dedicated that painting to a hummingbird trait of Goldie's that she admired."

"Goldie's the hummingbird," he said again slowly, as if he'd just been given a secret password. He put his head back and laughed, rocking back in his chair for a moment.

Abby frowned.

He looked at her and stopped. He picked up his fork and began to eat again and promptly changed the subject, asking Abby about the parade of boats that was to take place on Christmas Eve. But he seemed restless through the rest of breakfast and took off on his moped as soon as they left the Springhouse.

Abby felt much relieved. Tony had opened up. He'd told her quite a few things about himself.

The feeling of relief lasted only until she was inside her car and was pulling out of the parking space. When she thought back over the conversation she realized that again she hadn't gotten all that many answers to her questions. In fact, Tony had extracted a lot more information from her than he'd volunteered about himself. He was very good at that. In any case, she really didn't like the idea of him spending so much time at Goldie's. Especially with Goldie letting him into her life so unquestioningly. That was worrisome.

Abby had grown very fond of Goldie since she'd had a chance to get to know her through Mary. Goldie definitely marched to the beat of her own drummer. But that only made Abby admire her all the more. It had taken a lot of patience and attention to coax Goldie out of her self-imposed isolation. Abby couldn't bear to think of her getting hurt by trusting someone too much.

Abby resolved that she was just going to have to live with the guilt of not being a warm or accepting person if it meant she could protect Goldie from possible harm.

EMMA WAS SITTING UP IN BED, surrounded by pillows and working a crossword puzzle when Abby knocked on the doorframe. Both Emma and Janet, who was sitting in a side chair reading the newspaper, looked up and smiled.

"Doug said you were accepting visitors," Abby said.

"Yes, we certainly are," Emma said, holding out her hand to Abby.

"And she means the royal *we*," Janet said. "You'd think she was the queen mother—she's had so many people coming by to pay their respects today."

"Oh Janet, don't be impertinent," Emma said.

Abby squeezed the older woman's hand and sat down on

the side of the bed. "That's the second time in less than twenty-four hours I've encountered that word," Abby said.

"What word is that, dear?" Emma asked.

"Impertinent," Abby said. She told them the news about the paintings and about what she'd read in Sylvia's notebooks.

"Oh, what a sad story, Goldie losing her sister like that," Emma said. "I never knew. But of course, you know Goldie. She keeps her business and her thoughts to herself most times. How wonderful that the paintings were found after all this time."

"And I have good news to share too," Janet said. "I got a call this morning from the Medical Center. One of the grounds-keepers found my bag and turned it in. With every single thing—including every cent of the money from the craft fair—still inside."

"Oh Janet, that's really good news. It's great to know there are still honest people out there," Abby said.

"Yes, and I found out the poor man is working two jobs to stay afloat. He and his wife have three children and are barely getting by. I'm sure that money looked very tempting. I'm going to do something special for that family for Christmas, you can be sure of that. I don't know what yet, but something."

"I'd like to help with that too. Let me know what you come up with and how I can contribute. Mary will want in on it too, I'm sure. And probably a lot of other people from the church once they hear about it."

"It's a heartwarming story all right," Emma said. "Seems we all have our angels watching over us this year."

"So, how are you feeling, Emma?" Abby asked. "You're looking well."

"I'm fine, really just fine. I'm sore, I can tell you, and I look like I've been in a prizefight," she said, covering her mouth with her hand and scrunching up her shoulders as she gave a little laugh. "But I got off light. I don't need to be in this bed, but Janet's insisting on pampering me."

"Well, you deserve a little pampering," Abby said. "That was quite an ordeal."

"Not something I'd want to do every day of the week," Emma agreed. "I have to tell you, I was sinking pretty low by the time Tony came by and heard me calling out. I prayed and I tried to keep my spirits up, but I think I was pretty close to going under when I looked up and saw Tony at the head of those stairs. I don't know if I was hallucinating or what. I thought maybe I was having the kind of dream Jacob had in the Bible. Except I wasn't looking up at a ladder, I was looking up the stairs. And I didn't see a host of angels like Jacob did, but just the one. That's what he looked like to me, just like an angel with those blond curls and that sweet face."

"In that moment he definitely was your angel, Mother," Janet said. "And ours too. Do you know, Abby, he came by yesterday and repaired the window he had to knock out to get into the house to get to mother? Can you believe that?"

"He's something, isn't he?" Abby said, vaguely. "What has he told you about himself?"

"Well, I know he's from Seattle," Janet said, then frowned. "Or was it Spokane? And I know he'll be here on the island until after Christmas and that this vacation was a gift from . . . who did he say, Mother?"

"I can't recall," Emma said. "I believe he just said someone close."

"Any idea what he does for a living, or who he works for?" Abby asked.

"Yes," Emma said. "Well, no, actually," she frowned again. "When someone asked him at the hospital if he was the one who repaired the clock, he said he'd always been good with his hands, but I don't believe he said exactly what he does for a living."

"Rick says he knows his way around tools," Janet volunteered. "Tony's helped him with a couple of projects around The Bird Nest. Why are you asking?" Janet said, narrowing her eyes at Abby. "What aren't you saying?"

"No reason, nothing," Abby answered with a small shrug. "I'm just curious is all." She smiled a bright smile. No sense in poisoning people against Tony. What if she was wrong?

And she hoped, for once, that she was completely off base on this one.

MARY'S FLOWER SHOP was teeming with activity when Abby arrived just before lunchtime. As she parked her car, she could see Candace through the window, moving quickly back and forth from the cooler to the worktable. She was boxing up the orders Abby had promised to help deliver.

Henry was coming out of the shop as Abby hit the sidewalk, and he greeted her with a broad grin.

"Hey, Henry," she said, "you look like you're in the Christmas spirit."

"Guess I am," he said. "How about you?"

"I'm getting there," Abby said.

"Something holding you back?" Henry said, cocking his head to one side.

"No, not really," Abby said, waving a hand.

"Okay, out with it," Henry said sternly. "I know that look all too well. What's on your mind, Abby?"

Abby found herself spilling all her worries about Tony right there on the sidewalk. "He hasn't done a single, solitary thing to deserve this, Henry. I want to make that clear. It's just that he seems too good to be true. And all this attention to Goldie has got me worried. What if he's trying to run some kind of scam on her?"

"Don't underestimate Goldie," Henry said. "She's a lot tougher than she looks."

"I know," Abby said. "But she's been out there by herself for such a long while. She's just now starting to mix with people more. Plus I think she's especially vulnerable right now, what with the holidays and all. I don't want someone taking advantage of that."

"And you think that's what he's doing?" Henry asked. "How, exactly?"

Abby sighed. "By helping her in the greenhouse. By helping her get things down from her attic and by listening to her talk about her sister." She looked up at Henry and pursed her lips. "Some crimes, huh?"

"Not exactly felonies as far as I've heard," Henry said.

"I don't know, Henry," Abby said. "Maybe I'm being totally paranoid. "The thing is, I really like him. And I hope what he *seems* to be is just what he is."

"And maybe I'm not being suspicious *enough*," Henry said. "I'm a pretty happy man these days," he said, glancing back through the window and waving to Mary as she looked up from where she was attaching tiny silver glass balls to a potted Norfolk Island pine. "Maybe it's making me soft."

"My Christmas wish is that you're right and I'm wrong on this one," Abby said. "It's a strange feeling to be rooting against yourself. But this is one time I'd really love to be completely off-target."

"Then that's what I'll hope for too," Henry said. "On the other hand, if you see any reason that I should become involved, or be checking this guy out, you'll call me, right?"

"Don't I always?" Abby asked.

Henry tipped his hat and walked away, whistling softly. "Deck the halls . . ."

CHAPTER ❦ FIFTEEN

Terza Choi met Abby at the front door and swung it wide open to allow her to come through with her box filled with floral arrangements.

"Oh, they're beautiful," Terza said. "Mary and Candace do such nice work."

"Where would you like them?" Abby asked.

"Just set them there, Abby," Terza said, pointing to a large coffee table. "The large one goes on the piano over there and the others are for the tables in the dining room."

"Well, here, let me help you put them out," Abby said.

"Okay, sure," Terza said, glancing at her watch. "I've got most of the rooms freshened and it's not time to start dinner just yet."

Abby took the larger arrangement out of the box and carried it over to the piano. A Christmas songbook was open on the easel.

Terza grabbed a shallow ceramic dish from the front hall closet and trotted over with it. She put it in the center of the piano and motioned for Abby to set the planter on it. "This is just the right touch," she said. "Our guests have been gathering around the piano and singing carols at night. Tony's our pianist."

"Really?" Abby said. "So we can add musician to Tony's list of talents?"

"Well, I wouldn't go that far," Terza said. "He's a little rough, but he's a good sport, and we all stumble along together. We have enthusiasm, if not skill," she said with a smile. "Oh, but we have been so lucky to have Tony staying here with us. He's the sweetest boy. And so helpful. Really, I feel that we should give him a full refund on his room. He's earned his keep."

"I heard he's been helping out," Abby said, picking up the box and heading for the dining room, eager to keep Terza talking. "Where is it Tony's from now? I forget."

"He's from Spokane," Terza said.

"That's what I thought," Abby answered. "And what made him choose Sparrow Island as a vacation spot, do you know? He's apparently not a birder. Nor a boater. Or a fisherman."

"I'm not sure exactly," Terza said, hesitantly, a slight frown forming on her smooth forehead. "He just said he'd always heard a lot about Sparrow Island from different people and wanted to see it for himself."

"He came out to the museum a couple of times, but I don't think he had a chance to hike at the conservatory. Has he been out to the lighthouse or seen any of the sights?" Abby said, trying to keep her voice conversational.

"I think he's seen some things," Terza said, the frown returning. "He rented a moped so he could get around. He seems to like being around people though. I don't think he's much of a solitary person."

"No, guess not," Abby said.

"He has a nice way with people," Terza said, as if she hadn't heard Abby. "Martin and I have enjoyed having him here so much. We've talked to him a lot. He was very interested in our life back in Hong Kong and how we came to end up here." She stopped fiddling with the cut flowers she'd just set on the table, finally satisfied that they were perfectly centered on the table. She looked over at Abby, her eyes becoming unfocused and her thoughts seemingly far away. "And it's strange, you know. That's a part of our lives neither of us really likes to talk about— the part before we came here—but we found ourselves sharing even the painful parts with Tony."

Abby realized that in all the time she had known Martin and Terza, she'd never given too much thought to their past. They seemed to her like hummingbird people too. So content in the present and so much a part of the community here that it was hard to think of them ever having been anywhere else.

"I don't know if we've ever told you," Terza said. "Years ago we lost our only child in an accident back in Hong Kong. That's when we decided to come to America. Too many painful memories there."

"Terza," Abby said, the word coming out in a soft whisper. "I never knew. I'm so sorry."

Terza looked up with a sad smile. "We don't like to dwell on it, Abby," she said.

"Tony seems to have a profound curiosity about people," Abby said.

"Not just that, Abby," Terza protested. "I think he has a gift." She set another of the arrangements onto a dining table and turned to Abby. "Like you, Abby. He has a good heart and he really listens. He cares about people."

Abby wondered for a moment if her continued suspicions of Tony could possibly be rooted in a case of plain old green-eyed jealousy. Everyone took to him so immediately and seemed to confide in him. That was something people tended to do with her. Did some part of her feel that he was usurping her role? Could she really be that petty?

She soon dismissed the thought. She was certainly aware that she had her share of human foibles, but she was pretty sure this wasn't one of them.

"He's interested in everyone," Terza continued. "Everyone on Sparrow Island, it seems like sometimes. He's always asking about this one or that one."

"Did he ever ask about Goldie?"

"Well, yes, he did," Terza said. "He was concerned about her having all those plants to care for at Christmas and wanted to know if I thought she would let him help her out. I told him she probably wouldn't take any help if she thought he was feeling sorry for her or thought she couldn't handle it herself. But if he said he wanted to learn about the plants, she'd probably welcome that. You know how Goldie is. And that way he could help her out without her really realizing it."

"Yes," Abby said, biting her lip. "That was just the right approach. He's been helping her out in the greenhouse. And at her house too."

"See. See what a thoughtful young man he is. How many others, especially those his age, do you know who'd spend their vacation time that way?" Terza shook her head wonderingly.

"Not many," Abby agreed. "Not many at all."

ABBY FINISHED HER DELIVERIES and headed to Rick's. She'd been thinking all morning of how Mary's wedding ring had looked, nestled in a little compartment in her jewelry box, right alongside Jacob's. It didn't seem right to closet them away like that.

Then she'd been struck with a sudden inspiration. She would make a shadowbox frame and put Mary and Jacob's wedding picture in it, along with their wedding invitation and other mementos of that happy day. Then she'd attach both their wedding rings tied together on a pretty gossamer ribbon. Mary could hang it up in her room where she could see it every day.

RICK WAS IN THE WORKSHOP, building a shelving unit for the storage room at Little Flock. Abby smiled, thinking that Patricia had wasted no time in getting a plan of action in place to get the room organized.

Rick was working in the middle of the floor and assured Abby she could work at the bench without being in his way.

She pulled the paper she'd scribbled her rough sketch on from her vest pocket and set to work measuring the frame molding she'd picked up at Holloway's Hardware.

"Rick, can I ask you something?" she said, trying to figure out the most direct way to ask the question.

"Sure. When have you ever needed permission?" Rick said.

"Not permission to ask, but I guess permission to be blunt," she said, leaning against the worktable. "Do you find anything suspicious about Tony? Do you think it's possible he's here running some kind of scam?"

Rick looked at her and frowned. "And you're asking me this because . . . you think it takes a crook to spot a crook?"

Abby almost gasped. "Of course not. I think no such thing," she said. "You're no crook, Rick."

"Well, I was the next best thing to it and you know it," Rick said, and Abby saw a spark in his eye.

It hadn't occurred to Abby that Rick might take her question that way. She was one of the few on the island that he'd confided in about his prior life as a wealthy high-powered stockbroker. It had been a shallow life that had brought him little satisfaction, and he'd left it all behind him when he'd given away the money and had come to Sparrow Island to begin a new life as a handyman.

"I didn't mean it like that, Rick," Abby said insistently. "I just value your judgment, that's all. You've got a lot of street smarts and you're a good judge of people. Also I feel like I can tell you what's on my mind and you won't think worse of me. Honestly, that's all I was thinking."

"Okay," Rick said finally, going back to using the hand planer to smooth the edge of a shelf. "What makes you ask this about Tony? You have a reason to ask or you just got a hunch?"

She told him her concerns about Goldie and about how Tony seemed to evade questions.

Rick listened and, to his credit, he didn't brush aside her concerns or try to make her feel foolish. "I can see why you might think that," he said at last. "As far as evading questions, I can tell you that Tony's a cabinetmaker, a really good cabinetmaker. He works for a company in Spokane. He's got no family—but really wishes he did—and he's in love right down to his toes with a girl named Angela. That much I know."

Abby smiled. "That's more than I could get out of him."

"Guy talk," Rick said. "He's been in here a couple of times futzing around with me doing little projects. As far as running a scam, I don't get any bad vibe from him, but then again, that might not mean a thing. If he's a con man—a *good* con man—

he'd fly right by me. I'm not looking for that kind of thing any-more. It does seem a little strange, his being so attentive to all the older ladies. But maybe he's just really that nice a guy. Or maybe they remind him of his grandmother. I know she died a few months back. Maybe he misses her."

"Maybe," Abby said. "Maybe that's what it is. I hadn't thought of that."

WHEN ABBY HAD FINISHED the shadowbox she went back to Mary's, intending to assemble the pictures and artifacts inside it, then spend the rest of the afternoon reading more of Sylvia's journal.

But when she got home the weight of responsibility of having Sylvia's journal in her possession started to fall heavy on her. What if something happened to the book? Careful as she tried to be, things did happen.

She couldn't relax about it. She called Goldie and asked per-mission to make copies of the notebook's pages and got her approval. "I don't think Patricia has turned one up at the church yet, and even if she does, I'd like a copy to keep, if you wouldn't mind," Abby told her. "So I'd like to make two copies."

"Sylvia would be pleased that you're interested," Goldie said. "That her work still means something to someone after all these years. You surely have my permission to make as many copies as you wish."

"Are you okay, Goldie?" Abby asked.

"Yes, I'm fine, Abby," Goldie said. "Why do you ask?"

"Just checking," Abby said. "I know you've been working hard. And you know you're still recovering from that bad bug you had last week."

"Oh, I'm over that," Goldie said. "I'm feeling fit as a fiddle."

"Good, good," Abby said, still wary. She sensed something strained in Goldie's voice, something beyond her words.

"You had any visitors today?" Abby asked, trying to keep her voice casual.

"Yes," Goldie answered. "Tony's here now. He's learning about the Christmas plants. We're having a nice visit and then he's going to help in the greenhouse."

Abby suddenly felt a pressing need to go out and check on her. "I'm going over to make the copies now," she told Goldie, setting up an excuse. "Would it be okay if I return the journal to you after that? It'll be mid-afternoon before I get out there."

"That'll be fine, Abby," Goldie said. "But please don't feel like you have to do that. You know I trust you to take good care of it."

"Yes, I know you do," Abby said. "But I'll feel better getting it back to you where it belongs. I know how precious it is to you. And I can see why. It's very special."

"She was a special girl," Goldie said.

ABBY HEADED FOR THE MUSEUM to use the copy machine. She was a little sad when she pulled into an empty parking lot. It was dismaying for her to think of the museum just sitting there empty without people inside enjoying it.

As she let herself in the front door, she thought of how she'd been spooked the other night when she was here alone, and she glanced impulsively toward the tree at the spot where the dove ornament had been.

She couldn't remember when she'd felt so much inner turmoil. She'd meant what she told Henry. She wanted very badly to be wrong about this. What a gift it would be to find out that Tony was what he appeared to be. Abby had an image of his slow smile and his quiet way of speaking, and it made her feel hopeful about the world. But, on the other hand, she'd never forgive herself if anything bad happened to Goldie . . . if that smile masked a more sinister nature.

Abby made two copies of each page of the journal and used her computer scanner to copy the colored pages. She dutifully made an entry on a chart beside the copier noting how many copies she'd made so that she could reimburse the museum. While she definitely intended to work some of Sylvia's information on bird lore into her lectures, this was not strictly work-related.

As she went back out the door and double-checked to make sure she'd locked up tight, Abby had to resist the urge to take off down the trail to the conservatory. Her first instinct whenever she felt troubled was to seek the answer in communion with nature. But today she wanted to get the notebook back to Goldie. Sooner rather than later, with Goldie out there alone with Tony.

Goldie was in the greenhouse when Abby arrived. And Tony was nowhere to be seen. Goldie's cheeks were flushed and her eyes seemed to flicker.

"Goldie, are you sure you're okay?" Abby asked. "You look like you might be running a fever."

"I'm fine, Abby," Goldie said, giving out the most full-bodied laugh Abby had ever heard from her. "Come see."

She led Abby into the greenhouse where a riot of color was issuing from practically every pot in the place.

"They bloomed!" Abby exclaimed.

"Boy, did they bloom," Goldie answered, laughing. Every

single one has at least one blossom and plenty of buds. They're going to be even more spectacular by Christmas morning."

"And you were worried about your green thumb! Just look at this, Goldie," Abby said.

"Wish I could take the credit," Goldie said. "It was Tony. He read up on it on the Internet you people are all so crazy over. He found some information that's not in any of my books. They're all a little outdated I guess. Anyway, we force-fed a little fertilizer and turned the heat up another two degrees, and look at this." She spread her arms wide and gestured around the greenhouse.

"Amazing," Abby agreed.

"And not only that," Goldie said, striding briskly back toward the door. "Come out here. I want to show you something."

Abby followed along, and when they were outside the greenhouse, Goldie led her to a low-lying shrub growing along the greenhouse border. "Do you know what this is?" Goldie asked.

"I'm not sure," Abby admitted. "It looks like red-flowering currant. But I know they don't bloom this time of year, and this has definitely bloomed out."

"That's exactly what it is, red-flowering currant. I've been running an experiment on trying to force them, but I wasn't getting anywhere. Tony looked that up for me too. I didn't think it would be possible. You can't usually do this with berry bushes, but it worked. I may have to change my mind and get one of those computers. Seems there's some good things you can learn on that Internet."

"Yes. Unfortunately, there's also lots you can learn that isn't so good," Abby said, laughing. She looked at the currant bush again. "That's really something," she said. She looked along the row and saw the brown stems of other currant bushes still dormant. Only this one was showing life. "I half-expect to see a rufous hummingbird come swooping in," she said. They usually arrive just about the time the first bloom appears on the currant bushes, eager to get at that sweet nectar."

"Don't you worry, we won't be confusing your birds," Goldie said. "But I am going to try growing a few in the greenhouse now. For Mary, so she can have them to use in her arrangements year-round. You know how she loves using native things."

"I do. That'll be nice," Abby said. She smiled, then looked back at the tiny scarlet-pinkish pendant bloom, so incongruous under this cloudy winter sky. "Tony," Abby said softly, almost to herself. "Everything he touches seems to turn out rosy—literally and figuratively. Maybe he is an angel." She turned to Goldie who looked at her solemnly, then burst out laughing.

"Yes, I think he might be," Goldie said, then succumbed to another laughing spasm. "He's an angel, Abby, but a very human one—a flesh and blood one. In fact, he's my flesh and blood."

Abby frowned, wondering if perhaps Goldie *was* feverish. "What do you mean by that, Goldie?" she asked.

"Tony is my flesh and blood," Goldie repeated slowly, as if perhaps English was suddenly no longer Abby's mother tongue. "He is my great-nephew. He is Sylvia's grandson." She smiled broadly at Abby.

Abby felt her head swimming. Then she felt alarmed. "What has he told you, Goldie? You know that can't possibly be true. Sylvia died when she was a girl. He cannot be her grandson. Goldie, he's trying to con you."

Goldie smiled the same patient smile and put her arm firmly around Abby's shoulders and pulled her toward her tightly. "Don't you worry, Abby. Do you imagine I didn't *think* of that?" Goldie laughed again, throwing her head back and letting it rack her tiny body. When she'd gotten control again she reached down to cup the delicate blossom of the currant bush between her fingertips. "Oh, he's family all right," she said, her voice a whisper. "My family."

CHAPTER ❦ SIXTEEN

Goldie," ABBY SAID, THE words coming out sharper than she'd meant for them to, "you haven't promised Tony anything have you? Or signed anything? Any papers or anything?"

"Signed anything?" Goldie asked, frowning. "Like what?"

"Any papers having to do with your property here or with any of your finances, or anything Tony might have put in front of you?" Abby said, her voice rising.

"No, Abby, I haven't signed anything," Goldie said, the frown deepening. "Tony hasn't asked me to sign anything. It's not like that."

"Goldie," Abby said, patiently, "you know he can't be Sylvia's grandson." She put a hand out to touch the older woman's arm. "I mean, think about it. That just can't be true."

Goldie looked at Abby for a long moment and tears pooled in her faded green eyes. "Not only *can* it be true," Goldie said, as a teardrop overran its rim and ran down her wrinkled cheek, "it very definitely *is* true. It's my Christmas miracle, Abby."

"Oh, Goldie," Abby said, feeling as if her heart would break. "Let's talk about this. Why don't you tell me exactly how you've come to believe Tony's related to you? What has he told you?"

The stillness in the air was broken by the sound of a moped puttering up the long drive from the roadway. Tony, his gold metallic helmet gleaming in the sun, pulled up beside the greenhouse and he got off the bike. He smiled broadly and held up a hand in greeting to Abby. In the other hand he was carrying a Willoughby Pharmacy bag. "Got your medicine, Goldie," he called.

Goldie beamed and waved back. Abby put up a reluctant hand and tried to think of the best way to handle this situation. Goldie was going to be heartbroken when the truth came out. How could she expose Tony without making things worse?

"Abby," Tony said, "we meet again." He walked over to where they were standing. "Can you believe this worked?" he asked.

"No, I certainly can't," Abby answered coldly, then realized he was talking about the flowering currant. She looked to where he was pointing then stared him full in the face. "It's always difficult to believe it when things happen out of their time and place," she said pointedly. She needed to let him know she was onto him. Maybe that would be enough to discourage him from trying anything else, and he'd simply go away and leave Goldie alone.

"Yes, but we have a word for it when they do," he said, smiling at Goldie. "It's called a miracle."

"There's another phrase that comes to mind," Abby said, moving slightly toward Goldie to try to force Tony to look at her. "A mirage. Sometimes we want a thing to be true so badly, we see what we want to see."

Tony turned toward Abby and frowned. "Are we having an argument or something?" he asked, seemingly perplexed. "What exactly is it you're trying to say?" he asked, his voice gentle.

"That's enough," Goldie said, swiping her hand through the air. She drew in a breath and reached up to put a hand on each of their shoulders. "Let's go into the house and have a cup of good hot coffee and hash this out."

Abby kept a sharp eye on Tony as they helped Goldie put on the pot and arrange cookies onto a platter. He glanced Abby's way occasionally, but wouldn't quite meet her eyes.

Goldie directed them to sit down at the dining room table, still spread with the artifacts of Sylvia's life. She moved a few things out of the way at one end of the table, and poured a steaming mug of coffee for each of them, then made a production of offering cream and sugar. Abby thought she would burst. The social niceties seemed to pale in comparison to what she feared was really going on here.

Tony had been friendly with several women in Goldie's age group since he'd arrived. Had he been looking for the perfect mark and found it in Goldie? Goldie, who had freely admitted that being without family at Christmas was difficult for her. Goldie, who spent so much of her time alone and who confided in so few people. She'd be far less likely to tip anyone off if Tony ran a hustle on her than some of the other, more social women would be. At least until it was too late.

Goldie sat down and placed one hand over the other on the very edge of the table. "Now then," she said, "let's start over again. "Abby, I'd like you to meet my great-nephew, Tony Malachy."

"Oh, that explains it," Tony said, letting out a little chuckle.

"You told her. I thought you wanted to hold off on that. Now I see why you're acting this way," Tony said, turning to Abby and grinning.

Abby opened her mouth to protest, but Goldie held up a hand to silence her.

"I'm going to tell you the story of how this came to be," Goldie said. "I only found all this out a little while ago myself, so saying it out loud will be fun. It's hard for me to get my mind around it still." She flattened her palms on the tabletop. "A lot of it is confusing, but the one thing I have no doubt about— no doubt at all," she said firmly, turning toward Abby, "is that Tony is my family. And I'm so grateful that he's found me."

It took every ounce of willpower Abby possessed to sit by and watch as Tony reached over and covered one of Goldie's hands with his and gave her that trademark winsome smile of his.

Goldie cleared her throat and sat up straight in her chair. "Here's what I know," she began. "As I told you, Sylvia was a girl with a lot of romantic notions. And she and Jimmy really did love one another. I believe that. But they were both so young and their judgment wasn't very mature, I'm afraid. When I look back on it, knowing what I know now, it all makes sense, but I didn't understand it at the time. . . ."

Goldie's voice trailed off and she got that dreamy look in her eyes as if she were seeing a scene on a movie screen. "Sylvia tried to tell me. She hinted and she tried to work her way around to it, but I was impatient and wrapped up in my own business and I didn't understand what kind of pain she was in. Sylvia had discovered she was with child. How terribly upset and frightened she must have been," Goldie said, her voice going soft.

Abby watched as Goldie's face contorted. "Goldie, are you okay? You don't have to do this right now unless you want to, you know?" she said.

Goldie took in a deep breath. "No, I want to. I'm fine. It's just . . . so many missed opportunities. But there's no sense dwelling on that, there's nothing to be done about it now, is there?"

"No, Hummingbird," Tony said. "Nothing except look ahead to the future."

Abby gave him what she hoped was a withering look, but he didn't even flinch. He was shameless, Abby decided. The sure sign of a con man—no conscience.

"Anyway, that's why they decided to elope," Goldie said. "Apparently they thought they'd stay gone until the child was old enough not to raise questions and then they'd return to the island to live. Sylvia didn't want to bring shame on our family," Goldie said, her voice going tight.

"But Sylvia died that night, when they tried to cross the water," Abby protested. "You told me so yourself."

"That's what everyone had always assumed," Goldie said, putting up both hands. "And, of course, that was the logical conclusion. But it didn't happen like that."

Tony took over the narrative and Abby's mind raced as she listened intently for inconsistencies and holes in the story.

Sylvia had been rescued by the crew on a fishing boat. Weak and unable to tell her rescuers anything about herself, she was taken to an Anacortes hospital. When she stabilized and came to the realization that Jimmy had not made it, she was distraught. She couldn't go home and bring shame on her family, especially under those circumstances. She gave a false name and claimed to have no family. She asked for a minister and he visited her every day while she was in the hospital. His church adopted Sylvia, or Sarah as she was known there, and when she was ready to be released from the hospital, a woman named Constance Goodson took her in.

"And have you talked to this woman?" Abby asked Goldie.

"I wish she could," Tony said. "But my grandmother is deceased." He looked to Goldie and smiled, his Adonis face touched with sadness. "My adoptive grandmother," he amended.

Abby fought any sense of sympathy she might ordinarily feel toward a person in that situation. She certainly didn't want to be cruel. Maybe he really had lost a grandmother, but she wasn't buying this story. It was all too improbable. And she didn't want to be taken in by emotion.

Tony went on. Constance Goodson took care of Sarah/Sylvia for months as she was confined to bed rest. Sarah passed her time writing in her journals and making sketches. Constance and her husband Howard had not been blessed with children, and Constance saw Sarah as a gift. She spent long hours sitting beside her bed and listening to her talk about where she'd grown up, a little island in the San Juans called Sparrow Island. It became almost a mystical place in Sarah's memory and it seemed to make her very happy to talk about it. Sarah told Constance about all the people she'd known growing up and about the natural beauty of the island and the generosity and kindness of the people there.

Constance had asked her once, holding her breath while waiting for the answer, if she wanted to go back to Sparrow Island. But Sarah had told her that with her family all gone, it would be too painful. And Constance, greatly relieved, had never brought up the idea again.

Sarah/Sylvia slowly improved in health as the time approached for her to have her baby, but she became increasingly worried about what would become of the baby if something happened to her. She made Constance promise that she would take the baby and raise it.

As it happened, her worries were well founded. She developed an infection shortly after the delivery of a healthy baby girl who she named Hannah Elizabeth. She went into a steady decline and passed away before the baby was only six months old.

"And, true to her word, my grandmother Constance took Hannah to raise. Nobody could have had a more loving home. My mother was a very happy, healthy, wonderful person. She and Grandmother were always very close."

"Tell me about your father, Tony," Goldie said. "What was he like?"

"The best," Tony said. "He and Mom were so happy together. And he was the best dad a kid could ask for. He was really good with his hands. He was a cabinetmaker too. He used to let me hang around the shop with him and build little things. He was mechanical too. He could fix about anything. He used to buy old motors at the junkyard and encourage me to take them apart and figure out how they worked."

"It must have been devastating for you to lose them so young," Goldie said.

"Yes, yes it was," Tony said, clearing his throat before he went on. "We'd always lived near my grandmother's house. I went there every day after school while my mother was still at work." Tony turned to Goldie. "I forgot, did I tell you Mother was a teacher? She taught art."

Goldie beamed an almost beatific smile. "Well, that's fitting, isn't it? Was she talented?"

Tony laughed. "You're asking the wrong person. I'm not exactly unbiased. But I certainly thought so. I have some of her work I'll bring to show you next time."

Abby didn't like the sound of that. Tony seemed to be insinuating himself further into Goldie's life at every turn. He was already talking about another visit. And so far, Abby hadn't heard anything in his story that could easily be substantiated. He could have made it all up based on what he'd gotten out of Goldie over the course of the previous days.

"Anyway," Tony continued. "Grandmother always told me stories about Sparrow Island. It was our own version of a fairy tale. In fact, I thought it was all made up until I was half-grown." He laughed. "You know, like Camelot or something. I had no idea it was a real place until one day in geography class we were studying the island formations off the coast and there it was, right there on a real map. I rushed to my grandmother's after school and asked her about it. She laughed and told me that it was not only real, but that it was my ancestral land. That's the way she put it, my ancestral land. That really got me going. I went to the library and read everything I could put my hands on about Sparrow Island."

"So that's why you wanted to come here?" Abby asked.

"Well, that's certainly one reason," Tony said.

"He came for me," Goldie said, now positively grinning. "To find me."

Tony nodded. "It took a while. But I found you. And I have you to thank, Abby."

"Me?" Abby asked, staring at him blankly. What had she done to contribute to this charade?

"I'll get to that," Tony said. "But first let me tell you how I came to be here in the first place. After my parents died, it was a tough time. I went to live with Grandmother and Grandfather, and within a year after that my Grandfather died. So for a long time it was just Grandmother and me. Some people thought she was too old to be raising a kid approaching his teenage years, but they were wrong. She was great," he smiled now, reliving his own memories. "She listened to rock music with me, and we used to dance around the kitchen while we made supper. She kept me centered and showed me what was important. And one of those things was definitely family."

"Did you know your mother was adopted when you were growing up? That Constance was not your biological grandmother?" Goldie asked.

"Oh yes," Tony said. "Though I guess it was pretty common back in that day to keep it from kids that they were adopted. But Grandmother Constance didn't take to that practice. She thought it was important to be honest. She also wanted to make sure that she honored Sarah's memory." Tony stopped short and tilted his head in Goldie's direction. "I mean Sylvia's memory," he said solemnly.

"A rose by any other name," Goldie said softly.

"My mother always knew she was adopted. Grandmother told her a lot of things—all those same stories about Sparrow Island that she told me. But for some reason, maybe because my mother was so content, I don't know, but she never had much curiosity about it. Maybe it skips a generation," he said.

"And what was it that propelled you here, again?" Abby asked, still probing.

"My grandmother died a short time back," Tony said, pursing his lips and lowering his head again. She and my Gramps were both only children, and so were Mom and Dad. So that was it for me in terms of family—blood or adoptive. And like

I said, family was a big thing for her. She left me a letter and a check to cover my expenses and told me to come to Sparrow Island and see if I could find any family left here. It was her last wish, so here I am."

"That's a really touching story," Abby said, meaning it sincerely. He was inventive. She'd give him that. "But if the girl gave a false name, what makes you so sure it was Sylvia? And what would have made you believe she had a sister left here?" She turned to Goldie. "Don't you see how unlikely this all is, Goldie? I know you want to believe it, but it's all so far-fetched."

Abby turned back toward Tony. "Okay, let's just put the cards on the table. I like you, Tony, but I just can't be sure this story is to be trusted. I mean, maybe you think it's true and you're just deluding yourself. Or maybe you have other motives. I hope that's not the case, but I need to tell you here and now that, for Goldie's sake, you're going to need more than fairy tale stories to back you up."

"Abby!" Goldie said, her voice sharp.

"It's okay, Goldie," Tony said with a smile. "I'm glad you have friends like this who have your best interests at heart. It just reinforces everything I've always heard about this place."

Goldie huffed and Tony reached over to pat her hand.

"Goldie, I'm sorry," Abby said, feeling like she'd just stuck a pin in a child's balloon. "I didn't mean to upset you. But if we're to accept this—as wonderful as it would be that you two have found one another—we need something more tangible. Some proof."

"And do you imagine I didn't ask for it?" Goldie said, her voice steely. "I'm an old woman, but I'm not doddering, Abby."

"Of course you're not," Abby said. "Goldie, please forgive me if I've overstepped my bounds. I do that sometimes."

"Well-known fact," Goldie said, but then her face softened and she smiled as she got up from her chair and retrieved a box sitting in the corner of her dining room. "I'm sorry, Abby. We're all lucky to have someone who's willing to stick her neck out for us," she said as she set the box on the table and turned to Tony. "Why don't you explain what this is," she said, stepping away from the box and motioning for him to come and open it.

Tony smiled and got up to open the flaps of the box. "I found this when I was cleaning out my grandmother's house. Apparently, she'd saved it for my mother. But, as I said, Mom never had much interest in looking into any of this. But it was like finding a family treasure for me. My girlfriend went through it with me, and she convinced me I had to come to Sparrow Island right away, even though we'd planned to spend Christmas together this year."

He reached into the box and brought out a notebook similar to the one Sylvia had kept about the angel paintings, the one Abby had just returned. That one still sat on the opposite end of the table where Abby had put it when they'd come into the house and she glanced now from one to the other. Tony put the notebook he'd taken from the box in front of her and carefully opened the front cover.

"I got a little excited about this when we got all those things out of Goldie's attic," he said, nodding his head at the piles of artifacts on the end of the table. "But I couldn't go by the handwriting. She never wrote the same way twice. And I didn't know how common these kinds of notebooks were. Maybe every young girl had one back then. The way she put things seemed to fit. But still, I liked Goldie so much, I thought maybe it was wishful thinking. I didn't want to go building castles in the air, not for either of us. Not until I had a foundation to put under it anyway."

"What is this, exactly?" Abby asked, frowning down at the page. Then she noticed the other notebooks in the box.

"These are all of Sylvia's notebooks. She wrote them when she was bedridden and Grandmother Constance was taking care of her. She writes all about Sparrow Island and the people here. It's clear she was very homesick—and now I know she was missing her family. She doesn't mention them by name. Pity, it would sure have made my search a lot easier."

Abby had to admit these notebooks bore a striking resemblance to the ones Goldie had brought down from her attic, but she still was not entirely convinced. There was always the possibility of clever forgery. Tony had certainly gathered enough information from Goldie to pull that off. Not only that, but it was clear from the dove ornament he'd made that he had above-average artistic talents. She closely examined the paper and the inks. They looked old, but she knew there were ways to artificially age paper. If he could look up how to force flowers to bloom, he could look that up too.

"So if she doesn't use names, you can't be absolutely certain she was Goldie's sister. I mean, other young women must have left the island during that time period too," Abby said.

"Oh, a few," Goldie said. "But these notebooks *are* Sylvia's."

Goldie's tone left no room for argument. Abby fell silent. For a few moments, as she looked back and forth from Goldie to Tony standing before her shoulder to shoulder, it began to occur to her that there was a very strong physical resemblance. Their faces had the same shape and they both had the slight upturn at the edges of the mouth. The eyes—though Tony's were blue and Goldie's were green—had the same almond shape.

"You see it, don't you?" Goldie asked. "The kinship in us?"

Abby nodded. "Maybe it's the power of suggestion, but . . ."

"It's the power of genetics, Abby," Goldie said.

Abby took in a deep breath and smiled at Goldie. The last thing in the world she wanted to do was disappoint her, to snatch away something that meant so much to her. But none of this constituted proof.

"Okay," Goldie said, standing up. "I see we're going to have to do this the hard way. Come over here, Abby." She slid the box down to the middle of the table and took out another notebook. "There are seven notebooks in here. *Sylvia's* notebooks," she said, with emphasis. She took them out of the box and lined them up along the table. "I've looked through every page since lunchtime. And unless Tony is some kind of mad scientist who has learned to steal my memories right out of my head, these are authentic. Sylvia talks about things in here, things we did together, that only she could have known. And before you suggest that I may have told Tony about them, I'd forgotten half of these things myself. Sylvia's writings jogged my memory. There's simply no way anyone else would know some of these things."

"Are you certain?" Abby asked, feeling something in her flutter—maybe it was hope.

"Certain," Goldie said, her tone leaving no room for doubt. "Here." She flipped through the pages in the second notebook. "She writes about a time she and I went clamming down at Keyhole Cove. She asked me that day if I'd ever kissed a boy."

"What did you tell her?" Tony asked, in a teasing tone.

"The same thing I'll tell you, that if I had, I wouldn't kiss and tell," Goldie said, with a laugh. "There was no one else there that day—only the two of us. She writes about a time when we found baby kittens in the loft of the barn at the neighbor's house. About what each one looked like, about the smell of the kittens mingled with fresh cut hay. About how we had laid there, each of us stretched out on a bale of hay and watched the tiny, helpless creatures and listened to their soft mewing protests until the mama cat came and curled around them. No one else could know about this. We didn't even tell our parents. We were supposed to be out berry picking you see, while we were lazing there on a summer afternoon watching the kittens."

Abby looked down the row of notebooks and something in her seemed to release. She felt relief flood over her.

"These notebooks are full of such stories," Goldie said. "Sylvia just about wrote our entire lives during that time when she was so homesick. It must have helped her feel connected to us."

"But, I don't understand," Abby said, turning to Tony. "If that's the case, why didn't you know right away it was Goldie you were looking for?"

"Like I said, she didn't use names. She had a code," Tony said. "That's where *you* came in. I told you earlier I had you to thank for helping me find the last piece to the puzzle. She used names for some people on the island, but for others she used nicknames or code. I guess to keep anyone from locating her family. I figured that out by reading the notebooks. I studied them like a scholar. I can just about quote them directly. I figured out that she had a sister—a living sister—and that Sylvia-slash-Sarah was missing her very much. That made me begin to doubt the story that her family was all gone. Eventually I pieced a lot of the story together."

"And you say you only got these notebooks after your grandmother died recently?"

"Yes," Tony nodded. "I figured the odds were pretty good that her sister would still be alive. But I didn't have any names to go by. Only a general age range and the few things I could glean as clues from the journals. Her parents, she only refers to as Mother and Dad. And her sister was always referred to as . . ." Tony paused and tilted his head back, "Hummingbird," he said, drawing out the word.

Abby looked at them both as they stood side-by-side looking so much alike and so happy. She suddenly felt an enveloping warmth spread over her. She smiled as one after another her doubts evaporated. "Oh, Tony, I'm so sorry . . ."

He held up a hand. "You don't have anything to apologize for."

"Yes, yes I do," Abby said. "I've been harboring some very harsh judgments about you."

"I'm not offended," Tony said. "In fact, it just reinforces everything I've ever believed was true about this place. People here really do look after one another. And I'm happy Goldie's had friends looking after her."

"Well, I feel terrible," Abby said. But then a laugh escaped her lips and she found she couldn't stop laughing. "And wonderful, all at the same time. What a fantastic thing that you've found one another."

"I told you. It's our Christmas miracle," Goldie said. "Special delivery from Sylvia's angels."

CHAPTER ❦ SEVENTEEN

CHRISTMAS EVE DAWNED bright, but by mid-morning it had slipped under the spell of a gentle haze. Tony took in a breath of air and stood on the porch of The Bird Nest, looking down toward the water.

So much had happened since he'd first set foot on the island. He'd gotten what he'd come for. Goldie was the one. He had family. He had roots here. He felt like the richest man alive.

He couldn't say he'd ever felt neglected or unloved. His Grandmother Constance had seen to that. But he had always felt like something was missing. That was the one thing he'd found wanting in his life, some sense of family history and belonging.

Goldie would give him that. Sparrow Island would give him that. It was everything that Sylvia's old stories had promised. And more.

Tony couldn't wait to get back to Spokane and tell Angela about the trip. He felt like a different man than the one who'd stepped off the ferry less than two weeks ago. Now, on this beautiful winter Saturday morning, he felt complete. Ready for new beginnings. Ready for a family of his own if Angela would have him. The future held all the promise and hope of the Christmas season.

ABBY WAS STILL FEELING both exhilarated and ashamed when she thought about the previous day's events. She was so happy for Goldie, and for Tony too. That such a great thing could have come from a long ago tragedy was truly uplifting.

She had stayed at Goldie's house for a long time, looking through the notebooks Tony had brought with him. In the back of one of them, apparently the last one Sylvia had used, there was a letter she'd started, obviously intended for Goldie. As she had throughout her writings, she referred to her only as Hummingbird. Goldie had invited Abby to read the letter and it had brought her to tears.

By then Sylvia must have sensed that she wasn't going to make it. She begged forgiveness for all her bad decisions. She told of her love for her family and of the kindness of the woman who had taken her in and of her hopes that her child would someday know the love and the peace that she had always known on Sparrow Island.

"I sometimes wonder if my grandmother didn't suspect," Tony had said when Abby had finished reading. "That Sylvia had a family somewhere, I mean," he added. "She'd become so attached to her and she loved Hannah, my mom, so much. I think maybe she chose to believe what she wanted," he said. "Maybe that's why she kept telling me the Sparrow Island stories. I think she wanted to leave a trail for me to follow, obscure and overgrown as it was."

No matter how much Tony and Goldie had both told her that no offense was taken, Abby still felt a twang of guilt when she thought about how she'd thought the worst of the young man with only her own overactive imagination as evidence. She felt bad, too, about how antagonistic she'd been toward him when he and Goldie had tried to tell her the story.

As she stepped out the door onto the back deck at Mary's house, she breathed in the moist air and made a conscious decision to dwell on the positive. On this day, of all days, with its promise of hope and salvation, she was not going to let anything negative in. It had all turned out happily and that's what mattered.

Abby settled into one of the chairs on the deck and pulled the blanket she'd grabbed off the kitchen bench around her shoulders. She opened her devotional guide and smiled as her eyes fell on a few lines of the Biblical passage for the day. "And there were shepherds living out in the fields nearby, keeping watch over their flocks at night. An angel of the Lord appeared to them, and the glory of the Lord shone around them, and they were terrified" (Luke 2:8–9).

Abby took heart. Even though the shepherds hadn't understood, even though they had been frightened and disbelieving, they had been invited to be among the first to visit the newborn babe. They'd found him in swaddling clothes and lying in a lowly manger.

Though Abby had been afraid and disbelieving, she'd had a visit from an angel too. Seven of them in fact—Sylvia's angels. She'd spent the past evening pouring over her copy of Sylvia's notebook about the angels. In addition to the hummingbird and the sparrow, Sylvia had used bluebirds, a dove, robins, canaries and a nightingale.

Sylvia had painted the dove, according to her notes, just before what would have been her last Christmas here on Sparrow Island. Abby had closed her eyes after she'd read that passage and called the painting up in her mind. Then she remembered the ornament Tony had brought with him to the museum open house. She'd had that same feeling of peace and comfort when she'd looked at it. Obviously, some of Sylvia's talent—and some essence of her—had traveled down the generations.

Mary rapped on the sliding glass door and Abby realized she'd been sitting there for quite a time, lost in her thoughts. Her nose was numb and her limbs were growing stiff. She got up out of the chair and gathered up her books.

Mary slid the door open a crack. "I didn't mean to disturb you," she said. "I just wanted to make sure you were okay. You've been out there a long time and it's getting cold."

"I'm fine," Abby said, sliding the door the rest of the way back and stepping inside. "I was just wool gathering."

"Well, I hope you're not still beating yourself up about Tony," Mary said.

"Thank you, Mary," Abby said, meaning it sincerely, "for not having a big I-told-you-so waiting for me."

"Of course not," Mary said, giving her a sly grin, "though I did tell you so." She gave a little chuckle and turned to wheel into the kitchen. "Seriously, Abby," she said, "you were absolutely right to be concerned about Goldie. And I'd have probably jumped to the same conclusion you did. That is if I'd been smart enough to follow the warning signs the way you did."

"Well, it turns out it wasn't too smart. I know better than to jump to conclusions before I have the facts to support it, but I did it anyway because I got into a negative mindset. But what's done is done, and I am truly *happy* to have been wrong on this one occasion. *And*, I've made up my mind that I'm only going to think of all the good things and blessings of Christmas today," she added emphatically.

"Me too," Mary said. "I won't pretend I don't miss the kids. That wouldn't be honest. But I have so much to be grateful for, and I'm so thrilled for Goldie about this new development in her life. And Mom and Dad are in good health and Emma's doing well. So many, many blessings. I could go on and on." She glanced at her watch. "But I'd better not. I've got to get going. I promised Candace I'd be there to help with the last-minute orders. She's leaving on the noon ferry to go visit her boyfriend's family for Christmas."

"I'll go with you. I can play delivery person again," Abby said. "But first I've got something I want to give you. It's not a Christmas present," she said as Mary opened her mouth to protest. Mary took a dim view of the early opening of presents.

Abby went into the kitchen and brought in the shadowbox she'd put together and carefully wrapped late last night after Mary had gone to bed.

As she'd expected there were tears. Those from Mary, and her own. "Oh Abby, it's perfect," Mary said, her voice breaking. "Just perfect. Thank you."

"You're welcome," Abby said. "Here, I'll take it to your room. You can show me where you want me to hang it later. And then, like true hummingbirds, we get going, right? We'll get our work done at the shop then we can drop by the marina and see if Dad and Bobby are all set for their big premier at the Parade of Boats."

"Absolutely," Mary said, trying to get some resolve into her trembling voice. "I think this project has been good for both of them," she said, as she busied herself putting Finnegan's working cape on. "I just hope Bobby isn't still fixated on winning the prize."

"I think that's all gone now. Lately he seems to be just enjoying the process. Especially since they scrapped the Rube Goldberg contraption and started working on the design that Tony inspired." Abby stopped and put a hand to her forehead. "There it is again," she said. "Something Tony touched that came out better because of him. He really is as wonderful as he seemed. Oh, Mary," she said, turning a circle in the middle of the kitchen floor, "how *splendid* that I was wrong."

Finnegan started to bark and Mary laughed. "Yes, how nice for you Abby," she said. "And how rare. I'm glad you're enjoying it."

BY THE TIME the last order had been delivered and the flower shop closed down for the holidays, it was lunchtime. Abby and Mary found a note attached to the tarpaulin stretched over their Dad's fishing boat. GONE TO LUNCH, MERRY CHRISTMAS AND ABSOLUTELY NO PEEKING it read.

"Well, you want to go look for them or go on home?" Abby asked.

"I think we'd better get on home," Mary said. "We'll come back later in the afternoon. I want to get a shower and get dressed up in my Christmas duds. And you, my dear, still have gifts to wrap."

AS THEY TURNED OFF the main road and headed down Mary's driveway, Abby saw a frown settle over Mary's face. She slowed and Abby followed her eyes to see the big fir tree in her front yard glowing with strand upon strand of big-bulbed, multicolored lights.

"Who do you suppose . . ." Mary started. "Did you get somebody to do this, Abby?"

"No," Abby said. "Wish I could take credit. I did think of it, but one look in the storage shed was enough to discourage me. Maybe Dad?"

"Oh, I hope not," Mary said. "He's got no business in the world up on that ladder at his age."

"Henry maybe?" Abby suggested.

As they drove closer to the house, more and more outdoor decorations came into view. The wreaths on each window, the lighted manger scene in the front yard, the twinkling nets of lights over the shrubs surrounding the house, the icicle lights hanging from the eaves. It looked beautiful lit up against the gray sky.

Mary pulled up into the driveway and Abby pushed the garage door remote. Once inside the garage, Mary parked the van and shut the engine. She and Abby got out of the van and as they opened the door that led into the house, Finnegan began to bark, softly at first, then on full alert. There, in the kitchen, standing in a row, each wearing a Santa hat and holding their own section of a big banner was Mary's entire family. Plus Lily. The banner read: MERRY CHRISTMAS & GOD BLESS US EVERY ONE!

Mary put both hands to her cheeks, unable to speak. Then everyone converged on them both and Abby couldn't remember when she'd heard so much chatter or been passed around for so many hugs.

Even Finnegan, the most disciplined of dogs, was excited by

all of the commotion. His tail switched back and forth so vigorously it smacked the back of Mary's chair repeatedly.

The questions flew. "Grandma, may we play with Finnegan?" "Were you surprised, Mom?" "Aunt Abby, did we get this one past even you?" "What did you think when you saw Dad's lights on the front yard tree?"

They all managed somehow to move into the family room. Mary could hardly catch a breath. She was laughing and crying, both at the same time. Finnegan became concerned and nudged her arm with his nose.

"It's okay, boy," Mary told him, her voice thick. "They're happy tears." She took off his cape with trembling hands. "Off the clock, boy," she said, wiping at her cheeks.

Finnegan gave her one more scrutinizing stare before going off to greet Lily with unrestrained enthusiasm. Then he flopped onto the floor and allowed himself to be petted and adored by Nicholas and Emily.

"So, did we surprise you, Mom?" Zack asked. "You didn't suspect?"

"Not a clue," Mary said, fanning herself with her hand. "Were you in on this, Abigail?" she asked, turning to Abby with accusing eyes.

Abby put up her hands in protest. "I'm just as shocked as you," she said. She turned to Nancy. "Was this a last-minute thing or have you guys been scheming all along?"

"I was planning to come all along," Zack said. "And Lily's parents have gone on a trip for Christmas, so I convinced her to come to Sparrow Island with me."

"I didn't take much convincing," Lily said with a laugh. "I wouldn't have passed up the chance."

"When we heard Zack and Lily were going to be here, we

really wanted to come, too, but it just didn't seem like it would be possible," Nancy said. "But then we figured it out. We used Ben's frequent flyer miles, and a couple of friends from church donated their own miles to the cause, so we were able to get the tickets."

"I'm a lucky man," Ben said. "My wife doesn't need diamonds and extravagant presents. All she wanted for Christmas was to spend it here on Sparrow Island."

"And you're all here in time for the Parade of Boats tonight," Abby said.

"Yeah. I can't wait to see what Grandpa and Bobby have come up with for Grandpa's old fishing boat." Zack said. "Are they still working on it?"

"Yes," Abby said. "But it's all very hush-hush. They won't unveil it until the parade tonight."

"We can't get a sneak peek?" Nancy said. "Not even family?"

"Let's go down and try," Zack said.

"Let's call Mom first," Mary said. "She's going to be so surprised that you're all here."

"No, actually she won't," Nancy said. "Grandma and Grandpa have been in on the whole thing. We all stayed at Stanton Farm last night."

Abby made a shushing noise. "I cannot believe that. I must be losing my touch. Bamboozled by my own mother and father. I can't believe they didn't let it slip."

"Oh, they're wily," Zack said.

"So it would seem," Abby said. "I'm going to have to keep a closer eye on those two."

"I tell you what," Mary said. "Let's fix a little early supper, then we can all get dressed up nice," she gave a disdainful look at Zack's grubby jeans. "And then we'll just go down to the marina and see if we can see Dad's boat before the parade begins. Now, let's see, what do I have that I can fix quick?" she said putting her fingers to her lips.

"How does a hearty chicken noodle soup with sliced turkey on sour dough bread sandwiches sound?" Nancy asked.

"Delicious," Mary said, "but I'm not sure we have time . . ."

"Look, Grandma," Emily said, standing in the dining room doorway and motioning toward the table.

Mary wheeled over and found the table set with her favorite Christmas tablecloth and the Christmas dishes she had used when her kids were growing up. She frowned and sniffed the air. "Is that fresh bread I smell?" she asked.

"Thanks to Grandma," Nancy said. "Lily, Emily and I did our magic on the inside while the males in the family were putting the decorations up outside. Everything is ready when you are."

"Such pampering," Abby said to Mary. "Let's milk this for all it's worth."

THE CLOUDS HAD GATHERED in earnest, but brought only early darkness, no threat of rain. The entourage parked the van, Abby's car and Ellen Stanton's borrowed Lincoln in the front of Island Blooms, and everyone disembarked and set out for the marina.

Along the way they passed carolers decked out in Victorian dress. They were tuning up their voices and adjusting top hats and bonnets and flouncing out long, hooped skirts. A little girl, about five- or six-years-old, thrust her hand into a fur muff and seemed puzzled to see it emerge from the other side.

All along the streets Emily and Nicholas kept tapping one another and pointing out one site or another in the spectacular show of lights and tinsel. Their laughter blended with that of other children out with their parents waiting for the festivities to begin. The smell of wood smoke and evergreen filled the air.

Ellen Stanton was standing on the dock as they approached. She caught sight of them and walked briskly out to greet them.

"Grandma Stanton!" Emily squealed as she ran ahead and clasped the older woman around her knees.

"Hello, Emily," Ellen said, reaching down to push the girl's long blonde hair behind her shoulders. She took her by the chin and tilted her face up. "Did you surprise your Grandma and Aunt Abby?"

"We sure did," Emily bragged.

Ellen looked over to Zack. "Did you find the decorations all right?"

Zack started to answer, but Ellen was already busy asking Mary and Abby if they were surprised.

"I'll say we were. We both were," Abby said. "I didn't know you were that good at keeping a secret, Mom."

"Well, I'm not the only one in the family," Ellen said. "Do you know your father won't even let *me* see the boat before the parade?"

"Well, that means we sure don't stand a chance," Nancy said.

Just then Abby saw Tony emerging from the cocoon of tarps covering the fishing boat. "Hey, Tony," she called, walking quickly down to him. "What's this? How do you rate a preview?" she asked teasingly. "He won't even give the family a look see."

Her father stuck his head out the opening. "He's a collaborator," he said tersely. "Hadn't been for him, we never would have thought of this idea. Now, Bobby and I have got things to do. We'll see you all after the parade." He stuck an arm out of the opening far enough to wave to the family, then pulled it back inside.

"Is Goldie coming into town for the parade of boats and the tree lighting?" Abby asked as she and Tony walked back up the dock.

"You bet," Tony said, looking at his watch. "I'm going out to drive in with her in a few minutes. We got all the flowers delivered to the church this morning. Wait until you see how they look."

"They can't be blooming any brighter than Goldie is." Abby laughed. "I want to tell you again, Tony, how wonderful it is that you found her. And how sorry . . ."

He stopped her, palm extended. "No more of that, Abby. I mean it. I told you that your concern for Goldie's welfare is a good thing. You were standing in for my Grandmother Sylvia, being Goldie's guardian angel," he said, throwing his arms out wide and grinning.

"Come and meet the rest of the family," Abby said, tugging him along by the elbow.

"THIS IS MY FAVORITE," Emily said as she stood in front of Bayside Souvenirs gaping at the front window display. Donna Morgan, the owner and operator had chosen the theme "A Teddy Bear Christmas" for her window. The centerpiece was a fireplace and mantle. It appeared Donna had constructed the fireplace from cardboard and different colors of cellophane. Articulated teddy bears stood in front of it hanging their teddy bear stockings. In the corner more teddy bears decorated a small tree with—what else—teddy bear ornaments of all shapes and sizes. A sleeping teddy dressed in a red and white striped nightgown and matching stocking cap was nestled into a small bed in the corner.

"My favorite," Nicholas said, pointing to the Springhouse Café a short distance away, down Shoreline drive.

Mary laughed delightedly. "Isn't this your second or third absolute favorite, so far, Nicholas?"

The Springhouse was done up as an edible wonderland. Giant candy canes were crossed to form an arch over the doorway. The lights that were strung across the front of the building were replicas of peppermint swirl candies. A giant gingerbread man waved a welcome on one side of the door and a gingerbread girl waved from the other. The wreath on the door was made from fruits and nuts and was lit by a spotlight. More lights bordering the sidewalk and the entryway looked like gumdrops.

Abby had to admit both these businesses would be hot contenders for the prize in the theme category. Or perhaps Donna's would win best window. That was the nice thing about this contest. There were lots of categories and the winners invariably ended up giving the prize money to charity.

In the distance Abby could hear the carolers. Their singing carried on the light breeze and mingled with the laughter and excited chatter coming from all the people milling about. The weather was crisp enough to be seasonable, but not cold enough to be uncomfortable. Abby felt so much energy she could barely keep her feet on the ground.

"Shall we go on down to the ferry slip?" she asked, as she heard the horns from several boats signal the lineup for the Parade of Boats. "We want to get a good viewing spot."

Tents had been set up well back from the shoreline near the ferry slip in case of bad weather and to protect onlookers from the cold night air. Few had taken advantage of them, most people preferring the unobstructed view closer to the shoreline. Some people had brought along folding chairs, but Abby had just tossed a couple of blankets into the back of her car. She was getting ready to spread them out when Henry came along.

"I've got you a place right up here," he said after everyone had greeted him. "Mary can get up closer with her chair."

"Are you going to watch with us, Mr. Henry?" Emily asked, her blue eyes looking adoringly at him.

"For a little while, Emily," he said, leaning over to get eye-to-eye with her. "I'm on duty right now," he said. "That's why I've got on my uniform. But I can watch with you until your grandpa's boat comes by. Deal?"

"Deal," Nicholas interrupted, reaching over to touch the gold seven-pointed star on the left side of Henry's shirt.

Henry directed them to a spot at the far corner of the parking lot where they had a clear vantage point. "You all can spread your blankets right down here if you want." He motioned to the area of grass just adjacent to the end of the lot. "And I dragged this bench over from the front of the transit building for you, Mrs. Stanton," he said, touching his hat as he gave a little bow in Ellen's direction.

"Why thank you, Henry," Ellen said, settling on the bench next to Mary's chair. "You're not going to get in trouble for moving it, are you?"

"I don't think they'll mind, Mrs. Stanton," Henry said. "If they do, they can call the sheriff," he smiled and turned to Zack. "If you would, you and Ben can just set that back where it belongs when the parade's over," he said, moving over beside Mary's chair and squatting down to her level.

"Were you surprised?" he asked Mary, his voice low.

"You knew too?" Abby blurted, her voice rising.

"Yes, I did," Henry said, winking at Nancy. "And believe me," he said, taking Mary's hand, "it was all I could do to keep from telling you. Especially when you were so down in the dumps. But I didn't want to spoil the surprise."

"Look!" shouted Emily, turning from where she and Nicholas were sitting on the blanket, their arms wrapped around Finnegan. "The boats are coming!"

The first to come into view was the Blackstones' Bayliner. They had outfitted the boat with lights strung around every line of construction so that it stood out as a connect-the-dots boat against the dark night sky. The lights bounced off the ripples in the water and it seemed to produce an evanescent trail in the wake behind it.

Nicholas clapped excitedly. "It's a pretty boat," he said. "Look, look."

The boats made a wide arc out into the harbor and then turned about and headed back toward the marina, skirting the shoreline. Abby squinted to see if she could see her father's fishing boat, but they were still too far away on the turn. His was slated to be among the last boats in the lineup.

Next came a cabin cruiser with white icicle lights hanging from all around the cabin. They swayed and flickered as the boat gently rocked along, the movement adding to the dazzle. All the boat's railings were also wrapped in white lights. The water around the boat twinkled as if strewn with diamonds.

"I'd say the competition's pretty fierce," Zack said. "I hope Grandpa and Bobby don't have their hopes up about winning this thing."

"No, no," Ellen said. "Not anymore. In the beginning I think they did, but lately they've just been in the spirit of it.

George has enjoyed himself so much. And I think Bobby has too."

All around her Abby was hearing *oohs* and *aahs* of the sort she usually heard at fireworks on the fourth of July. Nancy tucked an afghan she'd brought around the shoulders of the children and her tender way with them gave Abby a lump in her throat.

Her thoughts went to Sylvia's painting of the angel and the nightingales, the one she had dedicated to her mother. The nightingale, the plaintive mother, the patient teacher of melodious song. Abby thought of Sylvia's mother's sorrow at the loss of her daughter. Then she looked at Mary's face and saw her sheer joy at having her children and grandchildren with her. Two sides of the same coin.

"Look, there's Grandpa Stanton's boat," Emily cried, jumping up and throwing off the blanket. She bounced up and down on her toes, clapping her hands together.

Abby looked up and saw her father's fishing boat just making the turn to come along shore. No wonder she hadn't been able to spot it in all the razzle-dazzle. There were no twinkling lights. Nothing blinked or chased. The boat was completely filled with hay and in the center was a simple feeding trough. Abby recognized it. It belonged in the barn at Stanton Farm. In this manger was a lifelike baby doll wrapped in blankets. A single golden light mounted on a mast shined down on the baby. A twin light shone upward to where an angel in flight was mounted.

"Isn't that your garden angel?" Abby asked her mother.

"Yes," Ellen answered slowly, her eyes wide. "But she's acquired a very large set of wings and a lot of gossamer garments," she said.

Bobby and George had taken the statue and given her yards of flowing organza and a set of iridescent wings. The light wind lifted the strips of fabric and caused the wings to flutter with each motion of the boat. As the boat passed, the *oohs* and *ahhs* gave over to soft murmurs and reverent whispers.

"Baby Jesus," Nicholas said breathlessly. "It's His birthday, right, Grandma? Tonight's the night He was born."

"Yes, Nicholas," Mary answered softly. "It's a very special night."

CHAPTER ❧ EIGHTEEN

THE PARADE OF BOATS WAS followed by a tree lighting ceremony in the Public Park and the presentation of the awards for lighting and decoration. It was announced that a new award would be established this year for the best neighborhood display. There was little doubt about which neighborhood would win the award. Trevor Carlson and his daughter Stacey accepted on behalf of Pelican Court's residents and announced that over three hundred dollars had been donated for the food bank.

The large Douglas fir in the middle of the town square was simply a shadow tree against the night sky. Everyone had seen town workers putting strands of lights on it. That had been going on for days. But in Sparrow Island tradition, the tree stayed dark until tonight.

Rev. James had been invited to lead a prayer and the honor of lighting the tree had gone to Janet's Good Samaritan, the grounds worker at the Medical Center who had found and returned her purse with the craft fair money inside. He came forward, seemingly embarrassed by all the attention.

When he flipped the switch, the tower of lights rose into the night sky and the carolers led off with a resounding "Joy to the World."

Nicholas pulled on Abby's hand. "Aunt Abby, Aunt Abby."

"Yes, Nicholas," Abby said, bending down to pick him up. "What is it?"

He pointed a chubby finger toward the tree and followed it from the ground to the sky. "It's my favorite tree," he said.

"Mine too, Nicholas," she said. "My favorite tree on my favorite island. Maybe I'll have a chance to tell you some stories about Sparrow Island while you're here this time."

"Good," Nicholas said, his face screwed up into a serious expression.

George and Bobby took the award for best traditional presentation in the parade of boats, but they hardly noticed. They were too busy listening to people tell them how moved they had been by the sight of it. George gave Bobby the small trophy and the boy held it proudly. "I can't wait to see the video my dad took," he said. "Everybody says it looked really cool from the shore."

"That it did, Bobby," Abby said. "I'd like to see it again too. You'll have to bring the videotape over to show it to us."

"I will. I will," Bobby replied before running off to find his friend Katia Keranovic to return the doll they'd borrowed to be their baby Jesus.

The last stop of the evening was at Little Flock Church hall for hot cocoa and cookies and the candlelight reading of the nativity story.

Abby was delighted to see Goldie's reaction to Sylvia's angel paintings, cleaned and hanging in a row along one wall, each with its own easel light shining down on it. They had finally been given a proper setting.

Rev. James made an announcement about the paintings and what had been learned about them and said how happy he, Patricia and the whole church community were to have them. "Now I'd invite Goldie to say a few words, but you all know she's shy, so I won't put her on the spot," he said, lifting his hand in Goldie's direction. She held her hand over her face and color crept into her cheeks.

"But she's asked me to introduce someone very special to her. Most of you have met him already, but what you probably don't know, what he and Goldie themselves didn't know until recently, is that Tony and Goldie are family. And that these truly remarkable angels," he gestured across the row of paintings, "plus some regular, living Sparrow Island angels masquerading as friends, are what brought them together. So let me introduce you all to Tony Malachy."

Tony came to stand beside Rev. James and made a few short remarks about how much his visit to Sparrow Island had meant to him, and how proud he was that he and Goldie were family. Then he asked everyone to be sure to take a close look at the paintings in light of the fact that Goldie had been the model.

"Oh, but don't expect I'll always be angelic," Goldie blurted, then quickly put a hand over her mouth, drawing laughter from the crowd.

Abby now saw layers behind what was on the canvas. Patricia, not yet having had the opportunity to read Sylvia's notebook, had hung the paintings in an order that best showcased the poses and coloration of each. But Abby viewed them in their chronology. The one featuring the canary was the one

Abby thought of as the troubled one. This was done at about the time Sylvia would have come in conflict with her parents about seeing Jimmy. A canary can signify joy or it can bode ill, being the bearer of gossip or bad news. It had also become a sign of warning, probably from the practice of miners taking canaries down into the mines with them. If the canary was found dead, that was a sure sign that dangerous gases were present and the miners knew to get out.

In Sylvia's canary painting the angel stood atop a large rock, her arms uplifted to the sky. The canaries circled above, their beaks open as if in song—or as if issuing a warning cry. It could have been either.

Tony came alongside Abby and looked at the painting with her. "She had a lot on her mind, didn't she?" he said.

"Yes, she did," Abby answered. "I was just thinking that. You know, if she'd been able to continue painting, there would be five more of them. She had them all sketched out in her notebook. Maybe she'd have added even more later. I feel sure your grandmother, your adoptive Grandmother Constance, would have been one of them."

"I think so," Tony said, his brow pleated in thought. "She was a very good woman. Imperfect, but kind and loving and she had a good soul."

"We're all imperfect," Abby said, looping her arm through Tony's. "But we keep trying to do better."

Tony lifted his cup of cocoa. "With a little help from our friends," he said. He took a step and pointed to the painting that featured a multitude of robins and an angel in a forest setting. "This would have been the last one she did before she left the island, right?"

"Yes, I think so," Abby answered. "The robin stands for

new beginnings. The coming of spring, new opportunities. And also for patience. Have you ever seen a robin sit and wait patiently for his lunch worm to emerge from the ground?"

"Can't say I've ever seen that," Tony said. "I told you, I'm pretty lost when it comes to birds. I've never paid much attention."

"We'll definitely have to remedy that," Abby said. "Your next trip to the island, I'll take you bird-watching. There will be another trip, right?"

"Oh, you bet," Tony said. "You won't be able to keep me away now that I've found Goldie. And now that I've made so many new friends on the island. I mean, like Grandmother said, this is my ancestral land."

"ARE YOU SURE Santa will know we're at Grandma's house, Mom?" Emily asked, trying to suppress a yawn.

"I know he will," Nancy said. "You see? We've already got your stocking and Nicholas' hanging on the mantle. And I know Santa got your letter. He'll know where to come."

Ben turned and winked at Nancy then went up the stairs carrying a soundly sleeping Nicholas to bed.

"Can I leave out cookies for him?" Emily asked, rubbing her eyes.

"You bet," Mary answered, wheeling her chair over to the cookie jar. "And I'll leave a light on in the living room so he'll be sure to see them." She turned and whispered to Abby, "If Finnegan or Blossom don't get to them first."

Abby watched Mary's face as Nancy took the child into the living room to leave the milk and cookies. She positively glowed.

She turned to Abby and clapped her hands together, much as Emily had done when she'd been so excited about seeing the boats. "How wonderful to have Santa coming to this house again," she said.

"There've been lots of wonderful things happening this Christmas, Mary, haven't there?" Abby said. "Even some of the challenges have been blessings in disguise."

"That's often the way," Mary said. "The Christmas story certainly teaches us that. You know, I just can't get over Dad's boat. Wasn't that moving? So simple, so humble, yet it perfectly portrayed the true meaning of the holiday."

Abby and Mary watched as Emily knelt beside the crèche Mary had set up on the side table in the living room and said her night prayers. "... and thank you for the baby Jesus. And God bless my family and all the families everywhere."

"Amen," Abby whispered.

EPILOGUE

ZACK WAS AT THE PIANO serving up soft background music as Lily and Nancy set the table at Stanton Farm for Christmas dinner. Emily was helping by setting a small bell at each place, and Nancy was explaining this Stanton family tradition to Lily.

"Grandma's been collecting these bells for years. See, there are tiny brass ones, some larger ceramics, those in glass—those are fragile, Honey," she said suddenly to Emily, lunging to put a protective hand underneath the bell the child was carrying. "Why don't you set that one at Grandma Stanton's place?"

She turned back to Lily and widened her eyes before continuing. "Then there are the little silver and gold ones over there and the big one—the cowbell, that goes at Grandpa's place. They are not to be rung until everyone is seated at the table and we're ready to ring in Christmas," Nancy said. "And Grandma says when."

Emily was being very careful to place the bells gently so that the clappers didn't brush the sides of the domes. Abby saw Mary sitting in the doorway watching approvingly as Lily and Nancy went about the task, laughing and talking like old friends.

"Stop that," Abby told her, leaning down close to her ear and whispering. "I can see those wheels turning. You think you've found Nancy the sister she always wanted."

"Not me," Mary answered with a bright smile. "Zack found her."

"Maybe so, but I know you'd surely like this to be a case of finders keepers."

"Guilty," Mary said with a laugh.

Abby opened her mouth to tell Mary not to count her chickens before they hatched, then thought better of it. This was the season for hope.

"Ho, ho, ho," came a low voice from the doorway. Henry came in wearing his uniform. But his campaign hat had been replaced by a Santa cap.

"Mr. Henry!" Nicholas cried, squirming down from his Dad's lap to run to Henry.

"I think I've got a couple of gifts here for someone," Henry said. He held one of the packages in his arms away from his face and pretended to struggle to read the tag. "Let's see, is there a Nicholas here? How about an Emily?" he asked, holding up the other package.

Serena and Rick arrived, adding more noise and confusion to the mix. Serena pitched in to help with the table and Rick wandered into the living room to talk football with George and Ben.

Abby walked by the doorway to the living room on the way to the linen closet for more napkins a few minutes later and had to stifle a laugh. She tiptoed away and went to get Mary. "Come look at this," she whispered.

They inched back and put their heads around the jamb just

far enough to see one of San Juan County's top cops sitting cross-legged on the floor putting together LEGOs with Nicholas and listening to Emily read one of the books he had given her.

He caught sight of them and gave a sheepish grin.

"Good thing your deputies can't see you right now, Henry," Abby said. "Then they'd know you're really an old softie."

Henry put his finger to his lips. "Our secret," he said.

Goldie had gone to considerable trouble to get dressed up, Abby saw when she and Tony arrived a few moments later. Abby had never seen her looking so nice. Her white hair, usually worked into a simple plait down her back, was done up into an elaborate braided chignon. She had on what looked like a new red wool suit, though not with a skirt, but with trousers, which were more in keeping with Goldie's style. Her shoes even had a little heel.

There was something else about her too. A change in her countenance. A spring in her step. Abby had always thought of Goldie as a contented person. She'd always struck Abby as satisfied, but not given to many highs or lows. Now she seemed happy.

Abby looked on as platters and bowls were being paraded out to the sideboard in the dining room. She hoped everyone had brought a big appetite. It was a good thing the whole family was here to help eat up the leftovers. No meals would be delivered around the island today. Between the efforts of the churches and the generosity of the islanders, everyone on the island had Christmas dinner taken care of.

Abby grabbed her digital camera and began taking pictures to remember the day by. It occurred to her that they were all having a Christmas touched by angels—celestial and earthly.

She thought back over all of the events of the last couple of weeks, of all the things that could have turned out badly if people hadn't cared enough to get involved and help one another out.

Tony had found Goldie, at long last. Serena had found the perfect project for her thesis. Emma had been saved from dire harm. The church money had been recovered. Bobby and George had put together a boat display that had inspired people. A neighborhood had bonded and found purpose by way of tinsel, silly decorations and strings of lights. Even the town clock worked again. And Abby had learned a valuable lesson and had come away with a renewed faith in the human spirit.

At long last they all gathered at the table and joined hands to pray. Abby silently gave thanks for all the many blessings she had been enumerating in her mind. She wanted to hold this moment in her heart forever.

They all served their plates high with turkey, dressing, salads galore, fresh cranberry sauce and a selection of side dishes. The breadbaskets began to work their way up and down the table and the sound of forks against plates created a gentle percussion underneath the conversation and laughter.

"So, Tony," Henry said, "now that we know you're Sparrow Island family, are we going to be seeing more of you?"

"You bet," Tony said. "And speaking of family," he said, leaning his head in Goldie's direction. "I want you to come visit soon and meet my girlfriend, Angela. I know you'll love her. She may be your family soon too. If she says yes to my proposal."

"Tony," Goldie said. "How exciting. So many new things all at once."

"Can I count on you to be at the wedding?" Tony asked.

"Right down front and center on the groom's side? Can I get you to venture off Sparrow Island for that?"

"Oh, I wouldn't miss it!" Goldie said. "I'll be there with bells on."

Nicholas dropped his fork onto his plate with a clatter when he heard the last words. He quickly snatched up his bell and started ringing it as fast as his chubby little hands could work it. "Bells, bells, bells," he urged, pointing around the table.

"Yes," Ellen said, standing. She picked up her own glass bell. "It's time to ring in Christmas." She laughed, and to Abby's ears her mother's laughter sounded as pure and lovely as the peal of the crystal bell.

Abby picked up her own brass bell and raised it high. "Merry Christmas to all gathered here—and to all the angels among us."

A NOTE FROM THE EDITORS

THIS ORIGINAL BOOK WAS created by the Books and Inspirational Media Division of Guideposts, the world's leading inspirational publisher. Founded in 1945 by Dr. Norman Vincent Peale and his wife Ruth Stafford Peale, Guideposts helps people from all walks of life achieve their maximum personal and spiritual potential. Guideposts is committed to communicating positive, faith-filled principles for people everywhere to use in successful daily living.

Our publications include award-winning magazines like *Guideposts*, *Angels on Earth*, *Sweet 16* and *Positive Thinking*, best-selling books, and outreach services that demonstrate what can happen when faith and positive thinking are applied to day-to-day life.

For more information, visit us online at www.guideposts.org, call (800) 431-2344 or write Guideposts, 39 Seminary Hill Road, Carmel, New York 10512.